# THE HAVEN STONE

## ASHLEY BUNDY

The Haven Stone

Copyright 10/01/2024, by Ashley Bundy.

This book is a work of fiction. Names, characters, places, and incidents are either the product of the author's imagination or are used fictitiously. Any resemblance to actual persons, living or dead, or actual events or locales is entirely coincidental. This book, both in its entirety and in portions, is the sole property of Ashley Bundy.

The Haven Stone Copyright © 2024 by Ashley Bundy all rights reserved, including the right to reproduce this book, or any portions thereof, in any form. No part of this text may be reproduced, transmitted, downloaded, decompiled, reverse engineered, or stored in or introduced into any information storage and retrieval system, in any form or by any means, whether electronic or mechanical, without the express permission of the author. The scanning, uploading, and distribution of this book via the internet or any other means without the permission of the publisher is illegal and punishable by law. The only exception is by a reviewer, who may quote short excerpts in a review.

Cover by Sleepy Fox Studio

The Haven Stone

Also by Ashley Bundy

*Blackwood Manor*

For my childhood besties, Candace, and Julia Ashley. You ladies helped me realize my love for writing. I love you both.

PART ONE

# CHAPTER ONE

The door to Blackwood Manor snapped shut behind Richard Price, echoing ominously throughout the abandoned house.

Richard had only taken two steps inside the house, then stopped to survey his surroundings. He was two months past his eighteenth birthday, though he looked much older. He stood six foot four and rail thin. His dark face was covered with a spattering overgrowth that couldn't claim to be a five o'clock shadow, and his chocolate brown hair was long and growing every which way. He wore a wrinkled, red button down and dirty, loose-fitting jeans. He stood with a confidence that he didn't feel, because before the door even finished closing, his childhood fear came washing over him like a flood.

The air was thick and heavy, making it difficult to breathe, and his heart thumped violently in his chest. His mouth was dry, and he didn't even consciously realize that his palms were sweating, even as he wiped them against his dirty jeans.

"*Go,*" a feminine voice thundered insistently inside his head. His mom? His sister? Aunt Claire? He wasn't sure. He'd been so young when they died in this house, and he didn't remember their voices, but it still felt vaguely familiar.

He looked around the rooms he could see from the entryway. The dining room to his left with its walls covered in obscene graffiti. The stairway straight ahead, looking as it always looked, like a dark hole wandering into dread. Then there was the parlor to his right. The open doorway gave him a clear view of the destruction within, and he hadn't been mentally prepared. His breath hitched and tears threatened to fall from his eyes. The room was charred from the fire that killed his family ten years before. What was left of the walls was covered in more graffiti, the magnificent fireplace in the corner was completely smashed in, and the curtains hung from the windows by a thread. The curtains that his Aunt Claire had so painstakingly made herself on an old antique sewing machine were charred and ripped, showing nothing of the love and beauty that had been poured into them.

He forced down the lump in his throat and walked into the parlor to kneel over a large burnt section of the floor and tenderly touched it. "You never came out of here," he said under his breath. "What were those last few minutes like? Did you know what was happening to you?"

Blackwood Manor was known for unexplained things happening. It was a hub for the paranormal, crawling with spirits and they'd all been greatly affected. He wasn't sure what exactly happened that night, but he knew that the fire never left the parlor... and that it went out on its own. He had his suspicions, and he was determined to figure out if he was right.

His thoughts were interrupted as the front door burst open, slamming against the wall of the entryway and he heard bags being dropped onto the floor.

"Hey, dipshit!" came a voice from the doorway to the parlor. Richard rose to his feet and turned around to face the three people looking in at him.

"You could have waited for us," Rod Owens said, surveying the room as he spoke. Rod was Richard's best friend. They'd met two years ago when they'd ironically both been looking to steal food from a convenience store. They'd teamed up and had each other's backs ever since. He was shorter and stockier than Richard with dyed black hair that was gelled up and spiked, making his green eyes glimmer.

"I thought I had time to bring my stuff and get back to the airport. Sorry."

"No big deal," Jamie Allister stepped forward and took Rod's arm. She was Rod's girlfriend and had been ever since Richard had known him. She was younger than them...only sixteen, but it didn't matter. Her folks split when she was thirteen, leaving her to fend for herself. She'd been homeless, bouncing from place to place until Rod found her and decided to help her. When Richard asked them to come with him, they immediately said yes.

Jamie's hair was bleach blonde with streaks of purple throughout and heavily dipping the ends. Her brown eyes were heavily lined, making her appear almost ghostly.

Remi was another story. She stood to the side with her arms crossed over her chest. She wasn't like the rest of them. She was always perfectly presentable, to the point that Richard was sometimes afraid to touch her, lest he wrinkle her perfect outfit or smudge her make-up. She was also freakishly smart, as the result of an impeccable education.

So, when Richard told his friends he'd inherited Blackwood Manor and would be coming back, asking for volunteers to come with him, he hadn't expected Remi to enroll in a community college near Blackwood and join them.

"This place is a little creepy," Jamie mumbled. "So, it's all yours, huh?"

"Yep," Richard said. "The house, the grounds, the money. Basically everything."

"Well, I'm sure it'll look nice when it's fixed up," Remi smiled at him, ever the optimist.

Richard snickered. "That's what Aunt Claire thought. It did for a while, but we know how that ended."

Jamie approached a graffiti addled wall, tilting her head to the side to try to take in the artwork. "Is it just me or does this look like…"

"A dick," Rod agreed. "It's a giant dick."

Richard snorted and sneered. "At least it isn't false advertisement."

There was silence as no one knew how to reply. The air was thick and suffocating, and the silence was suddenly deafening.

"Yeah, that's right!" he yelled out. "I brought reinforcements. Did you think I'd come back alone, you Big Bitch?!"

"Dude," Rod said. "It's a house."

"It's an evil fucking house," Richard replied and narrowed his eyes. "Look. I warned you guys what you were getting into but if you want to leave now that you've seen it, I get it. Last chance though. Just don't bail on me in a month."

"We're not going anywhere," Remi said, and the others nodded in agreement.

Around two am everyone was finally getting ready to call it a night. They'd claimed rooms upstairs and had been hard at work cleaning them up until the moving trucks arrived with their things.

Richard chose Donovan's old room because he had the best view of the grounds from there. He'd swept up the floor, wiped the grime off the windows and put his bed next to the dumbwaiter. He placed a dresser on one wall but otherwise the room was bare.

Rod and Jamie took Aunt Claire's old room because it was the biggest and didn't need significant changes. They'd lifted the mattress back on its frame and put new sheets on the bed, but that was the only thing they'd done. They didn't have anything of their own to bring other than their clothes, and a few personal items small enough to fit into a bag.

Remi, on the other hand, already had her room set up nice and cozy and looked like she'd been in it for years. She'd swept and mopped the floor until it shone bright and glossy, hung hot pink curtains in the window, and had her furniture already set up. Bed under the window, a night table on either side with lamps sitting atop them. One wall had a desk for her schoolwork and a dresser. The opposite wall featured bookcases from one end to the other, already lined with books. All the furniture was white. The bedspread, like the curtains, was hot pink, providing a splash of color in the room.

Ashley Bundy

Richard said good night to the others and went into his room, and sat down on his bed, popping open his laptop. He typed in *Blackwood Manor 2009* into the search engine and pulled up articles about the fire that killed his family. They'd called it faulty wiring, but Richard knew better. Their names were eventually all released, but one article specified that there was also an unidentified female child. This was something Richard never knew about. He opened a blank Word document and typed in *Find out who girl was*. There were a lot of other articles from that time period too. People speculating Aunt Claire was crazy for buying Blackwood Manor, and then that she was crazy for wanting to open a bed-and-breakfast, something that never came to light.

He was startled as his bedroom door creaked open and he jerked towards it, prepared for some ghostly activity but it was only Jamie.

"Hey, Richard. What do you want to do with this stuff?" She was holding a large cardboard box.

"What is it?" he asks.

"Cameras and film and stuff like that. It was in the closet." She sat the box down on his bed and Richard's breath caught in his throat as he picked up a camera. How many times had he seen Aunt Claire shooting such beautiful shots with this?

"Thanks," he says.

"Don't mention it," she answered as she closed the door behind her.

He waited until he heard her footsteps plodding down the hallway before getting up and digging a bottle of vodka out of his bag.

# CHAPTER TWO

Remi

As the clock struck three o'clock in the morning Remi began to toss and turn in her bed. Her brain was shooting her down a long tunnel, deep into her subconscious. At the end of the tunnel were swirling nightmares full of flashes of gruesome sights. She saw flashes of screaming and blood, shooting guns, fire, and bursts of light in bright shades of red, blue, purple, and white.

Finally, the swirls all turned into one succinct image. A girl crawling out of the fireplace in that creepy downstairs parlor. She had horns coming out of her head, scaly blue skin, hooves for feet, and unnatural black eyes.

"Lucy, no!" a woman's voice screamed as the girl creature began to grin. Then the room erupted into flames.

Remi shot up in her bed, breathing heavily and sweating profusely. She placed her hand on her chest, feeling her heart beating erratically beneath her palm. She took deep, slow breaths, trying to slow her heart rate down to a less dangerous level. Finally, after a minute, her heartbeat was normal, but she was still covered in sweat, her bed sheets sticking to her skin. The room was like an oven.

She pulled herself up and onto her knees and turned around to open her window. It was stuck. She pulled at it with all her strength, grunting with the effort it took but it still held tight.

"*Is the damn thing nailed shut?*" she thought to herself.

Finally, she gave up on the window and sunk back down onto the bed. She pulled her pajama bottoms off and tossed them aside.

When she looked up, straight ahead of her she thought she saw a shadow for a split second. She shook her head. *"Your eyes are playing tricks on you,"* she thought. *"Unfamiliar house. Get it together."*

But the shadow moved closer and now she knew something was really there. Her eyes fixed on the shadow, unblinking. It moved towards her slowly, coming out of the shadows and she could see that it was a woman. A tall woman with blonde, curly hair and grotesque burns covering the right side of her face, trailing down her neck and disappearing under her shirt. Her right eye was burned shut.

Remi's chest felt tight, and her heart beat erratically. She kept eye contact with the woman for what seemed like forever.

The more time that passed the more unsettled she felt. This woman stared at her, unblinking. She cocked her head to one side and Remi's fight or flight came crashing to the forefront. She jerked her body back until she hit the headboard.

She was about to make a dash for the door when the woman's mouth twisted up in a ferocious grin and she lunged for Remi.

Remi heard a terrified scream seconds before realizing it was coming from her own mouth.

## Richard

Richard was looking through a photography textbook down in Aunt Claire's darkroom, trying to figure out how to develop the film, when he heard the shrill screams coming from upstairs. He dropped the manual and darted towards the stairs, flying up them, and up around the grand staircase to the second floor.

Remi. The screams were coming from Remi's room. Terror filled his chest at the shrill tone, and he picked up his speed. He ran down the hall and saw that Rod and Jamie were already inside trying to calm her down and console her.

The light was on now and the bedcovers were crumpled on the floor. Remi was thrashing in the bed with Jamie's arms wrapped around her, sobbing uncontrollably.

"Remi, what happened?" Richard asked breathlessly. He ran to the bed and tried to reach for her, but she screamed out, "Don't touch me! Don't touch me!"

A momentary sting of rejection filled him, and he stepped back slightly.

"Okay. I won't touch you," he said in the gentlest voice he could muster and held up his hands to show her he meant no harm. "Can you tell me what happened?"

She didn't answer, just continued to shake and cry in Jamie's arms.

"I need to know, Remi. What happened? Are you hurt?"

She still sobbed uncontrollably but shook her head no. She stopped thrashing but lay trembling in Jamie's arms. Jamie looked at him with wide eyes that reminded him of a doe caught in headlights. He recognized the question in those eyes because he felt it himself. This was Remi acting so erratically. *Their* Remi. She was normally the composed one of the group, the one who had her shit together when it seemed like the world was ending. What could have possibly happened to make her lose her cool like this?

"What happened? Was it a person?"

"W—woman!" She pointed a finger towards the corner and then suddenly launched herself towards him, throwing her arms around his neck. He instinctively felt arousal at the feel of the half-naked woman wrapped around him, then disgust as she was clearly mid crisis.

He pulled her close to him, trying to still her trembling and simultaneously turned his head towards the corner she'd pointed at. There was nothing there. He was disappointed but managed to keep that out of his tone as he comforted her with soft proclamations of safety.

"Umm...Dude?" Rod said, turning to Richard, his face ashen.

"What?"

Rod pointed down to the floor where there were footsteps on the hardwood made of ash.

No one got much sleep for the rest of the night. Remi eventually calmed down, but she hadn't wanted to discuss whatever she'd seen. Richard couldn't stop thinking about the ashy footsteps. Could it mean fire? Someone in his family, maybe? But if it were one of them, Remi wouldn't have been so scared. Would she?

Once daylight broke, Richard headed outside to further survey the work to be done. He was examining the front columns when he heard a familiar voice behind him.

"Ghosts and demons, stay away," said the gruff voice.

Richard turned around and grinned when he saw Brad Morse. "Don't push us, we won't play," he continued.

"If you insist on torment, well,"

"We'll cast you down to the bowels of Hell."

Brad laughed, smiling broadly. "Good to see you, Richie." Brad didn't look any different from how Richard remembered him. He was dressed like an old cowboy, complete with hat, faded denim jeans, and white t-shirt.

"You too, man," he allowed the short laugh and looked back as he pulled away. "It's Richard now."

"Richard?!" Brad guffawed. "That's an old man's name."

"Well, I'm no little boy either," he laughed.

"Holy shit, you grew up," Brad let out in his gruff voice. "I wasn't sure I'd ever see you again."

"Me either," Richard admitted. "I just found out I inherited it a couple of months ago. Took a little bit to plan to come back."

Brad nodded. "I knew it was put in a trust and it's been vacant ever since y'all lived here. When I started hearing talk in town about utilities getting turned on, I figured it was you. Is Callie with you?"

Richard paused and his smile faltered. "No... she passed."

"What?" Brad let out in shock. "How?"

"She… she swallowed a full bottle of sleeping pills."

"God, Richard. I'm so sorry."

"She never found a way to deal with what happened here. She talked about it in therapy several times and kept getting locked in a psych ward. It didn't help that we really weren't treated well by our family."

Brad nodded grimly with understanding. "Your dad's side?"

"Yeah. They never approved of his marriage to Mom and were even more appalled when they started having kids."

"I can't believe I'm actually saying this, but why the hell didn't he just let you go to foster care?"

Richard shrugged. "I never understood that, honestly. I know a judge placed us with him and as far as I know, he never fought it. He made a comment once about us being the last thing he had of his brother, but he just couldn't look at us and not see Mom. That it made him sick."

Brad snarled. "Disgusting. I'd like to knock his block off."

"Yeah, well. It was a no brainer when I found out I inherited Blackwood. Got me out of there."

"He must have been a royal prick if you'd rather come back here than be with him."

"Well, that wasn't the only reason," Richard sighed. "Come on in. Let me get you some coffee."

Richard led Brad into the house and back towards the kitchen. He didn't see Brad looking around in disgust at the graffitied walls.

Once they got into the kitchen, they both took a seat at the island and Richard poured a cup for Brad.

"Claire must be spinning in her grave at the sight of this place. She worked so hard to restore it and here it is looking damn near as bad as when she got it," Brad mused.

"Yeah, you're probably right about that," Richard absently ran his fingers along the rim of his mug.

"Well, we'll get it fixed up again. For her. I'm more than glad to help you."

"Thanks, but I'll be honest with you. I will, of course, make it habitable, but I'm not going to any great lengths to fix it up. Not like she did. That isn't the goal here."

"Then what is the goal?"

"To find out what happened."

"There was a fire, Richard."

"You and I both know there's more to it than that."

There was silence for a moment, then Richard continued. "Were you there that night?"

Brad nodded. "Morning, actually. It was around two am. Your dad called me and said Bailey was lost in the woods running from Margaret. He asked me to get the crew together. He was so panicked. Somehow, I managed to get everyone, and we were out combing the woods. I smelled the smoke before I saw it. By the time we were able to get out of the woods it had already burned itself out. It was the most bizarre thing I've ever seen. We didn't go in. I just called the fire department. They said the fire hadn't spread beyond the parlor but that there were...*bodies*...inside. My heart dropped."

"So, you don't know what caused the fire?"

"They said it was faulty wiring, but I know that was a crock of shit. I wired that place myself. I'm also the one that came out and checked it when they began getting it ready for you, to make sure it still met code and was safe. Not a goddamn thing wrong with the wiring."

"I never bought it either. Something happened. I can feel it in my bones. Bailey wasn't even supposed to be there. She was supposed to be in that psych hospital."

"Your mom broke her out the day before."

Richard looked at him, surprised.

"Yeah, she called me and asked me to meet her at my grandmother's nursing home. Bailey was with her, and she was being extremely covert about it. I knew she hadn't gone through the proper channels to get her out. She wanted to talk to my grandmother about Bailey's episode, the attack on Callie, and about these blue crackles of electricity that were shooting out of Bailey's fingers. I don't know what happened after that. I had to go back to the hospital for my daughter. Caroline had been in a bad state. I didn't hear anything else until your dad called me at 2 am and it was pure chaos over here."

"God, I'm sorry. I can't believe it's taken me so long to ask," Richard's voice dropped low and became soft. "Caroline, is she…"

Brad dropped his chin gravely. "Three days after the fire here."

"I'm so sorry, Brad."

"It's okay. Really. She's in a better place now. That poor baby was suffering so badly. As much as I miss her, I was also relieved that she wasn't in pain anymore."

"I understand that. That's how I feel about Callie. Sometimes I get so mad at her for what she did, but other times I totally get it. She was tortured. She'd been through so much. And no one ever believed her except for me. But I was a little kid too. What was my word worth? At least no one can hurt her ever again."

There was a moment of silence and Richard saw the look of utter sympathy and kindness in Brad's eyes. He couldn't believe he was in the same room as someone who'd witnessed the same things. That for once someone would *believe* him.

"So..." There was a reluctance in Brad's voice as he asked the dreaded question. "How was your first night?"

"Bizarre," Richard snorted. "Seeing all our things again, the same but different all at once; aged and destroyed. It about broke my heart."

"And what about—" Brad's voice broke before he could say what they both knew he meant. "The other thing?"

Richard sighed. "It was quiet for me. The air is heavy. It always was. Something happened to my friend, Remi though. She woke up screaming and was hysterical when we went to her. She wouldn't talk about what happened but there were ashy footsteps on her floor. The only thing we got out of her was one word. Woman."

"Already?" Brad furrowed his brow. "I would have thought something would've happened with you."

"Nope."

"Have you been out to the cottage yet?"

Richard's heart tanked. The cottage that Brad was talking about was the building that was behind the manor house at the edge of the property. It once served as servant's quarters and at some point, was converted into a three-bedroom apartment. It was used as a storage shed before Aunt Claire bought the place. When an unexplained fire destroyed his family home, Aunt Claire graciously offered to let them move in. His mother didn't want to live in the manor house, so they'd compromised, and his family set up in the cottage.

"Not yet," he admitted, feeling as though he were a small child once again. "I almost did, but I couldn't…"

"Go alone?" Brad asked gently.

Richard nodded.

"Want me to go with you?"

Again, Richard nodded, and the men headed out the kitchen door and walked towards the cottage. The grounds were overgrown but not as badly as he remembered. Still, stickers and thorns bit into his calves, and he hissed through his teeth at the sting of the pain but just kept pushing.

When they approached the cottage, it looked remarkably okay from the outside. It needed paint and there were a few shingles missing on the roof, but the condition appeared to be better than the main house.

When they approached the door, Richard twisted the knob on instinct and was surprised when it turned easily and swung inward. It hadn't even been locked.

He took a step into the living room and the air left his body. It was exactly as he remembered it. The couch was on the wall with his mother's favorite blanket curled up on the end as though she'd just gotten up and left the room for a quick minute. The remote still sat on the coffee table pointed at the TV. Their family photos still adorned the walls, untouched.

He turned toward the kitchen. There were still dishes in the drainboard next to the sink. There was no musty odor, in fact, he would later swear that he could smell the cleaner that his mother favored. It was like standing in a time vortex and time held still for this moment. The moment when he would finally come home. He opened the refrigerator and was surprised to find it empty.

"I... uh... I came and emptied it out and the trash too right after everything happened," Brad said quietly. "I hope you don't mind. Didn't seem right to leave it there to rot."

"No, it's fine," Richard closed the door and turned towards the hallway that led to their bedrooms and the bathroom. He stepped into his old bedroom. His bed was still a wad of unmade covers and sheets. He'd been very bad about making his bed back then, a habit his uncle knocked out of him. His mother, however, had been lenient about it. She'd told him she didn't care how his bed looked as long as the mess didn't trickle out to the rest of the house.

He stuck his head into the bedroom that had belonged to his sisters. Twin beds on opposite walls, a table between them, Callie's toy box at the foot of her bed, a dresser in the corner. He didn't like the energy in here, which surprised him. It was dark and heavy, which he didn't remember from childhood. The manor house is what always scared him; the cottage had always been a safe haven where he'd felt nothing but peace.

Finally, he stepped into his parents' bedroom. It was exactly as he would have expected to see it, the bed neatly made, a laundry basket in the corner full of clothes waiting to be washed. He was about to step out when he spotted something on the bed he'd almost missed. He approached it and was astonished to see a very old leather-bound book. He sat down on the bed and gently picked it up. He could feel the material cracking underneath his touch, and he heard the pages crackle as he gently opened the cover. The pages were yellowed, and the writing was so faded it was almost illegible. One thing was certain. This was not his mother's diary.

"Maybe you want to leave that alone," Brad said gently as he approached with caution.

"Why?"

"Well, your mama got real obsessed with that there book before she died. It was Josie's. She lived and worked in the manor house during the Civil War."

"Are you saying there is something in here that killed my mom?"

"I don't know. I never read it. I just know she got obsessed with it. Was always talking about things she would find. Something about it scared me. Claire never said anything, but I could tell she didn't like it either."

"It might give me answers."

Brad sighed and sat down on the bed next to Richard. "Look, it's your choice. I can't make you not read it. But hear this, everything in that book is a hundred and fifty years old. There may well be answers to the house in there but there aren't answers to your family. Fear is what will get you in the end. It always does. Fear is a fickle, fickle bitch and it gets into your bones and your thoughts, and it rots everything away 'til there's nothing else left. Your mama was terrified of Blackwood Manor, and she was obsessed with the book. I don't want to see it happen to you."

"Then give me something!" Richard suddenly shouted. "Give me a fucking answer! I know you know something I don't, Brad. You were here. I'm not a child anymore. I can take it. Don't give me a bunch of bullshit about fear if you can't give me a reason."

Brad looked at him hard, and for a moment Richard thought he wasn't going to say anything, but finally he drew in a long breath and answered him. "Alright. I don't know everything, so I don't have all the answers. That book belonged to a slave named Josie. She detailed her years of service to the family, the house, and her secret relationship with Margaret Blackwood."

Margaret Blackwood. This was the second time Brad mentioned her name and it seemed familiar, but Richard couldn't put his finger on how.

"I feel like I've heard that name."

"I'm sure you did. She was at the height of the investigation that Claire and your mama were doing. She was the mistress of the house during the Civil War. She was once warm and giving but grew dark and cruel. Many thought it was the house that made her that way, but Claire and your mama came to believe it was something that happened to her.

"Me, I'm somewhere in the middle. Margaret went through a tragedy no woman should have to experience, especially at that point in time, and it ate her up. I think the house latched on to that and fed on it. It fed on that fear, on that anger, and chewed her up 'til she couldn't remember love anymore."

"So, you believe the house is haunted?"

"Son, there ain't no believing when you see it with your own two eyes. The stuff I saw in this house, the stuff others would tell me they saw...there are no earthly explanations for those things, and I have a hard time believing one woman's tragedy is enough to spoil the land."

"The land?"

"My grandma was a Seer, God rest her soul, and she worked in Blackwood for a while for the owners before Claire. She told me things. Arms sticking right up out of the ground out back. Hundreds of them. Dark auras on anyone who was here too long. She told me after everything was all said and done, she knew your mama was marked for death when she met her, but Claire surprised her. She really thought Claire could put an end to things. We all thought that. But we were wrong."

"So how can you be here and be so calm knowing all that?"

Ashley Bundy

"Because I don't let the fear in," Brad put his hands on Richard's shoulders and looked deep into his eyes. "I leave them be. Just because they're dead doesn't mean they don't leave a mark, and it don't mean they won't be defensive if we stir up their bad feelings. That's why I strongly believe you should leave that book alone. The less you acknowledge Margaret, the safer you'll be."

"The others?"

Brad thought about this carefully for a moment. "I think the others are fine. For the most part. Most of them are just stuck, but..."

"But?"

"But...I don't think I would trust it enough to test the theory. Bad things still happened that involved other spirits. I couldn't tell you how much of it was intentional. I don't have the gifts my grandmother had."

"But my *parents,*" Richard looked at Brad, his eyes full of desperate hope. "What if I see *them*?"

"Richard," Brad sighed. "I know your parents were good people, and I know they loved you. But it's been ten years. This house changes people. Even if they are still here—and keep in mind I can't tell you if they are— even if they are still here, they'll be...different. Not what you remember. It probably isn't worth it, honestly."

"But the diary is Josie's," Richard insisted. "If Margaret is the danger..."

"Josie was Margaret's lover," Brad sighed. "So, it's probably a safe bet you should stay clear of her too."

Richard's face broke. The tough guy image he tried so hard to maintain faded away and left in its place was the scared, broken expression of a child. "I just need answers. I don't even want to live here. There are too many bad memories. But I have to know. I *need* to know. It's my whole family, Brad. Literally everyone. Callie may not have physically died here, but she was haunted. This house killed her as much as it did them."

The tears fell before he could stop them. Brad put an arm around him and pulled him into his chest just as he would to console a small child. Neither of them knew how long they sat like that, crying in silence over a century's old diary.

# CHAPTER THREE

"The old guy sounds like he has a few screws loose to me," Rod said as he leaned back to allow the waitress to put his plate down in front of him. The four friends had agreed to go into town for dinner at a Mexican restaurant with excellent reviews online.

"No, Brad's great. He probably knows more than anyone. I think he just doesn't want me to meet the same fate so many other people have there."

"Yeah, but telling you to ignore your parents when finding out what happened is the whole reason you came back to Blackwood? That's fucked."

Remi averted her eyes and dipped a chip into the bowl of salsa, quickly shoving the whole thing into her mouth.

The waitress paused as she set Jamie's plate down in front of her, not pulling her hand back from the plate.

Jamie looked at her hand and then up at the girl who was completely drained of color. "Umm...is there a problem?"

The girl snapped back to herself and pulled her hand away, straightening her spine up. "No, I'm sorry. I was just surprised. Did you say Blackwood? As in Blackwood Manor?"

"Yeah," Richard nodded. "Do you know something about it?"

"Not me, personally," she shook her head and absently ran her fingers through her hair. "It's been vacant forever. I know someone briefly lived there a few years ago…"

"Ten years ago," Richard confirmed. "That was my family. There was a fire, and they died. I wasn't home. I inherited it."

"So, you've moved back?"

He nodded, but he was growing irritated by this interrogation, the butting in on a personal conversation.

"It sounds like you're talking about the rumored spirits," she persisted.

"Not rumored," he said it a little more harshly than he intended but he wanted her to just go away.

"I'm sorry. I'm not trying to be nosy. I think I can help you. My roommate has connections to the property, and she's a little psychic. I figure if you believe in the ghosts, you'd probably believe in that too."

Remi's eyes widened with anxiety as she quickly glanced from the waitress to Richard.

"What kind of connections?" Richard's irritation was gone, and he was now filled with curiosity.

"Well, I don't think she's ever been there, but her family either lived there or worked there at some point in time. She's brought it up before."

"Great, I'd love to talk to her."

The waitress looked up. "I have to go. My manager is giving me the evil eye. I'll write my number on your receipt later and we can talk about it then."

She then scurried off.

Remi immediately started in. "Richard, this is a horrible idea. Brad told you not to acknowledge them or you'll make it worse. You want to bring in a psychic?"

"I just want to find out what happened to my family, Remi," Richard told her gently.

"We can do that without being confrontational with spirits." she hissed. "Go through their belongings, talk to people that were here at the time."

"Hold up," Jamie held up her hand to silence her friend. "Richard isn't saying anything about being confrontational. The waitress says the girl's family has experience with the land, so she probably knows something. Her having psychic powers doesn't have anything to do with it. He just wants to talk to her. Her abilities don't have anything to do with it."

"Actually, her being psychic is a big reason why I want to talk to her."

"What?" Jamie let out in shock.

"Dude—" Rod began.

"Let me explain," he raised his voice slightly. "Brad's grandmother was a Seer, and she worked with my family a lot back then...helped them out. She's dead now so I can't go to her for help. But I figure it may be a good idea to have someone who can do something similar. My family learned a lot thanks to her. Maybe this girl can help me the same way."

"Has it escaped your attention," Remi hissed through clenched teeth, "that she helped your family and now they're *dead?*"

"That didn't have anything to do with Sadie."

"*How do you know that?*" there were tears in her eyes.

"Look," Richard gave out an annoyed grunt, "you guys knew this was a majorly haunted house with a dark history when you agreed to move here with me. I gave you an opportunity for an out when we arrived and it was you, Remi, who said you weren't going anywhere. Did you really expect me to do nothing?"

"To be fair, I was expecting there to be more activity from the way you talked about it," Rod said. "I didn't experience anything. No sounds, no funky smells, nothing."

"Me neither," Jamie nodded in agreement. "It doesn't seem that bad. It might be okay. Maybe it was so terrifying to you because you were so little."

"I did! I experienced something horrifying last night! Or did you guys forget that?" Remi cried.

"To be fair, you didn't exactly tell us what happened," Jamie shrugged.

"Maybe it's what Brad was saying," Richard said. "If the house feeds on fear, maybe you experienced something because you're afraid."

"Oh, and you're not?"

"No," he growled. "I'm fucking angry."

"Well, will you do me a favor and at least call her *away* from the house?"

"Fine," Richard snapped and angrily stabbed his fork into his enchiladas.

Later that night Richard sat perched on his old bed out in the cottage staring down at his receipt from dinner. True to her word, the waitress scribbled her number on the bottom. "Okay, time for some answers," he mumbled to himself as he punched the number into his cell phone.

It rang briefly before being answered by a breathy, "Hello?" Someone was just doing some intense cardio.

"Hi, is this Dani?"

"No," the breathy voice answered.

"Oh, umm... my waitress at Alessandro's gave me this number tonight."

"Dani is my roommate."

"Oh, I'm sorry, she led me to believe she was giving me her number. She said her roommate...I'm guessing you... may be able to help me."

"Yeah, she does that," the woman chuckled. "I'm Natalie. So, what is it this time? Need a fortune read? Missing child you need help finding?"

"You do that?" Richard asked in surprise.

"I hate the fortune teller thing, but I have been known to save a child or two from the woods."

"Wow. Well, I own Blackwood Manor now and Dani said you have some sort of connection to the property so I was hoping we could work together."

There was silence on the other line, and Richard thought for a moment he'd lost her. Finally, she spoke again.

"My advice is to run as far away as you can and never look back."

"I'm afraid that's not an option. I lived here as a child with my family, and everyone was killed in a fire. They said it was the wiring, but I know better. I need to know what happened."

"Wow, you're one of the family members that lived there ten years ago."

"Yeah, only my little sister and I made it out alive and she...well, let's say it's just me now."

"Jeez, I'm sorry."

"I don't need your pity, no offense. I need your help. Surely you understand why. Dani said you know things. Will you help me, Natalie? Please?"

She sighed. "I don't know a lot of details. My family worked there for generations. In fact, my dad was a part of the crew ten years ago. I overheard things here and there over the years, but the conversations were always shushed as soon as they realized I was listening. I was never allowed to set foot on the property."

"What kinds of things did you overhear?"

"Well, I know that the property attracts the gifted. It sucks in those with gifts and rejects normals. Those are typically the people who run out screaming in the middle of the night or after only a few hours.

"I know it stands vacant for years at a time and when it does get occupants, no one lasts long. I know there have been endless tragedies on the property. I know there is a mass graveyard near the woods. I know for sure of one evil spirit but judging by the track record, I'd say there's more."

"So, is it a good thing or a bad thing I haven't experienced anything yet?"

"Nothing? It just feels like a normal house to you?"

"Not exactly." Richard leaned back against the pillows. "The air feels heavy in certain areas, like it's kind of hard to breathe. I haven't seen anything, but I swear when I got here, I heard voices in my head telling me to leave. I could have imagined that though. But my friend Remi said she was attacked last night. No one else experienced anything."

"Interesting," there was a slight cadence to her voice.

"What?"

"It sounds to me like the spirits are present. That's what you're feeling. But they are choosing to *not* communicate with you."

Richard's heart sunk. If what Natalie was saying was true, his family was consciously ignoring him. "Why would that happen?"

"I don't know," she said. "I've never experienced that before. It is interesting, though, that a location that is as notorious as Blackwood is being deliberately docile. What about when you were a child?"

"Well, my mom was pissed when my aunt bought the place. Us kids were excited because we knew the stories, and anything related to ghosts was so cool. I'm sure you know what I'm talking about. I personally had a bad experience shortly after she moved in that caused friction between everyone for a while."

"What was the experience?"

"You know, I barely remember it. I remember it had something to do with a servant's staircase just off the kitchen. I remember going into it and the darkness but then...nothing. The next spot in my memory is my mom and Aunt Claire at each other's throats. They argued a lot over whether I was attacked or simply got locked in."

"We need to unlock that memory. It's almost impossible to know how to proceed without knowing if it was violent or not. Do you know if anything else violent happened?"

"Well, the adults didn't tell us too much. My family's home burned down in a fire, and we ended up in the cottage behind Blackwood. My older sister had a seance with her friends and something went wrong. She was *never* the same, but she never told me what happened. And later she was sent to a mental institution for attacking my little sister."

"Attacking her?"

"Yeah, but I didn't know that until later. Mom just said Bailey was sick and had to go away for a while. Later, my little sister told me that Bailey came at her with a knife, but she was different. She couldn't really explain to me how. She was only three at the time."

"Sounds like possession," Natalie sounded confused.

"Is that unusual?"

"Depends. I was always told there were plenty of angry spirits at Blackwood, but no actual demons. Which does make possession strange. You said your family home was burned down, which forced you onto the property...was this before or after your sister's seance?"

"After. Right after, actually. It was the same night."

"Okay, here's what we need to do. We need to find out exactly what happened at the seance. I need you to try to contact your sister's friends who were there. We need to unlock your memory. Sometimes revisiting the location helps. I would say go back to that staircase and see if anything at all comes back to you.

"I'll also need to investigate. My gift works through touch, so I'll need to come to the property. Was there ever a formal investigation? Do you know?"

"Well, I don't know if it would be considered an investigation, but I know my aunt had a medium walkthrough at some point. I think they ended up not using her because she was too 'commercial', and they didn't want a media circus."

"Probably Nadine Lewis. We'll need to contact her as well. It'll take me a little time to compile a team. In the meantime, see to the tasks I've laid out for you." She hung up without saying goodbye.

Richard sighed as he put down the phone and reached for the bottle of vodka stuffed under the pillow.

## CHAPTER FOUR

Richard was down in Aunt Claire's dark room later that night, going through a box of her things. This room was once a cellar before she'd converted it. He picked up her old camera, blew the dust off it, and smiled to himself as he lovingly ran his hands over its surface. He remembered that she always had it with her and was lining up brilliant shots. It was rare to see her without a camera in her hands. Until Blackwood Manor began to eat her.

She'd still taken shots at first, shooting everything in sight in typical Claire style. Slowly, as she'd become more and more invested in the house and its mysteries, she'd stopped carrying her camera completely. As a child, he thought nothing of it, but now, as an adult, he realized how completely bizarre and out of character that really was. Not only was it strange in general, but she was a professional photographer. How was she even getting away with it? Had she lost her job? He tried to think back, but he simply couldn't remember if anyone mentioned it.

Still, she'd used it, however briefly, since moving into the house. This room *had* been used as a darkroom. But where were the photographs? There weren't any in the room that he could see, and they hadn't been in her old bedroom either.

He took another look into the box of things from her room. Her laptop was at the bottom. Luckily, the charger was there as well. He removed them, along with a notepad, and lined them along the bench, preparing to take notes. He plugged the laptop in, patiently waited for it to boot up, and prayed that it wasn't password protected.

He was able to easily log onto the computer once it started up and he navigated to her email first. He scrolled through and saw plenty of communications with a magazine editor. That must have been the one she'd worked for. He jotted down the name and kept scrolling. There were emails to two different email addresses with the same woman's name. Jennifer Carter. He wrote down her name as well as the email addresses. One appeared to be business and the other personal.

The business one was full of technical talk he learned quickly were about the magazine. He then navigated to the personal. The first one he read caught his eye immediately.

*C: What do I do about Emma? She hates me. She blames me for buying the house with its history and the stories. But it's just a house. Houses don't have feelings of hatred. I'm sure horrible things happened here...it's expected in a building this old. I just want things to go back to normal.*

*J: This is Emma we're talking about. She doesn't hate you. She loves you. She's just scared something is going to happen. And the statistics are against you. Plus, Richie got stuck in the staircase. You can't blame her for being protective. Just give her a little space and she'll cool down.*

*C: I hate that he got hurt! I can't believe she doesn't think more of me than that. He had a panic attack. And that is a spooky old staircase, so I don't blame him. But I just don't understand how that turned into me being selfish and irresponsible.*

Richard's blood ran cold. So, he *had* been hurt in the staircase. But to what extent? What *happened?*

Ashley Bundy

His vision flooded with flashes of intense darkness and moving shadows, the slightest swish of white.

No, he stood up suddenly, jolting himself from the memory. He didn't want to think about it anymore. He closed the laptop and picked up his notes, carrying them upstairs with him, hoping to tuck the day away with the sweet release of sleep.

## CHAPTER FIVE

Richard was awoken by a bloodcurdling scream, and he shot to attention. He didn't know what time it was...the room was flooded with soft light from the big windows. He jumped from the bed and ran out into the hallway.

Jamie stood on the landing with a hand over her chest taking slow, deliberate breaths.

"What, what is it?" he asked her as he ran up to her.

She pointed towards something sitting in the shadows. "I'm such an idiot," she said. "The light hit it just right and all I saw was the eyes."

He approached the space she was pointing to and saw what she was talking about. Sitting against the wall, almost completely veiled in shadows, was an oil painting of a little girl. She was blonde, had piercing blue eyes, and a bored expression on her face. Richard couldn't explain exactly what made him uneasy, but it seemed for a moment as if this child were staring directly into his soul. Suddenly, he felt like he was being watched from every angle.

A memory flooded his mind of his mom and Aunt Claire discussing oil paintings. He remembered them mentioning that the little girl in particular would always move around, but no one ever seemed to know how she got to this location or that. They'd discussed it openly, but he didn't think he'd ever seen it before. Until now.

"Well, there you are," he muttered, running his hand along the frame.

"What was that?" Jamie asked, snapping him out of his funk.

"Nothing," he smiled back at her. "I just remember hearing about a little girl painting, but I never saw it with my own eyes."

"You won't tell Rod I freaked out, will you?" she blushed slightly. "He'd never let me hear the end of it."

"Of course not," Richard straightened up and walked over to her to put a comforting hand on her shoulder. "It's our secret."

She gave him a grateful smile.

"Where is he anyway?"

"He said he was going for a run."

Richard briefly furrowed his eyebrows. A run. That was unlike Rod.

"Remi already left for the day?"

She nodded. "I get the feeling she won't be hanging around much."

"Did she have an okay night?"

"Nothing happened if that's what you mean. She had a hard time sleeping though. I think she was scared that whatever she saw the night before was going to come back. She came and woke me up and asked me to stay with her."

Richard looked at her, aghast. "You spent the night in her room?"

"Not the whole night," Jamie answered. "She came and got me around two in the morning. Begged. Said she couldn't sleep by herself, and she had an early class and needed to get some sleep. I told her it was just for the night. She fell asleep quick after I set up camp."

"I wouldn't have thought that one little experience would upset her so bad. I mean, maybe if she was unaware but I did warn you guys."

"I think she's a little sensitive."

"What like a Seer, psychic?"

"No, she's never said anything to me to indicate that. But she always seems to know when people are in pain or angry and it affects her. Remember how she cried for a week when Danielle Lawson's grandma died? She wasn't friends with Danielle, and she never met her grandma. Maybe she's picking up on all the sorrow from the spirits here, and she just didn't expect to."

"It's a theory. I never thought of that. I'm in a tough position, you know. I came here for answers, and I was upfront with you guys about everything, and she chose to come. I feel bad that she's scared, but I don't think I should have to give up on my goal when she knew what she was getting into. She was so angry at the thought of me investigating."

"I don't think she wants you to give up. She just doesn't want to interact with ghosts."

"I called the psychic."

"Oh," Jamie whistled. "She's not going to like that."

"No. She says we need an investigation. She's putting together a team."

"You better butter Remi the hell up before you tell her that."

"Do you think I should give her money to go back?"

"I think if you do that, you can kiss your friendship goodbye. She will see it as the ultimate insult and that you don't want her around."

"That's not true!" Richard ran his hands through his hair and took a minute to calm his tone. "I don't *want* Remi to leave. I love her. I just don't want to give up doing what I need to do to get answers, and I don't want her to be uncomfortable."

"You guys need to sit down and talk and see if you can find a compromise. I'm not the person you need to be telling this to...no offense."

"No, you're right," Richard thanked Jamie and went back to his bedroom to grab his phone. He shot Remi a text message, *"Hey, can I take you for lunch? I think we need to talk."*

She responded back quickly; *"I have a break in classes between 1 and 3."*

He told her he'd pick her up at one and then he began constructing emails to send in the meantime.

## CHAPTER SIX

Richard picked Remi up at one o'clock in the student union parking lot. He immediately felt bad for their argument the night before because he could see she wasn't doing well.

Her hair was frizzy and pulled back into a messy bun. There were dark circles under her eyes and smudged eye liner from makeup she never took off. She was wearing baggy sweats and flip-flops.

This was not the Remi he knew. She wasn't vain but she did take great pride in her appearance. She wasn't a shopper like a lot of girls he knew, but she still always looked her best. She said it was because she always needed to have her best leg forward and always appear professional.

The girl beside him was nearly unrecognizable from what she'd been only two days before.

He didn't say anything yet, not wanting to antagonize her before he had a chance to present his case. He drove them to a small diner a couple of blocks away from the school, and he waited until they'd placed their orders before attempting to break the ice.

"So, rough night?" he asked gently.

She shot him a look so sharp that he could practically feel the daggers piercing him. "Is that a polite way of telling me I look like shit?"

"No," he said, refusing to back away from her gaze. "It's a way of telling you I'm worried about you."

"You weren't worried yesterday."

"No, I guess I wasn't," he looked down as he fiddled with his napkin. It was like he was a toddler being scolded for being caught with his hand in the cookie jar. "I was an asshole. I was so caught up in my own thing that I didn't see you were suffering. I'm sorry."

The ice seemed to melt in her eyes a little, but she still sat in a defensive stance. "So, you're going to leave the ghosts alone?"

He held out his hands in a peaceful gesture. "I don't think I can, Remi."

She huffed, crossed her arms over her chest, and looked toward the window.

"Your friendship means the world to me. I need you to know that. But my childhood, Remi, was messed up. Callie and I were stuck with that shithead for way too long and he made our lives a living hell. We weren't allowed to mention our mother's name, and any pictures were destroyed. Basically, all I have left of them is here."

Richard's voice cracked, and he took a sip of water to soothe it. He wasn't used to being so vulnerable. "I remember little things about the house but not much. I was young and a lot of details were kept from me. This is where everything changed, it's where my life was forced down this hectic path that I didn't want. I need to know why, Remi. I need to know why what happened to me happened. I need to know why my family disappeared in a puff of smoke. I need to know why Callie died. I can't ever know who I really am until I know the truth."

Remi uncrossed her arms and leaned in against the table. "I'm scared, Richard."

"Did something else happen?"

She shook her head. "No... well, I don't know. I wasn't attacked again. But I keep hearing giggling in the hallway upstairs and I couldn't sleep last night. I didn't *see anything*, but my body was on alert. I couldn't shake the feeling that something awful would happen if I passed out. I had to get Jamie to come in with me."

She reached forward and grabbed his hand, squeezing it tight. "I know you feel like I want you to abandon hope of getting answers. I don't. I just don't want to do something to piss them off by nosing around too much. What happened that night...I thought I was about to die. I saw my life flash before my eyes and I thought, 'this is it.' It wasn't until I calmed down later that I realized that thing didn't leave a mark on me. How? How is that even possible? How could I feel so completely *done* and not have a single scratch? I honestly feel like it was a warning. 'Don't let there be a next time.'"

"Did it say that?"

"No," she let out a frustrated squeak. "It was more intuitive. I don't know how to explain it. That thing could have hurt me if it wanted to. Hell, it *should* have. It didn't want to hurt me. It wanted me scared. It got its wish."

He sighed. "Knowing Blackwood, it probably was a warning. But I don't see that we have any other choice. How can we find answers if we don't try to get to the bottom of everything they were doing? They were looking into the ghosts and the house's history, so I think we have to too."

"How about going through their things? Maybe they wrote something down that we can read on the sly. You know, don't bring it up out loud and acknowledge it. That guy Brad said to leave it alone."

"He also said don't let the fear in. Maybe that has something to do with it." He squeezed her hand and looked deep into her face. She bit her lip as if she were contemplating something impossible.

The anguish in her eyes killed him. He'd do anything to relieve it. Anything as long as he could still get his answers.

"You should know I called the psychic. The one that's roommates with the waitress from last night."

Her eyes went wide, and she opened her mouth as if to protest what he'd just told her.

"I promised I wouldn't call from inside the house, and I didn't. But I did call. Based on what I told her, she thinks we need an investigation."

"Of course, she wants an investigation!" Remi pulled her hand free. "That's what they do. It's all about self-promotion."

"No, I don't think so. She didn't ask for money or any other sort of payment. She just seemed...intrigued."

He went into detail about everything he'd discussed with Natalie the night before. By the end, Remi was invested.

"So, she has to come do an investigation because what you experienced back then and what is happening now doesn't add up?"

"Exactly. She's confused, and she can't tell me what to do without knowing what we're up against. She said she has to be there, and she's compiling a team. She didn't say exactly what that means, but I would assume equipment and stuff like that."

"I'm also trying to follow up some on Aunt Claire and some emails I found on her computer. The cellar was her dark room, but I can't find any pictures, and I find that extremely weird."

Richard felt better after his lunch with Remi. At least now he knew she didn't hate him and understanding her fear made him more willing to compromise. He was sure she understood his side a little better too and that was comforting.

When he returned to the house, he logged onto the laptop to check his emails. He found one almost immediately from the magazine.

*Dear Mr. Price,*

*Thank you for your inquiry. I'm afraid I'm unable to divulge any information other than confirming that both Claire Donahue and Jennifer Carter were employed in 2009. Releasing any other information is strictly prohibited, though I do sympathize with your case and wish you the best of luck.*

*You may be able to get back issues of the magazine if you contact our marketing division, though I can't make any promises. I'm not sure how or if that would even help you, but it's an idea.*

*Sincerely,*

*Abigail Wallace*
*Human Resources Manager*

Well, that was a bust. Richard got out his notebook and crossed off the note about contacting the magazine and added that he needed to find Jennifer Carter.

He took a moment to think before a lightbulb went off in his head. Social media. 2009 wasn't prehistoric days.

Ashley Bundy

MemoryBook was a thing then. He navigated to the website and quickly created an account. Once he was logged in, he searched for Jennifer Carter's name. Almost immediately, he grunted out his frustration. There were so many hits on the name, and he had no clue if any of them were the Jennifer Carter he was looking for.

Instead, he typed in Aunt Claire's name and quickly scrolled until he found her picture. Her account was private, but he could still see photos. He scrolled down, not sure what he was looking for, but certain he would know when he found it.

He found a picture dated 2008 of Aunt Claire not looking well at all. She was pale, and her eyes were puffy and swollen. Her face was plastered with a smile that was obviously not genuine. She was seated next to a woman who looked slightly older. The caption read, *Feeling heartbroken. Through the tunnels of darkness, a light waits at the end. Have the patience to find it. I will overcome this. Thanks, Jenny for pushing me toward the light.* The woman she tagged was Jennifer Carter.

He clicked the link to her page and had to bite back surprise at what he was met with. The page was flooded with RIP messages and memorial pictures. Dead. Jennifer Carter was dead. He sat back in his chair and let out a long breath. What was he going to do now?

# CHAPTER SEVEN

Natalie arrived unannounced at seven am the following morning. Richard was in the kitchen, brewing coffee, trying to make up for his lack of sleep, and nursing the hangover that was caused by a bottle of vodka he'd found at the back of a kitchen cupboard. He'd desperately needed a drink and there it was like the answer to a distant prayer. It was even his preferred brand. He'd wondered briefly if it once belonged to his father. He knew alcoholism ran in his family. But he couldn't recall ever seeing his father taking a drink. A loud, persistent banging on the door startled him and made him drop a mug.

He cursed as it shattered and he made his way to the front door, wiping his tired eyes.

"Dude, what the hell is going on?" Rod came down the stairs as Jamie and Remi peeked nervously over the banister.

"I don't know," Richard answered as he reached for the lock.

"Be careful, dude. It's too fucking early for this shit."

Richard unlocked the door and opened it only a couple of inches to peer out.

A surprisingly small woman stood on the opposite side of the door. "Richard?"

He nodded.

"Natalie."

He was surprised. This was not the image he'd pictured while talking to her on the phone. She was maybe five feet tall, and he could snap her like a twig, though he wouldn't dare due to the fire he could sense in her very essence.

Ashley Bundy

Luscious, fiery red hair framed her fragile face and cascaded down her back with wild, unruly curls. Her amber eyes burned him to his core as if she could see right through him.

A vivid tattoo of some kind of snake wrapped around her throat. Her black skeleton tee proclaimed, "Bitches Need Stitches", and ripped jean cut-offs showcased her toned thighs. They seemed to contradict the curves of her small frame.

Definitely not what he'd always pictured when thinking of psychics, mediums, or anyone else who claimed to have a connection with the other side. No flowy gypsy dresses or crystal balls here. He never thought he'd take one look at a psychic and find them utterly hot. He felt the flush to his cheeks as he eyed her body.

Rod wrenched the door the rest of the way open and scowled at Natalie. "It's seven in the fucking morning."

"So it is," she smirked up at him, crossing her arms in front of her.

Richard chose to play devil's advocate and interject. "Umm...Natalie, hi. Did you call? I didn't see a message."

Her eyes twinkled and the corner of her mouth rose up in a teasing grin. "Nah. The energy is better if no one has a chance to...interfere."

He looked behind her to see if he was missing something. "I thought you were compiling a team."

"I did. I always come along first to get a feel for the place. It helps with placing the equipment. Let's get to the first floor, shall we?"

Without waiting for a reply, she breezed right past him into the entryway.

Stunned, Richard closed the door and turned around to find Natalie already striding confidently into the parlor and

Rod crossing his arms over his chest and mouthing "What the fuck?"

Natalie stopped in the parlor and placed her hands on her hips as she surveyed the room. "Something awful happened here."

"Shit, you don't say," Rod muttered, eyeballing the scorch marks on the floor and walls.

If Natalie was aware of his sarcasm, she didn't let on. She placed a hand against the wall. "I sense this room was a central focus in past generations. It makes sense that it would have a level of activity predating the fire."

She turned, and her eyes appeared to be drawn to the corner fireplace as if by a magnet. The stone was crumbling, revealing a hole in the wall behind it. She strode across the room and put her hand to what was left of the mantle.

Richard had wondered about the fireplace. That was relatively recent, he knew. The fireplace was normal when he was a child. So, to see it not only looking burned, as everything else in the room was, but also looking blown apart puzzled him.

"This piece isn't original," Natalie said, her voice near a whisper.

"It's not?" Richard asked as he cautiously approached her.

"No, it was added later. It—" she broke off and stepped back suddenly, yanking her hand away as though it had been burned.

"What?" he asked.

Her face was ashen, and her eyes were wide with shock. It only lasted a few seconds, though it seemed like minutes. Her face neutralized, and she glanced over at him. "A child. A child was buried in the wall."

Richard's blood ran cold, and he stared deep into her eyes. He thought of the newspaper article he'd read stating that the unidentified body of a girl was found in the parlor in addition to those of his family. Is this what it meant?

Rod, not knowing about the article, yelled out, "Cut the shit!" and strode forward, dropped to his knees, and stuck his head in the hole. "Nothing in here but cobwebs."

"I did say 'was'," Natalie retorted, annoyance evident in her voice for the very first time.

"Oh, please. Like anyone is supposed to believe that. How would it even be possible? And what possible reason could there be?"

Natalie continued to look at Richard. "You know I'm right."

Somehow, he did. He trusted her. It's possible she read the same article he did and spun a tale around it, but he didn't believe that to be true. He believed her story. Rod posed good questions, but Richard still believed her, and he couldn't be sure of why. He intended to find out.

Was this why his family died in this very room? Had they discovered the body and a secret that someone didn't want to get out?

He thought again of the diary he'd found in the cottage. He hadn't read it yet, but Brad said his mother found that book and became obsessed with it. Did that lead her to the fireplace? Did the diary hold answers?

He was pulled out of his thoughts by Natalie breezing past him and back out into the hallway. She found her way to the cellar door, again almost as though a magnet were pulling her.

Rod walked up behind him and hissed in his ear. "This is horseshit. She's clearly been here before. Are you seeing this?"

"Look, I thought you supported me getting to the bottom of what happened? Wouldn't that mean you believe in the spiritual realm? If you believe that, why wouldn't you believe in psychics?"

"It's not that I don't believe, man," Rod insisted. "But I also know that there are a lot of kooks in this field. Phonies trying to scam people. It's hard to know who to trust, and I think this is just a little bit convenient."

There was a thump, and both jerked their heads toward the sound. The cellar door was open and there was no Natalie in front of it. It appeared she'd chosen to go down while they were squabbling about whether to believe her.

Richard rushed forward and down the steps. "Natalie! Natalie! Are you okay?"

"I'm fine!" she called out to him.

Richard turned toward Rod and jerked his head toward the steps, beckoning his friend to come down with him.

"Fuck this, man," Rod shook his head and headed toward the dining room. "I can't with this chick."

Richard rolled his eyes and descended the last of the steps and turned to see her with her palm flush against a shelf against the wall.

"What was that noise?"

"What noise?"

She didn't hear that? It seemed unbelievable. It was so loud. He looked around the space for anything that may have fallen. There was nothing. A chill ran down his spine when he realized it was a phantom noise.

"Never mind," he muttered.

Natalie pushed against the shelf. "Help me move this, 'kay."

He approached her and grabbed the opposite side of the shelf and began to tug. It wiggled only slightly but did not want to fully move, even with the weight of the two of them against it.

"Rod!" he called up the stairs. He heard his friend's footfalls as Rod began to descend.

"What?" he snapped as he reached the bottom.

"Help us move this?"

Rod approached and together, the three of them were able to move the shelf away from the wall. Behind it was a small metal door that rolled upwards and didn't reach the floor.

"What is it?" Rod asked.

"It's a dumbwaiter shaft," Natalie answered. "Old houses, especially big ones, often had them, so it was easier to haul things from one floor to the next. Mostly used by servants. Dishes and laundry. That kind of thing."

"I've heard of them, but I've never seen one," Rod mused as he reached for the handle.

"Wait," Natalie grabbed his wrist before he could touch it.

"Excuse me," he snarled.

"Let me check first," she pressed her palm against the door. "No, it's not safe. That's why the shelf was blocking it."

A memory flickered to the surface for Richard. He recalled a lot of talk regarding Aunt Claire getting stuck in a dumbwaiter. His mom always sent him out of the room when they were discussing it, but he would listen at the door.

"There's one in my room," he told the others. "It looks better than this though. I think my Aunt Claire got stuck in the shaft once. I remember everyone being all worked up about it. They would send me out of the room, but I listened anyway. She said something about tunnels and that she went in because she thought she heard my sister calling to her, but my sister wasn't home."

"Well, that's trippy," Rod shivered.

"Actually, it makes perfect sense," Natalie nodded. "If there was a girl stuck in the walls, maybe her spirit was down there. Maybe not. Either way, we shouldn't go exploring. I'm sensing it's dangerous. Unstable. It might collapse. I say we have professionals look before anyone goes poking around."

Both boys agreed.

Two hours later, they were all huddled around the kitchen island. They'd taken a thorough walk around the house and Natalie had some interesting insights that were leaving Richard excited to continue with a full-blown investigation.

Some rooms she hadn't picked anything up in, mostly upstairs bedrooms. It was agreed that those were most likely guest bedrooms back in the olden days that rarely got used.

She'd picked up on an overwhelming feeling of sadness in the cellar once she'd explored it further and mused that perhaps someone lived down there at some point in time.

If Richard had any doubts about Natalie's abilities, they were squashed in the upstairs bathroom. She'd been able to tell him in vivid detail about the attack on his sister, Bailey, so many years before.

She described the attack as beginning with water running on its own and then Bailey seeing a figure in the mirror behind her. The figure was wearing an emerald-green flapper dress from the 1920s. This woman grabbed Bailey's head and shoved her face into the mirror, breaking it.

This wasn't something that Natalie could have read in the papers. There was never any police report filed, no media coverage about the incident either.

He remembered Bailey having to go to the ER to get stitches in her forehead from the glass. He also heard that dress mentioned many times. *"Emerald-green flapper dress. But it felt like she was faking."*

He hadn't understood then. The way that Natalie explained everything to him though, it was almost like he was there, seeing everything through Bailey's eyes, and he felt her terror.

Now, as he really thought about things for the first time, he was seriously beginning to believe that Bailey was targeted by something. First, the seance, then the fire in their family home, then the attack in the bathroom, what she'd done to Callie. Something latched itself onto her, and Natalie basically confirmed it.

*"Hostile spirits tend to do one of two things. They either latch on to the weak and feed on their energy, or they latch onto those they see as a threat and try to drive them away. What happened with your sister was a series of cheap scare tactics right up until she became possessed,"* she'd said.

Now, they were all sipping coffee and getting ready to implement a game plan.

Natalie nodded toward the doorway on the opposite side of the kitchen. "Was that where it happened?"

Richard nodded his head as he stared at the space.

"How did you get stuck? There's no door."

"There was back then," he answered before taking a big gulp of coffee. "It was gone when we got here. I don't know what happened to it."

"Did you do what we discussed?"

He shook his head no and averted his eyes to study his cup with fascinated interest. It was like a child who knows they are in trouble for drawing on a wall and takes up an unnatural interest in everything around them.

"Richard," she said sternly as she set down her cup. *"Richard,"* more insistent this time, and he lifted his head to meet her gaze.

"If you want me to be able to help you, I'm going to need *your* help. I wasn't there. When I give you homework, I expect you to do it. Otherwise, we won't be able to work together. I can't help you if you hold back. I can't adequately tell you how serious the situation here is, what happened to your family, or even if you are currently in danger if I don't know what *happened* when there is an incident."

"I know," he admitted, "and I didn't mean to avoid. I just got filled with anxiety. I didn't want to be alone."

Her gaze softened. "I understand that. That happens, but when that's the case, you have to tell me, and I'll be here when you do it. But you have to do it, Richard. It's necessary."

He nodded. She was right, of course. She was going largely on secondhand information. She couldn't do her job if she wasn't given the full picture.

Natalie dusted her hands and rose to her feet. "Okay, let's go."

"What, now?"

She stared at him, and he suddenly felt as though she'd drilled a hole through his eye socket and straight into his brain.

"Okay, now." He rose to his feet and followed her to the entrance to the staircase.

"I'm going to wait outside the door," she told him "But if you need me just say so. I'm right here."

He nodded and stepped into the doorway. Instantly, it was as though his lungs constricted from the thick air. The atmosphere was heavy to him, and he sunk down to sit on a step.

There was a sensation as though he were being swallowed up into a fog of smoke, and his weight disappeared as he left his body. When the smoke cleared, he was in the same stairwell, further up.

His eight-year-old self stepped through the door and climbed two steps before the door slammed shut behind him.

A woman materialized directly in front of him, and he stumbled back onto his tailbone and began to scream.

This woman had every appearance of a monster. She was tall and slender, wearing a white maid's uniform, but she only looked half human. Peeking out from underneath her skirt were hooves, and her skin was covered in blue scales. There were the beginnings of nubs of horns on the top of her head.

She roared and leapt at him, seizing his shoulders, and shoving him against the door.

He was still screaming and wildly swung out, trying to push her away from him. He could hear his family on the other side desperately trying to open the door.

He went limp and dropped his weight to the floor, surprising the creature woman momentarily and turned, beginning to claw at the door and calling out, begging his mom to help him.

The creature threw him against the steps and leaned over him, hissing in his ear, "Don't release her."

"Who?" he cried.

A light shined down from the top of the steps and the woman disappeared in a flash of white from her skirts. Then the door opened.

"Richard! Richard!" Someone was calling out. His weight dropped back down into his body, and his focus returned.

Natalie knelt before him, peering into his eyes with concern. He noticed then that he was in a cold sweat and slumped against the wall, still seated on the same step.

"You're okay. You're back," she put the back of her hand to his forehead and then pulled it away. "You're hurt."

He shook his head adamantly. "No, I'm not. I'm fine." He went to stand and was met with a searing pain in his back. He cried out and slumped against the wall.

He automatically raised a hand to the pain in his back, and Natalie raised his shirt to look. He was riddled with bruises and three long scratch marks.

# CHAPTER EIGHT

Richard was quite happy with the progress they were making. Natalie's insights were extremely reassuring to him, and she'd promised to return the next day with her team.

Now, it was time to tackle the house.

Richard had no plans to go to the same extent as Aunt Claire to fix the place up, but he did need to make it livable and sellable. He didn't plan on being at Blackwood for long, after all.

It had been agreed to start in the parlor, not only because it was at the front of the house but because it sustained the most damage from the fire.

The group congregated in the parlor that Saturday morning. Brad was working as a contractor for him at an extremely discounted rate, which he was thankful for. He'd stepped around slabs of flooring that were stacked in the hallway on his way in.

The windows on the first floor had been replaced the day before, and now the large windows filled the room with impressive natural lighting, making it feel less intimidating.

"What's the verdict, boss?" he asked Brad, who gave him a big grin.

"Well, the good news is the damage is pretty minimal. The wiring and plumbing are completely fine as well as the framing. However, this wall," he gestured toward the wall that the fireplace had been on, "is severely damaged and will need to be removed. It's not a supporting wall, so that should be easily accomplished. Now we can take it out and make it one giant room, but the issue with that is the downstairs bathroom."

"Why is that an issue?" Remi asked.

"That bathroom was a late addition. I'm sure you've all noticed the matching fireplace in that room?"

They all nodded.

"Well, someone threw up walls to add in the decorative fireplaces. That room was probably something else before it was a bathroom. If we take this wall out, it's going to mean pulling out all the fireplaces, and the bathroom will be missing a wall."

"What a shame," Jamie said and raised a hand to her mouth. "Those fireplaces are so pretty. I mean obviously it was clear the one in here would need to be replaced because of the fire, but it would be such a shame to remove all of them."

"Can't we just put up another wall in the bathroom?" Rod asked.

"We can but it's going to be more expensive, and I know Richard wants to save money on renovations where possible."

"Let me take a quick look," Richard said, and he strode across the room to the sliding pocket door that led to the next room. He struggled with the door but finally got it to slide into the wall. He looked back at Brad.

"That's due to the internal damage."

Richard nodded and stepped into the next room. It was a small study or office with shelves affixed to the walls and its fireplace in the corner. Jamie was right. It was beautiful. He'd known this room was here, but he'd never spent any significant amount of time in here before. He'd cut through it a few times as a kid on the way to the bathroom. On the opposite wall was another set of sliding doors that led to that bathroom.

He walked back out to the parlor. "So, what are our options?" he asked Brad.

"Well, as Rod suggested, we can knock this wall down, pull out the fireplaces and put up a new wall for the bathroom. We can also replace this wall and fireplace and keep the layout exactly as it is now. Or we can take out the walls and tear out the bathroom to make it part of the parlor."

"I vote for keeping the bathroom," Jamie said. She looked at Richard. "I already think two bathrooms are not enough for a house this big anyway. If we take it out, all we have is the one upstairs, and that might not be appealing to buyers."

"I agree," Richard said. "The bathroom stays. I honestly like the layout down here. Tearing the walls out would mean losing the fireplaces and the pocket doors, which is a huge selling point for people wanting to buy a house like this. I say we replace the wall and the fireplace in here, but I would like the new one to look as much like the other two as possible."

"Consider it done," Brad nodded. "Now on to the next issue. The floor."

The group looked down at the floor with its harsh, black scorch marks.

"Now, all things considered, it's not so bad," Brad said. "It's not in danger of caving in or anything like that. But we're not going to be able to make it look pretty no matter what. Now, I already took the liberty of getting the flooring. I found a near perfect match to the hallway so it should look seamless once it's put down. So, today, I feel the best bet is to paint the walls that are not going to be pulled down before we tear out the floor."

Jamie strode to the window and grabbed hold of one of the curtains and gave it a tug. The curtain rod came falling down, leaving the curtains in a heap.

Richard's heart crumbled slightly. He could remember seeing Aunt Claire making those curtains herself with so much love and dedication. They had to go though. They were marred by ten years of dust, broken glass, holes from animals, and graffiti.

He grabbed them and pulled them out of the parlor to leave them in the entryway.

"Shouldn't we leave them as a drop cloth?" Remi asked, glancing down at the floor.

"Wouldn't do no good," Brad replied. "Floors gonna be replaced after."

Remi eyed the scorch marks on the floor. "Yeah, I guess that's true."

Collectively, they all began to work.

"So, Brad," Jamie opened the conversation. "Rich tells us you worked here before."

"Yep," Brad answered as he began to roll paint across one of the walls. "I worked for Claire. She hired me to do her wiring. I'm a licensed electrician. But she saw how hard it was for me to find work, and she offered to let me stay on 'til Blackwood was completed. Damn fine woman."

"Why were you having a hard time finding work?" Rod asked.

"I'm an ex-con."

Everyone stopped painting to exchange glances. They looked at Richard who seemed completely unfazed. He already knew this. It wasn't that they heard the word *con* and immediately wanted to run. After all, they'd seen their fair share of convicts on the streets. It was more that Brad did not fit the image that they'd grown so familiar with.

"What did you *do*?" Rod was nothing if not blunt.

"I defended a Black girl that a bunch of white boys were beating on."

Richard knew there was more to the story. It seemed though that Brad didn't want to go into too much detail.

"Wait. They were beating on her, and you went to jail?" Remi asked, appalled.

"It was the '70s," Brad shrugged as if it were no big deal. "And I pulled my gun. It went off and a boy got shot. He was okay but no one wanted to work with an ex-con. I did time and that's all anyone cared about. No one cared why."

"That's fucked, dude," Rod muttered.

"Do you still have the same kind of trouble?" Jamie asked.

"Not professionally. I'm mostly a homebody now. My old bones couldn't do it no more. Not full time. I'm only doing this to help Richard. His folks were good to me. Still get looks when I'm in town, though. Folks whispering behind their hands like I can't see them."

"That must be so frustrating," Remi's voice was full of sympathy.

"It used to be but not so much anymore. I'm over giving a damn what anyone else thinks."

"Well, at least you have more time now to spend with your family," Jamie said brightly.

Brad stopped painting for a moment and when Richard looked over at him, he saw pain in his eyes.

"Brad, you, okay?" Richard asked, concerned.

"I'm fine," Brad said gruffly. "Was just surprised to hear someone ask about my family. Ain't got one no more." He picked up his paint roller and went back to work, leaving Richard dumbfounded.

"What do you mean? You were such a family man."

"I don't want to burden you with this, Rich," he said solemnly.

"Tell me!" Richard insisted.

Brad sighed, put down his roller, and turned to face Richard. "Well, you know how my daughter died of leukemia?"

"Oh, that's awful," Remi exclaimed.

"Well, Sylvie was distraught. She was angry that I spent so much of my time here while Caroline was at her sickest. She even thought I might've brought somethin' back with me and that it made her worse. Sylvie was always more superstitious than me. She didn't want me to take this job, but I convinced her it was Caroline's best chance. So, when Caroline died anyway, you couldn't convince her of different. She divorced me and took our other daughter. She easily won custody. I have a record, after all. I never saw either of them again."

Richard's heart was heavy with guilt. His family was the reason Brad didn't have one anymore. "God, Brad. I'm so sorry. I—"

He was cut off by Brad putting his hands on his shoulders. "It's not your fault, Richard. It's not Claire's fault. It's not anyone's fault. Except maybe whoever gave this place its reputation in the first place. I wouldn't change anything."

"But if you weren't here working all the time, Caroline—"

"Would have been gone even sooner," Brad answered firmly. "We were able to fight so hard *because* I had this job. Claire paid me good. More than she should've. So, I don't want you to worry about nothing, okay? I don't have grudges. Your folks were good to me. All of them. You all were like a second family to me while I was here. Do you hear me? You're a son to me, Richard."

Richard broke down in heavy tears, his chest heaving from the force of it, from holding in all that pain and anguish for so long. He didn't even care that the others were in the room and may perceive him as weak. All that mattered was purging the despair.

Brad took him into his arms and held him while he cried. Rod and Jamie stood to the side awkwardly, unsure of what to do. Remi rushed forward and threw her arms around him from behind, burying her face in his back and whispering that everything was going to be okay.

Richard hid in his room for the rest of the day. He was embarrassed that he'd lost control and cried in front of his friends. It was just he'd never had someone tell him they considered him a son since his family died.

He knew he was being juvenile, but he couldn't let go of the hope that if he stayed in his room long enough, everyone would forget what happened, or at the very least he could come up with a response if they did mention it.

He pulled out his laptop, scanned his email to find nothing new, and then switched over to MemoryBook and searched for Bailey's friends who'd done the seance with her.

It was simple enough to figure out who they were. He'd only remembered one name, Alex, though the last name escaped him. A simple search of Bailey's bedroom gave what he needed. He found a single photograph in a shoe box. Bailey and two other girls making silly faces at the camera. He'd also found her yearbook from that year, issued just before everything went sour. He'd cross-referenced the yearbook with the picture until he matched names to faces. He'd found the girls. He scanned the autograph section of the yearbook to find only two signatures, a fact that made him instantly feel bad for his sister.

*Hey Bails!! I miss you! Call me! Alex*

*Bailey. It's us against them. Don't let them win. Jessie.*

He quickly discovered that Alex McCarthy owned a smoothie bar one town over, but he couldn't find Jessie Landry.

He looked up the phone number for the bar and dialed. It only rang twice before a breathy voice answered.

"Hi, can I speak to your owner? Alex McCarthy?" he asked.

"This is Alex. Is there an issue with a product or customer service?"

"No, nothing like that. This is Richard Price. You used to be friends with my sister, Bailey."

"Oh wow. Bailey. There's a blast from the past. How are you, Richie?"

"It's Richard now. I'm good. I inherited Blackwood Manor and I just moved back."

"Oh..." there was an awkward silence on the other end of the line.

"Listen, I know this will sound strange. I know you and Jessie Landry had a seance at Blackwood with Bailey and that something happened. I was too young to get too many details at the time, but I really need to know. I'm trying to figure out what happened to my family, and everything seems to be coming back to the house."

There was a pause and then she answered. "Hang on a minute."

Richard heard shuffling and then Alex called someone to watch the front. There was more shuffling and the unmistakable sound of a door closing.

"Sorry," she said. "I had to go back to the office. It's business hours, and I probably shouldn't discuss this in front of the house."

"That's okay."

"So," her voice was pained, "what do you want to know?"

"I was wondering if you could tell me about the seance and anything you might remember about how Bailey's behavior changed after. I personally remember her becoming withdrawn and there were some behaviors that were unlike her."

Alex sighed. "Well, we were all into that hocus pocus, and Blackwood Manor was always kind of a legend. You might have been too young to remember.

"Kids were always getting dared to go up on the porch and take pictures. I know a few who snuck in on dares and ended up leaving terrified less than an hour later. The mystique of it was very alluring. So, when your Aunt Claire bought the place, Bailey was fascinated. She would tell us about things that were supposedly happening in the house, and we begged her to take us there. We wanted to do an investigation."

Richard already knew this part of the story but something about the forlorn tone of Alex's voice pulled him in even more. It suggested she was strapping in for a wild ride. "Okay," he pressed her on.

"My father was a devout preacher, so I had to keep my interest in these things a secret. Especially when it came to Blackwood Manor. He always swore the place was a portal or an open doorway. Something along those lines.

"We'd done 'investigations' before but nothing too serious. Cemeteries, older looking structures. Nothing that actually had a real reputation though. We had cameras, though, so we thought we were tough shit. Bailey convinced your Aunt Claire to let us do an investigation, and she agreed to let us do it when no one was home. We were on Cloud Nine."

Her voice cracked, and she began to hesitate.

"It didn't go well?" Richard asked.

"No," she admitted. "It started off cool enough. You could feel it the minute you walked onto the property. The energy was just different. I could swear I heard a voice in my head telling me to turn back, but it didn't sound threatening. I was more intrigued than anything. First, we set up cameras everywhere we knew for sure there was an occurrence."

"And where was that?" Richard asked, scrambling for a piece of paper to write it down.

"The attic, the upstairs hallway outside the bathroom, in the kitchen pointed at the entrance to that servant's staircase."

"Do you know what happened in those areas? Why Bailey wanted to put cameras in those spots?"

"Well, the hidden staircase was because you were attacked there, the attic was because Claire saw a woman there, the hallway where Claire saw a little girl with her head bashed in asking her to be her mommy—she fell down the stairs when that happened. The bathroom was because something was creeping up on Claire in the shower, but I wasn't ever given details on that one."

"Okay. So, then what happened?"

"Well, Bailey was determined to solve the mystery of Blackwood Manor and put all the spirits to rest. She thought she had enough information to go off too."

Bailey had solid facts? Richard was having a hard time containing his excitement.

"The woman in the attic apparently told Claire to help someone name Gloria. We all assumed that meant help her into the light. Also, she kept talking about these oil paintings that Claire found and one of them, the little girl, tended to move around on her own. It was a painting of Lucy Blackwood."

Richard of course knew about the paintings, but he'd never known the identity of anyone in the portraits.

"Bailey wanted to find out who Gloria was, and why Lucy's portrait moved around. She wanted to put all the souls to rest. So, we set up an Ouija board in the parlor. Bailey asked if there were any spirits still there and how many of them there were."

"Do you remember how many?"

"Three hundred and forty-seven."

Oh, shit. Richard didn't know what he'd been expecting, but it certainly hadn't been that.

"She asked if Margaret Blackwood was still there, and we got a 'yes'. She asked if Josie was still there. We got another 'yes.' Then she asked if Gloria was there and that's when...when—" her voice broke, and it took a moment before Richard realized she was crying.

"What happened?" he asked gently.

"A gust of wind blew out the candles and all the doors started slamming shut on the second floor. We went up to investigate, and we saw this *awful* looking woman. She had blue scaly skin, hooves instead of feet. Horns materialized on her head before our very eyes, and she *flew* at us. Bailey and I got out of the way, but she slammed into Jessie, and she flew into the wall. This thing kept attacking her. I tried to stop it, but it threw me aside and I hurt my ankle. Then another ghost walked out of the wall, and they started attacking each other."

"Trippy," Richard was amazed. "They found each other. What did this new ghost look like?"

"That's the weird thing," she said. "They were dressed the same way, but the new ghost looked more human. No hooves, no weird skin. Her face was blank, like there was a veil over it. I had the distinct impression the first woman was *trying* to appear like this one but ended up this warped version instead."

"What happened next?"

"I don't know," Alex sighed. "While they were fighting each other, Jessie ran for the stairs, she was crying hysterically, and I went after her. I didn't realize until we were outside that Bailey wasn't with us. We sat out there a long time until your Aunt Claire and this guy showed up. He talked to us and calmed us down, gave me a cell phone to call an ambulance, and then they went inside to look for Bailey."

"What about after? Did she ever talk about what happened after you guys went outside? Did her behavior around you change at all?"

"I wasn't supposed to stay friends with her after that. My dad was very upset. He kept saying everyone there were devil worshipers and I needed to steer clear to avoid my soul burning for all eternity. In our class though, I noticed she'd changed. Started mouthing off, not doing her assignments, picking on people. She even dressed differently. Jessie told me later that Bailey's family believed us because they watched the camera footage."

Richard's heart skipped a beat. "All this was captured on camera? I thought activity like this messed with electrical equipment."

"So did I, but Jessie said that's what Bailey told her."

"Do you know where I can find Jessie to get her side of the story? Maybe she got more information out of Bailey. I couldn't find her on MemoryBook."

"Jessie was never quite the same after that. She attempted suicide multiple times. She started talking about seeing stuff that wasn't there. Like a lot. She's been in a mental institution for about four years now. She's her family's dirty little secret." There was a bite to her voice that hadn't previously been there, and Richard instantly got the impression that Alex was not the type of person you wanted to screw with.

"Do you know which one?"

"Smith Pines in Macon. I visited her a couple of times, but I couldn't keep going. It was too depressing."

"Were the cameras ever returned to you? I'd love to see the footage for myself and try to get a feel for things."

"No," she answered. "I never saw them again."

# CHAPTER NINE

"Brad?" Richard tentatively asked while the pair was painting the kitchen the following day.

"Yep?"

"You know when my sister and her friends had their seance?"

Richard noted the way Brad's shoulders stiffened, and it was what he'd expected. He almost didn't ask him at all, but Brad was the only person that could possibly provide an answer.

"Yes," Brad said sharply, a tone that was unusual for the sweet old man.

"Well, I know they set up cameras. I talked to one of the girls that was there, but she doesn't have the cameras, and I haven't found them anywhere in the house. Do you happen to know where they are?"

"I know about the cameras. Claire told me what was on them, but I never saw them myself. I would figure they'd be with her equipment."

Richard shook his head. "They're not. That's not all that's missing either. None of her developed photos are anywhere to be found. I can't find them. I do have her main camera, and it has a roll of film in it that may have something on it but none of her photos are there. The cellar is still set up completely like a dark room, but I can't find any evidence that she actually used it for that."

Brad furrowed his eyebrows, confused. "She did. I saw photos down there many times. We weren't allowed in *while* they were developing, but I was down there a lot. I mean she worked for a fancy magazine, and she worked remotely."

"I remember she was always photographing at first, but the more into the house she got, the less I saw of the camera."

"Yep, I'll agree with you on that one. Eventually, I never saw her holding a camera. I mean, she had to have been taking shots at some time because she wasn't in trouble at work 'far as I know."

"Did she ever say anything about getting rid of the pictures?"

Brad shook his head. "No, not to me."

They painted for a few more minutes, then Brad let out a frustrated grunt and turned back to Richard.

"I want to talk to you about something now."

"Yeah?"

"The drinking."

Richard paused. His chest tightened, and his blood turned to ice. "I don't know what you mean."

"Don't bullshit me, boy," he said sternly. "The smell is getting stronger by the day. Now, I didn't say nothing at first because it wasn't too strong, and I knew coming back here wasn't easy. But it's becoming a problem."

"It's nothing," Richard insisted. "Just a little to take the stress off. I'm under a lot of stress."

"I know you are," Brad reached over and took the paintbrush out of Richard's hand before steering him over to sit at the island. "But that's how it starts. I'm gonna tell you something that I don't like to talk about now. I developed a drinking problem after Sylvie left me. I told myself I was just stressed at the time. My daughter had just died, my wife left, I lost custody of my other daughter, and I lost the best friends I've had in years. All in a very short period of time.

"Eventually, I woke up in a fast-food bathroom four hundred miles away, and I'd lost three days. I don't want to see that happen to you, Richard. You're young. You've got your whole life ahead of you. I'd hate to see you screw it up."

Richard hung his head in shame. He'd been scolded by his uncle time and again, but he'd never felt as thoroughly disgusted with himself as he was feeling right now.

"Where are you getting it?" Brad asked, more gently this time. "Are you stealing it?"

"No," Richard insisted, shaking his head. "I mean, I have before, but not anymore. It's just...there."

"Just there?"

"Yeah, I found a bottle in the back of one of the cabinets and no matter how much I drink, whenever I open the cabinet again, there it is...full to the brim again."

"And you didn't think maybe you shouldn't touch it?"

"It's just vodka."

"Vodka doesn't magically rejuvenate, boy," Brad said as he got up and turned towards the cabinets. "Which one?"

Richard pointed to the upper cabinet closest to the refrigerator. "That one."

Brad strode over to the cabinet, pulled out the bottle, and instantly poured it down the sink.

"Cold turkey?" Richard nervously chuckled.

"I will not watch you waste away."

"It'll just refill itself."

"Then I'll just have to take it with me, won't I?" Brad stated as he stuffed the empty bottle into his knapsack.

"Isn't it just as bad for you to have it as me?" Richard asked. "I mean, if you're a recovering alcoholic?"

"I'll dump it when I get away from here," Brad gave Richard a little pat on the back. "I got you."

As Richard consulted his checklist the following day, he was astounded by how far things had come. His list differed greatly from the things Aunt Claire always had going, but he was making progress none the less.

He wanted to find some way to talk to Jessie Landry and get her point of view on the seance. Natalie was due to return with her team the following day.

There was a knock on the bedroom door, jarring him from his thoughts, and he looked up as he beckoned the person inside.

Remi strode inside and perched on the end of his bed. They'd been doing slightly better since their brunch together, but he hadn't been able to get a read on her with the upcoming investigation.

"How're you holding up?" he asked her gently.

"Nervous," she admitted, and she pulled the sweater she was wearing tighter around herself. "I don't like that all these paranormal people are going to be here, stirring things up."

"But you know..." he prodded.

"That it's necessary," she finished. "But I don't like it. They're going to have to investigate my room, aren't they?"

"Probably. I mean, that's where the only occurrence since we've come back has been, so I'm sure they'll want to.

It is your space though. You have the right to say no if you want."

"It's not the only occurrence," she laughed timidly and cast her eyes down to his comforter, fingering a hole in the threading.

"What do you mean?" he asked her.

"Jamie told me about the painting of the little girl."

"Oh, well, I don't really consider that an occurrence."

"Paintings don't move on their own, so yeah, it is."

"Fair point."

"I've seen it too."

This surprised him. "Really? When?"

"I didn't know that's what it was until I talked to her. I saw it leaning up against the wall when I was coming out of the bathroom. It was the morning after we got here. Maybe the morning after that. It didn't strike me as suspicious at the time. There was tons of stuff in the hallway and leaning against the walls. It didn't click."

"Was it there when you went into the bathroom?"

She shook her head. "I'm not sure. It was first thing in the morning, and I was exhausted because I hadn't slept. I just know it didn't send up any alarm bells."

"Well, that is good to know. It ties into my childhood. I never saw it myself back then, but I heard everyone talking about it. Aunt Claire saw it right after an incident in the bathroom."

"I'm glad I didn't realize it was a magical painting," she chuckled awkwardly, rubbing the back of her slender neck.

Richard gave a half smile, and stared at her, trying to pin down where her mind was at. He wanted her at his side for this but was too prideful to ask for that. Almost like she could sense his turmoil, she reached over to tentatively squeeze his hand. Each finger wrapped in his steadied nerves, almost calming him.

Her skin was so soft, not like his. Her apricot scent tickled his nose like it was playing with him.

The foreign emotions caressing his veins alarmed him. What was he thinking? Richard slid his hand from her grasp.

"You'll be seeing things soon enough, you know? With Natalie and the team coming, the activity is probably going to increase."

Remi's smile faltered and she nervously ran her hands up her arms. "I know."

"Do you want me to put you up at a hotel?"

She shook her head. "I don't want to be the only one taking off when things get real. But I'd like to keep the offer on reserve if that's okay."

"Of course," he reached up and ruffled her hair affectionately.

She laughed and then hopped up to her feet. "Well, I have a class. I'll see you later."

She made her way towards the door where she passed Rod who was peering in. She said goodbye to him, and he turned back towards Richard, raising an amused eyebrow.

"What?" he asked.

"Did you *ruffle* her hair?"

"So what?"

"Not the slickest come on, my man."

"Please!" Richard spat in disgust. "She's practically my sister."

"Dude," Rod grinned. "I know I never had a sister, but if I did, I don't think I'd be caressing her hand and smelling her perfume."

"I did no such thing."

"You did. You could cut the sexual tension in here with a knife."

Richard glared at him. "Don't make me kick your ass."

Rod laughed. "Like you could. Hey, man, don't sweat it. She's totally into you too."

Richard grit his teeth. "Did you need something?"

"As a matter of fact, I do." Rod glided in and plopped down on the spot Remi just vacated. "So, I *might* have gotten annoyed and busted the lock on that old desk in the attic."

"You did what? Rod, that desk is like two hundred years old. Maybe even three."

"Well, you should be happy I did."

"And why is that?"

"Because I found a shit ton of very modern-looking photos and rolls of film in it. I put them down in the dark room for you to explore at your convenience."

"Aunt Claire's missing photos?"

"Probably. They don't look nearly as old as everything else in this house."

"They were in the desk? The roll-top desk?" Richard asked again.

"Isn't that what I just said?" Rod rolled his eyes.

"Why the hell were they in the desk?" Richard muttered under his breath. "What about the cameras? You know the missing ones from the seance?"

"No cameras. But there was something else interesting."

"Yeah?"

"I saw a freaky chick up there. Totally dead. Smelled like rotten meat, skin hanging off her bones. It was disgusting. Totally cool."

"You're pulling my dick."

Rod stared at him, incredulous. "I promise you, I would never do that."

"So, what did she look like?"

"I told you. Skin hanging off bones. She was wearing a floor-length white dress. Looked kind of like a maid."

"Probably Josie then. Did she do anything?"

"Nah, just stared at me. Which was weird because she didn't have a face."

"Definitely Josie. Was there anything else up there?"

"I'm not your damn secretary. If you want to know what I found in the attic, I suggest you take your happy ass down to the cellar and look."

Richard got off the bed and muttered, "Dick," as he made his way to the door.

"It's taken."

When Richard got down into the cellar, he saw a huge pile of stuff on the workbench. Rod hadn't been lying.

He rushed over and went for the stack of already developed photos first. There were so many of them. There were pictures of Blackwood Manor overgrown and broken, not much different from how it currently looked. There was a picture of a carriage block, almost completely hidden from view by overgrown weeds.

There were pictures of the house and grounds at various stages during the renovation, including a stunning shot of the kitchen sparkling and looking like it belonged in a magazine.

Aunt Claire had serious talent, he thought to himself as he shuffled through, shot by shot. She had a way of making any image she shot come to life, looking vibrant and respected.

Ashley Bundy

The exterior shots made the house look positively evil, which wasn't all that surprising. The front windows always looked like giant eyes staring out and that was even more apparent in the photos, especially the ones where the front was center framed. It was a mocking, ferocious grin. There was no denying it.

Once he'd made his way through the stack of pictures, Richard reached over and ran a hand over the several rolls of undeveloped film.

What was on it? Why was all this locked away in the rolltop desk, somewhere it shouldn't have been? Why had everyone else seen or experienced something in the house except for him?

While the others might have been relieved in his shoes, Richard was dejected. It was *his* family; *he* was the one who used to live here. So, why hadn't he experienced anything at all?

Why were his answers, things as precious as photographs that could help to give him closure, being locked away from him?

Suddenly, with a heavy heart, he wondered to himself if they ever wanted him at all. Had anyone *ever* wanted him?

# CHAPTER TEN

Natalie looked radiant when she breezed through the door the following day. She was wearing a ballerina style skirt with fishnet stockings.

She directed her crew into the parlor and barked orders at them while Richard observed her. She had marvelous muscular, tanned legs, which was a personal weakness. And he loved the way she commanded any room she was in. There was something special about a woman with that ability.

He heard a huff from his left, and he took his eyes off Natalie long enough to glance in that direction. He found Remi staring at him with her nose scrunched up as if she smelled something foul.

"What?" he asked.

She rolled her eyes and crossed her arms in front of her, breaking the eye contact.

"Clueless bastard," Rod muttered on his other side.

Richard was about to snap at him but was stopped by Natalie turning towards them.

"Okay, now I need to know what has happened here and if you've done your homework," she grinned at Richard.

Briefly, he told her about the few experiences they'd had so far. Remi's experience the first night, the painting, and Rod seeing Josie in the attic.

"Okay, what about the homework? The other things we discussed?"

"I reached one of the other girls that was at the seance, and she gave me a pretty detailed account of the night, but she said the whole thing was captured on camera, only we haven't found the cameras yet. The other girl is in a mental institution, so that may be a little trickier. I'm still trying to track down Nadine Lewis, but so far everything I've found is outdated."

She waved a hand. "I'm not worried about Nadine. We have connections. We'll find her. We still need to speak to the other girl that was at the seance. I'll see if I can get a feel for the cameras. That would give us a leg up. Remi?"

Remi stared Natalie down and then gave her a curt nod to acknowledge she was listening.

"We're going to need to set up some equipment in your bedroom. At least for the first night. Night vision camera, EMF reader, that type of thing. You're free to stay in there if you want, of course, but you may be more comfortable in one of the other rooms."

"Fine," Remi snapped. "But only for one night. I don't want a bunch of strangers going through my things."

Natalie gave her an amused grin. "Nobody wants to go through your stuff, hun."

She then turned to Rod. "So, the woman you saw in the attic...you're certain that wasn't an illusion?"

He shook his head. "No, I didn't blink, and it was more than a few seconds. She was as solid as you and me."

"I'm pretty sure it's Josie," Richard cut in, wanting to feel like a part of the process. "I heard a lot from my family about her as a kid. She was a maid in the 1800s."

"Any clue why she doesn't have a face?"

He shook his head no.

"Oh well. We'll figure it out."

"You think that's important?" Jamie asked.

"It *could* be. It just depends on whether or not it has something to do with her death."

"So, you planning on introducing us to everyone here or are we just supposed to be cool with a bunch of strangers in our house?" Rod asked sharply.

"Well, it is my understanding this is *Richard's* house, and he asked us to come here," Natalie retorted. "But of course, I was planning on introducing the team. I'm not a heathen."

She gestured towards a young man who appeared to be in his mid-twenties leaning over the cameras. He had spiky blond hair and wore a dog collar. "That's Gus. He handles the tech. Don't touch his collar. He bites."

She pointed to a petite, middle-aged woman with hair cut into a pixie style. She wore octagon shaped eyeglasses and waved nervously. "That's Mel. She handles all our research."

"Do you guys have Wi-Fi?" Mel asked timidly.

"'Course," Jamie smiled.

"Great!"

Natalie pointed to a tall, intense looking man standing in the corner. He hadn't interacted with anyone since they got there, and he seemed particularly sullen, as though he'd been sucking on a sour lemon and the look froze his face. "You can basically ignore that brute. He doesn't know anything. He's the money. He funds us so we're able to make things like this possible, but he's not an active participant. He doesn't trust us though, so he likes to supervise. Wave hi, Baxter."

Baxter did not wave. He continued to stare ahead as though he never heard her talking.

"Great, now this creepy old house has a mindless monster. What's next? Vampires?" Rod whispered in Richard's ear.

"So, tech guy, huh?" Remi turned to Gus. "I thought the spiritual people and the tech people notoriously hated each other. It's interesting to see you guys teaming up."

Natalie gave an offhanded wave of dismissal. "Such a generalization projected by movies. I'm not saying some level of animosity never happens, but it's not the norm."

"Right," Gus nodded in agreement. "We find we balance each other well. We follow Natalie's feelings and urges to lead our investigation and set up the tech, and the equipment helps us to verify and document the things she feels. It's beneficial to have both on any team."

"That's so cool!" Jamie chimed in.

"Never trust the movies," Gus slowly shook his head bringing a belly laugh from Jamie. Rod glared at him.

Natalie cut off the tension before it became too intense by saying, "Mel did some research into the history of the property."

Mel nodded and pulled out a notepad before sitting down. "I'm not sure how much you know about the property."

"Not a lot," Richard admitted. "I was only eight when I lived here."

"Well, it appears that Gerald Blackwood built the property in 1809 for his wife Elizabeth. There were many strange incidents in the record almost from the very beginning, but it got way worse after it left the Blackwood family.

"That seems to be when the 'infamous' evil that everyone knows about began. Everything while the

Blackwood family was in ownership was swept under the rug for the most part, with the exception of a scarlet fever outbreak in the 1840's that killed many slaves."

"So, you don't have a record of incidents that happened while they were in possession?" Jamie asked.

Mel shook her head. "No. There is A LOT of word of mouth, however. Members of the Blackwood family would tell friends at neighboring plantations about strange occurrences. It seemed to be plagued by bad luck. Crops going bad when no one else's did, mysterious deaths, accidents."

"But they still didn't leave?" Rod mused.

Mel shot him a finger pistol. "Bingo. Although they had the opportunity. They lost ownership in the early 1900s because the owner at the time, Robert Blackwood, had a gambling problem. He owed a lot of money and there were threats being made toward his family. The only thing he had of value was the property. He sold it to his friend, Daniel Thompson. Thompson owned the neighboring plantation, Heaven's Estate. Thompson held the deed but allowed the family to stay on the property, so they never actually left. At least not for another two years. At that point, Robert packed up his wife and child and they moved. Daniel Thompson then sold the property and there became a revolving door of owners after that point."

"So, do you actually know of anything specific that happened once new owners took over?" Remi asked. "Or was it all speculation?"

"No one has held ownership and lived in the house longer than two years since then, although the average is about six months. That alone is suspicious. There are a lot of bad incidents documented, though I doubt we have them all.

Ashley Bundy

Multiple people dying during childbirth, a double suicide where the woman lost her mind and kept talking about seeing and hearing things before committing suicide. When her husband found her, he did the same. A young girl was thrown from a horse and broke her neck. People that were present said that the horse seemed to have gone crazy for absolutely no reason.

"The owners before your Aunt Claire lived here for six months before leaving, but they didn't sell. They owned the property for forty years and left it to rot before finally selling to her."

Richard sat back; his brow furrowed with confusion. "Why the hell would they keep a property for forty years that they aren't even living in? And why did they sell to her?"

"I don't know," Mel answered. "I'm planning on contacting them to see if they have a reason for that. But it gets even weirder."

Richard pulled in a big breath. "Lay it on me."

"During the period that the house was vacant, this would have been the '80s, a group of kids broke into the house on Halloween night. There was a mass murder. Three kids were found dead, and one was missing and never found. His name was Donovan O'Ryan."

"Wait," Richard held up a hand to stop her while his heart pounded dangerously fast in his chest. "That can't be possible."

"What?" Natalie asked, looking from Richard to Mel.

"A man name Donovan O'Ryan worked for my aunt. He was a drifter and showed up looking for work after finding out about the project in town. He lived here. I'm in his room. He was a real nice guy."

"Well, there was no Donovan O'Ryan found at the scene of the fire," Mel told him.

"We'll investigate in your room later. Maybe I can pick something up," Natalie said.

"You'd think the psychic would know that," Rod interjected.

"Okay, look," she snapped around to stare him down. "Let's just get this out of the way now because I'm not going to have time to address it every time you say a dumb ass remark. I don't just *automatically* know everything. My gift works through *touch*. I have to *touch* something to see anything and even then, it's brief flashes. I can piece things together over time. It's not automatically implanted in my brain."

"You're gonna watch that tone when you speak to me," Rod growled as he squared up his shoulders.

"Or what?"

"Knock it off, both of you!" Richard snapped.

"Anyway," Mel raised her voice to indicate she was not done sharing her information. "I didn't realize that you may or may not know Donovan so breaking the next part to you is going to feel like a double whammy."

"Okay, I'm ready."

"I investigated the teens that were found dead that Halloween night. One of them was named Donna Birch. She was your mother's sister."

"What?" Richard asked.

"What the fuck?" Rod yelled out.

"Are you kidding?" Remi asked.

Mel nodded. Her eyes shone with deep sympathy.

"So, you're saying that my biological aunt died here in the '80s before Aunt Claire ever even bought it? But Mom was always terrified of Blackwood. She would speed when we drove by. Before Claire ever moved here."

"Maybe there was a reason," Mel answered him gently.

Richard's heart was so sore. He couldn't think of any logical reason that his mom wouldn't just tell them that's why she didn't like Blackwood Manor.... especially when they had to move into it. He couldn't deny that he felt slightly betrayed. There had been secrets surrounding him his entire life and he just needed them gone.

"There are even more mysteries associated with your family. Did you know that your Aunt Claire was divorced when she moved here?"

Richard nodded. "Yeah. She'd been living in New York for years but moved here when she got divorced to be closer to Mom and us."

"Do you know why?"

"I assumed it just didn't work out. People get divorced all the time."

"Claire had laid some pretty serious abuse allegations towards her husband, Brock. She had a relatively extensive hospital record from consistently having to go to the ER following his attacks. He forced her to lie at the time of the visits, but she kept a record of her own. Photos and even a few audio recordings, and she used them in court when she finally divorced him. It ruined him financially. She reportedly hid out with a friend from work until the proceedings were finalized and then she moved here after. There was a colleague of Brock's that testified he'd seen him slap her at a party who ended up found in a ditch with his neck broken not too long after. Many people assumed it was Brock, but no evidence was ever found."

Richard had an epiphany. "Who was the friend?"

"What?"

"The friend she was staying with while they were in court. Who was that?"

"A woman by the name of Jennifer Carter. Who coincidentally was also found dead not long after your aunt moved. At that point, an investigation was launched against Brock, but he was reported missing. Two days before the fire here."

There was a deafening silence as everyone in the room began to put the pieces together for themselves.

"So…are you saying it's connected?" Richard asked. "That Brock was responsible for the fire?"

"I'm saying it's something we have to find out," Mel told him gently. "It is still strange that the fire was contained to one room and went out on its own. That doesn't sound natural to me. But there are a lot of coincidences that seem to be tied to either the property or the people living here."

Natalie rose to her feet. "She's absolutely right. So, let's get going."

# CHAPTER ELEVEN

Natalie wanted to start in Richard's room. They all stood in the corner as she walked through the room, running her hands over the walls and the furniture.

Gus set up a camera in the corner of the room that pointed directly at the bed.

Richard was crippled by sudden anxiety. He'd acknowledged that Remi may be uncomfortable with an investigation taking place in her own room, but he hadn't been compelled to stop it.

Now that everything was getting kicked off in his room, he couldn't shake the feeling that he was being silently violated. A person's bed was their safe space. That was where they could be vulnerable with no prying eyes looking and judging. That would be out the window with a camera in his room, rolling nonstop. Would the camera be able to pick up him getting undressed even if he did it on the other side of the room? He wasn't sure how wide of an angle this camera had. Hell, he couldn't even whack off in his own room anymore.

Natalie's fingers trailed the door to the dumbwaiter, and she stopped, her fingers frozen to the door. This one was in much better shape than the one in the cellar.

"You said your aunt was stuck in the dumbwaiter at some point?"

"Yes. I don't know the details, but I remember things were kind of chaotic around that time."

"She was lured down there. She thought she heard a child calling out to her...Callie."

The air went out of Richard's lungs, and he developed a pain that spread throughout the rest of his body. He'd told her Bailey's name, but not Callie's. "Callie is my sister. She was three at the time."

Natalie nodded. "She went in after Callie. She had to shimmy down the rope and then she got locked in."

"But who…"

If Natalie heard him, she ignored him. She turned toward Mel. "Mark it. I sense more than that in there. We need to explore the tunnels, but it isn't safe. We'll need help."

Mel moved forward with a giant roll of blue painter's tape and placed a giant X on the dumbwaiter door.

The group then moved to Remi's room and Richard couldn't help but let out a sigh of relief that the pressure and attention was now off him.

While Gus was setting up his equipment, Natalie asked Remi to tell her about her experience on the group's first night.

"Well, it started with a nightmare," Remi began. She stared at her feet, and Richard instantly knew that she was nervous. Remi was extremely introverted and hated attention being on her. He couldn't help but wonder how she expected to be a doctor if she couldn't handle looking people in the eye.

"What was the nightmare about?" Natalie asked her.

"It was kind of like a swirl of different things. Flashes. There was blood and screaming, guns going off, fire, a lot of flashing lights in different colors."

"You mean like wizarding wars in movies?" Rod asked.

"Kinda," Remi replied. "Except more. And it wasn't like a straight line. The room was just filled with the colors."

"What colors?"

"Red, blue, purple, white."

Richard noticed Natalie freeze. It was only for a moment, but she lost all her coloring, and her eyes glazed over in confusion but then she was back.

"What happened next?" she asked.

"A little girl climbed out of the fireplace downstairs, and someone was yelling 'Lucy, no,' then I woke up."

Richard thought his heart might beat right out of his chest. Hadn't Natalie said on the first walkthrough that someone had been in the fireplace? And wasn't the creepy girl painting supposed to be Lucy Blackwood?

"Was that the extent of your experience?" Natalie asked Remi. If she was aware of Richard's discomfort, she didn't let on.

"I thought so at first," Remi admitted. "The room was like an oven. I was sweating profusely, and it literally felt like I was cooking alive. I tried to open the window but couldn't. I remember wondering if it was nailed shut. Then I saw a shadow in the corner of the room, and it slowly moved closer. It was a woman. She was tall with curly blonde hair and was severely burned."

Richard's lungs were officially burning from lack of air. *Aunt Claire?* He wondered. She did fit the description.

"She stared at me for a minute and then she smiled in a real twisted way and lunged at me."

*What? No way. Aunt Claire would never try to scare anyone.*

"Were you hurt?"

"No, just scared. I thought I was dying though. She grabbed my arms, and it was like jumping naked into an ice-cold lake for a couple of seconds and then it got really hot, and I felt my skin sizzling. She just disappeared. Later, I realized there were no marks on me even though I'd been in pain and was afraid for my life."

"Is there any chance that this was part of the nightmare and just felt real?" Gus asked.

Remi shook her head. "No. I was definitely awake."

"She was," Jamie cut in. "She was screaming, and we all ran in to see what was wrong. There were ashy footprints on the floor."

"Where?" Natalie asked.

Jamie pointed out the spot and Natalie knelt on the ground and placed her palm to it.

"Claire," she said after a few seconds. "She wasn't trying to hurt you. She was trying to scare you."

"Why?" Richard asked angrily. "Why the hell would my aunt want to scare any of us?"

"It's hazy, but I'm getting the feeling from this spot that she's scared, and she wants you kids out, so nothing happens to you."

"Why me?" Remi asked in despair.

"She's a smart woman," Natalie answered. "There's a connection between you and Richard. She went after you because he's more likely to leave to keep you safe than himself. He doesn't care what happens to him."

Heat spread through Richard's cheeks. It was such a bold statement to make and especially in front of the entire group. It was true he didn't give a damn what happened to him. He'd given up on that a long time ago. Of course, he cared more about what happened to those he loved, but she was making this seem like a romantic entanglement.

He looked over to catch Rod and Jamie exchanging a look, and Rod with a big smirk on his face. God, he deserved a massive uppercut.

Remi looked up from her feet for the first time and her cheeks were bright red. The statement made her just as embarrassed as him.

"He didn't leave though. In fact, we argued about the whole thing."

Natalie waved a dismissive hand as she rose to her feet. "Technicality. You weren't in any real danger. If you were, it would be a different story."

Later that afternoon, after the entire group walked through the house setting up equipment, Richard excused himself to the kitchen. He was completely drained.

On top of how taxing the situation itself was, his skin crawled from embarrassment over what happened in Remi's room.

He grabbed a frozen dinner from the freezer and popped it in the oven and then went to grab a glass from the cabinet for water.

He froze when he opened the door. Right inside the door was a bottle of vodka, full to the brim.

*"No,"* he told himself. *"This isn't possible. Brad took the bottle. It can't be here."*

But it was there. He reached up with a trembling hand and pulled it out to further exam it. He knew he should be cautious. As Brad said, vodka didn't magically rejuvenate. It was bad enough that the bottle always refilled on its own, but for it to reappear after being removed from the home? He couldn't think of a logical explanation for that.

Still, it was there, right where he needed it. This had been a day from hell, and he could definitely use a drink. Just one would be fine. Just to calm him down.

He took one long swig from the bottle.

He let the warmth fill his belly and waited for the calm to overtake him. He heard a scream come from upstairs, and the thundering of footsteps from everyone rushing toward it. Instead of joining them, he took another swig.

# CHAPTER TWELVE

### Natalie

Natalie was startled awake that night by a noise. She wasn't sure at first if it was in her subconscious or reality. She snapped her eyes open and looked in the direction of the noise.

Her bedroom door was open, and a woman stood staring in at her from the doorway. She was a pretty Black woman with gorgeous chestnut eyes, and she was crying.

There was a flickering around her image similar to a movie projector.

Natalie sat up and slowly began to approach the woman, half expecting her to startle. She didn't run off though. She just looked at Natalie with overwhelming sadness in her eyes.

"Why are you crying?" she asked tentatively.

"You have to get him out of here," she answered in a shaky voice.

"Who?" Natalie said, and then she saw the resemblance. "Are you Richard's mother?"

She didn't answer. "Just get him away from this place. It isn't safe."

"He wants to help you."

The woman turned and began to disappear down the hall.

"Hey, wait!" Natalie called and tried to follow, but the woman vanished before her eyes.

Natalie couldn't help but feel a little unsettled. Was this how everyone else experienced the paranormal? Her gift typically worked differently. For as long as she could remember, she'd only experienced things through touch.

She would sometimes get bursts of emotion and sometimes would see things play out as if she were a spectator of the original events, but it only happened like this one other time. That was right after her grandmother died. She'd been twelve years old, and Grandma came into her room, and they'd had a full conversation about all of Natalie's accomplishments and how they made Grandma proud.

Natalie knew at the time Grandma was gone but hadn't wanted to admit it to herself. She'd lived in a nursing home for years and was senile for a while. The fact that she was so lucid was a dead giveaway. Her mother appeared within minutes of Grandma leaving to tell her she'd just received the phone call.

Therefore, interacting with Richard's mother in real time without touching anything was giving her bad vibes, and she wasn't sure how to handle it.

She made her way down the staircase and to the kitchen. She needed a late-night snack to calm her nerves. She opened the fridge and pulled out a strawberry shortcake and helped herself to a slice.

Remi made two cakes. One was served with dinner, and she'd told everyone to help themselves to the other if they wanted. Well, she needed that sugar rush now.

She was just sitting down to eat her cake when she heard creaking on the servant's staircase and turned her head slowly to peer into the darkness of the doorway.

Ashley Bundy

Richard walked into the light, rubbing the sleep from his eyes. She couldn't deny he was a good-looking man. He wore red flannel pajama pants slung down low on his hips and a skintight white t-shirt that did nothing to hide the tone beneath it. There was a smell of liquor emitting from him that was mixed with deodorant. He'd clearly been trying to cover the smell. She'd been meaning to talk to him about it, but the stress of the situation was evident in his eyes, and she couldn't help but feel bad for him. Still, she was disappointed he hadn't shown up to investigate the sighting earlier that night.

"Oh," he jumped when he saw her. "I'm sorry. I didn't think anyone would be up."

"It's your house," she laughed. "Cake?"

He looked at her, eyes wide with shock. "Wh—What?"

She gestured to the cake in front of her. "Do you want a piece of cake?"

"Oh!" he chuckled. "Sure."

She gave him a knowing smile. "What did you think I meant?"

"I didn't think you meant anything," he said as he took a seat next to her and helped himself to a slice. "So, why are you awake?"

She shrugged her shoulders. "Just trying to take everything in." It wasn't really a lie, but she wasn't sure he was ready to hear the whole truth. "How about you?"

"Insomnia."

"Have you always struggled with it?"

He shook his head. "No. I've been struggling since we got here though. I'm getting a couple of hours a night at the most. I think it's all the memories."

"Maybe you should go to the doctor and get a prescription until your nerves settle. A couple of hours isn't enough. It'll start taking a toll."

"I know, but I can't bring myself to do it. Callie died from taking sleeping pills."

Natalie's heart ached for him. She reached out and placed a comforting hand over his. "I'm so sorry to hear that. I know it's hard, but you have to remember she didn't die from taking one. If you take them responsibly, you'll be fine, and it's only for a short time. You have to take care of yourself."

He turned his palm up to hold her hand and gave it a gentle squeeze. "I appreciate the concern, but I'll be okay. I can't get too obsessed with what happened to her. It won't be productive."

"But it's productive to be obsessed with what happened here at Blackwood?"

He paused and his face fell. "Natalie, do you have any idea what it's like to lose family and not have any idea why?"

"I do," she admitted.

"You do?"

She sighed and gently pulled her hand from his grip. "My dad walked out on us when I was a kid. I never got an explanation. I grew up thinking I wasn't good enough."

"I'm sorry. That really sucks. People shouldn't have kids if they don't want to be parents."

"It's okay. It was a long time ago." She stuffed another chunk of cake in her mouth. "I still had my mom, and she was great. But we moved to Chicago not long after that. It was just the two of us. She worked hard for us, and she was always there. But I still always felt like a piece of me was missing."

"Then you do get it," his voice wasn't condescending, only full of wonder. "Most people say they do but they don't really."

"Yeah. They just expect you to be over it because it's been so long."

"Yes! Easy enough to say when you haven't experienced true trauma."

"My favorite…I know what you're going through. My dog died and it was so hard."

"I've gotten that too!"

"I mean, don't get me wrong, I love animals. I've had all kinds of pets, and yes it does hurt when they die. I'm not diminishing their pain. For some, that pet is the equivalent of a child. But don't tell me it's on the same level as abandonment."

"And abuse," Richard shook his fork in agreement before taking a bite.

Natalie blushed in acknowledgment. "I didn't want to pry."

"But you saw?"

She nodded. "When I touched your hand. Flashes of a belt and cigarette burns."

He shrugged his shoulders. "My uncle. Asshole."

"Was it just a resentment thing?"

"Maybe. But I think it was more a racist thing. My dad's entire side of the family was appalled when he got with my mom. They were all worried about their reputations. Fucked up thing is they were literally the only ones who even cared. Until my parents died, I'd only been around them once at a reunion. My grandparents even cut us out of the will."

"So, why did your uncle even take you two in?"

"It never made sense to me. He was always going on about duty. But then we'd get the business end of a belt, a smack, name called, belittled. And yeah, he burned me with a cigarette lighter a couple of times. Once, he even told a church lady who stopped by that we were the maid's kids."

"That's awful!"

"I lost track of how many times he had Callie committed."

"I thought that was because she talked about Blackwood in therapy."

"That didn't help, but he was greatly exaggerating things. He'd say she was getting weapons and threatening us and hallucinating. Her talking about possession just made it easy for the doctors to take his claims seriously."

Not knowing what to say, she gave him a halfhearted grin. In her experience, sometimes the best thing to say was nothing.

"Anyway," he let out a nervous chuckle. "So, you grew up in Chicago, huh? But your family has ties to Blackwood? How'd that happen?"

"Well, actually we're from here," she answered, thankful the conversation was shifting to safer territory. "My mom moved us to Chicago when I was about nine. She said there were too many bad memories for us here. I came back after high school graduation."

"You didn't like it?"

"It was fine, but I just didn't feel like me."

"Been there. How about the Blackwood connection? What's up with that?"

"I know of at least three generations who have worked here at one point or another. I guess we're drawn to this place like a moth to a flame."

"Well, you're not working here," he smiled.

"You think this investigation isn't work?" she laughed. "Honey, you got no idea the things that go through my head when I walk through this place."

Richard's face fell.

"What's wrong?"

"It's just that it seems I'm the only one not experiencing anything."

"The staircase…"

"Don't bullshit me, Nat," he said gently. "That wasn't an experience…unless you count when I was eight. It was a repressed memory. I mean, you see stuff constantly, even when you're not sharing it. I can see it in your eyes. Jamie has seen the damn teleporting painting. Remi got a visit from my Aunt Claire on our very first night. Rod saw Josie in the attic, the same place Aunt Claire saw her for the first time. But me? Dead silence."

"The staircase wasn't merely a repressed memory."

"What do you mean?"

"Repressed memories don't typically leave physical marks on you. Your back was covered in bruises and scratches. I'd be willing to bet that those marks were identical to the ones you got at the time."

"Well, then what does it mean?"

She sighed. "I wish I knew. The way you described it sounded more like you were witnessing it happen to someone else rather than simply remembering it. It's almost like a time vortex and somehow you got injured both times."

Richard took another bite of his cake. "Well, even if that is true, it doesn't change the fact that my family has basically been ignoring me."

"They're trying to protect you."

"From what?" His voice was so anguished.

"I don't know that yet. But your mom wants you to leave."

"You saw my mom?" He straightened up in his seat, looking at her intently.

Natalie nodded. "I'm pretty sure it was her. She just kept telling me I have to get you to leave. She seemed scared."

Richard looked at her with despair.

She leaned forward and took his hand again. "I will get to the bottom of it, I promise."

They stared deeply into each other's eyes for a moment and then a creak came from behind them.

They turned to see Remi standing in the doorway to the dining room. She turned abruptly and headed back in the direction she'd come from.

"Remi!" Richard called after her. He got to his feet and began to follow her.

Natalie watched after them, wondering how to tell him the rest.

# CHAPTER THIRTEEN

"Remi, wait!" Richard caught up with her halfway up the staircase and grabbed hold of her arm.

She stopped running and put her back to the wall, but she didn't look him in the eye. "I'm sorry. I wasn't trying to interrupt."

"Interrupt what? We were having a midnight snack. You would have been more than welcome to join us. You know, sometimes I just don't get you. You're my best friend, then you hate me. You forgive me, then you run out on me."

Fire flashed in his eyes, and he felt fury flowing from the tips of his toes throughout his entire body. She finally looked at him, and he automatically felt an anger that unconsciously made him ball up his fists.

"*Do it,*" a voice commanded inside his head. "*She deserves it. She's making a fool out of you. Are you going to let her get away with it?*"

For a split second he was startled by the voice. It was deep and smooth as silk, far inside his head. But then he thought of how much sense that the voice was making. She was making a fool out of him. Making him guess her emotions at every turn. Fuck those mind games.

"*Do it!*" The voice thundered in his head more insistently. "*It would be simple enough. Look where you are.*"

His hands were filled with a warmth, and he reached up unconsciously to put his hands on Remi's shoulders.

There was a loud roar from right up the stairs. It sounded like an unearthly guttural scream followed by a thump.

Remi jumped under his hands and jerked her head up to look up the stairs. Richard was broken out of his funk and followed her gaze.

Natalie appeared at the base of the stairs. "What was that?"

"It came from up there," Richard said, gesturing toward the stairs.

"Well, come on then." She rushed up, running right between them on her way to the second floor. Richard and Remi closely followed her.

As they reached the second-floor landing, they saw a smattering of books strown over the floor. The large bookcase that they'd adorned was laying halfcocked at the end of the hall.

Twenty minutes later, the group sat around Gus's computer monitors to watch what happened in the hallway. The hallway was still before the scream tore through the speakers, causing feedback. Then they saw the bookshelf lift itself up off the ground and hurl itself down the hallway.

"Holy shit," Rod murmured. His voice quiet at the sight. "That's a big ass bookcase. It didn't fall."

"It's clear it didn't fall," Jamie agreed, grabbing his arm and giving it a gentle squeeze. "It literally went all the way down the hall. It left the ground."

Richard exchanged glances with Remi, who was shaking next to him, and rubbed her shoulder.

"Well, Richard," Natalie said as she looked over at him. "There is definitely something here—and not just to sensitive people like me. It appears to be violent."

When everyone filed out of Gus's room for the night, Richard tugged on Natalie's shoulder and pulled her into his room before firmly closing the door behind them.

"What's up, Richard?" she asked him.

"I wanted to talk to you about something privately. Something I don't understand." He sat down on the bed and instinctively pulled a pillow to his chest.

"What is it?" she sat down with a look of concern on her face.

"Promise you won't tell Remi?"

"Richard, you know I can't promise something like that without knowing what it is. But if it has something to do with what happened tonight, you need to tell me. It could be important."

He nodded and took a deep breath. "I honestly don't know if it's related or not."

"Why don't you just tell me what happened?"

"Okay. Well, after Remi saw us in the kitchen, I caught up with her on the stairs. She apologized for interrupting us. It wasn't even a fight, but I suddenly just felt so incredibly angry at her. I wanted to hurt her. There was a voice in my head telling me to 'do it. Do it.' I literally reached out and put my hands on her shoulders. I think I was about to push her."

The concern on Natalie's face only grew. "Why do you think this might not be related to what happened?"

"Maybe it's in my blood," he admitted. "I mean, I grew up with an uncle who hated my guts. He was violent sometimes. Maybe I have some of that in me."

Natalie shook her head. "You don't. Do you hear me? You don't have that in you. Believe me, I'd know. You're a good person. Those thoughts, those urges—they weren't you. And think about it. You might have wanted to do it, but you didn't. You stopped yourself."

"That wasn't me," he disagreed. "I was interrupted by that roar upstairs."

"You're absolutely sure?"

He nodded. "Why?"

"Well, this is just my gut instinct here. I think there were two different spirits at work here. One was trying to get you to do something, and another acted to prevent you from doing it. It makes sense. Why cause a ruckus like that at that particular moment if they wanted you to do that?"

"Someone in my family?"

"That would be my guess, but I still wouldn't let my guard down just yet. The manner that bookcase was thrown was still concerning. Even if it is someone in your family, they may not be the way you remember them."

Richard nodded and hung his head. "So, do we have to tell the others? Remi?"

Her eyebrows furrowed together, and her mouth became such a tight line that it nearly disappeared. Finally, she spoke. "You didn't actually do anything, so I guess there is no reason to alarm them yet. I will be keeping a much closer eye on you though."

Relief flooded him. "That's fine. That's more than fine. That's exactly what I want. I don't ever want to feel that way again."

Natalie reached over and squeezed his hand. "I don't know what happened, but I promise you I will get to the bottom of it."

# CHAPTER FOURTEEN

Despite the warm weather, Richard had chills running up and down his spine. The group had been walking the property in the back of the house when they came across the cemetery. He'd known there was one. It had openly been talked about when he was a child. He just hadn't known where it was. Plus, he knew it wasn't uncommon for old properties like this to have their own cemeteries. However, he hadn't been prepared to find it completely cleared of weeds, and perfectly manicured, as if it were tended to every day. Natalie had mentioned wanting to investigate the cemetery anyway, and she didn't seem fazed at all. If there was one thing he could give her credit for, it was that she possessed a massive set of lady balls.

It was larger than Richard expected it to be, which was chilling enough. Then there was the grave in the second row that was uncovered. There were orange cones on each side of the grave, probably to keep anyone from accidentally stepping into it. There was a mound of dirt next to the grave, indicating it had been dug up. What kind of sick mind would do something so horrendous?

Remi shivered next to him and pulled her sweater tighter around herself, keeping her arms crossed as if she was attempting to hold in her warmth. She was looking at the grave with immense sadness on her face, a single tear rolling down her cheek.

Richard put his arm around her shoulders and pulled her into him. "I know," he whispered as he kissed the top of her head.

"What kind of a monster?" she sobbed out.

"Which one of you did it?" Rod snapped, glaring at the paranormal team.

"None of them did this, Rod," Richard said gently. "It's been like this for awhile. We just couldn't see it because it was covered with weeds."

"What makes you so sure of that?" Rod asked him. "We couldn't see shit yesterday. Now it's picture perfect."

"Look," Richard pointed around the edges. "The vines. Plus, the right side looks a little unstable, like it wants to collapse. This isn't a fresh dig."

Gus began to set up a camera on a tripod, pointing it directly at the open grave.

"Isn't that a little morbid?" Remi asked, looking at him incredulously.

"It is," Natalie answered before approaching the girl. She slid one arm around her back to give her a gentle squeeze. "But it's necessary. If someone dug up this grave, they had to have done it for a reason." She wiped away a tear from Remi's cheek. She made a silly face, pulling a reluctant laugh from Remi, who turned and put a hand over her face in shame at laughing over an open grave.

Natalie pulled her arm down. "Hey, now. No tears, okay? Look at it this way. The sooner we do this, the sooner she'll be at peace."

"Hey, did anyone notice the headstone?" Jamie asked, edging closer slightly. "Lucy Blackwood."

"That can't be a coincidence," Gus said excitedly.

"I seriously doubt that it is," Natalie agreed and moved forward around the cone. She stepped forward slowly and carefully, testing that the ground was steady as she went.

Ashley Bundy

When she was sure, she turned her back and sank to her knees. "Gus, give me a hand, would you?"

Gus stepped forward and knelt to offer Natalie a hand as she swung one leg into the grave.

"No, no! Good god, what are you doing?" Remi cried.

"Shh. It's okay. She has to," Richard said soothingly as he rubbed her shoulders. She sank against him, sobbing into his chest.

Once Natalie was all the way in the grave, she called up to the others that she was okay, and they all edged closer to peer in.

Baxter knelt next to the stone to look in, watching with a fierce intensity, and Richard couldn't help but notice it was the most interested he'd seemed in anything since he'd arrived.

There were loose leaves, vines, and dirt dropped in but what drew the eye was the sight of the tiny coffin. It was old and blistered and had been pried open at some point, though it appeared the perpetrator had at least slid the lid back over to conceal what was within.

As carefully as she could, Natalie pushed the lid off the coffin to look inside.

There was barely anything left of the small girl. Tiny bones splintered and appeared to be disintegrating. A brown rag of a dress draped the frame that was in tatters.

But it was her skull that seemed to interest Natalie the most. "Gloves," she called up to the group and Mel dropped a box of surgical gloves down to her.

Natalie put them on before gently picking up the skull. She slowly and tenderly examined it, turning it over in her hands. A large chunk at the back was broken.

Richard initially thought that age caused a crack but then he realized that the other piece was not lying on the bottom of the coffin.

"This isn't Lucy," Natalie said finally.

"But the headstone," Jamie protested.

"I'm telling you it's not her," Natalie sighed.

"Then who?" Gus asked.

Natalie gently placed the skull back down and then peeled her gloves off. She put one hand on the skull and the other hand on the tattered rag.

"I'm sensing a 'G'. The girl, the girl, the girl, and then 'G'. Ginny? Glenda...that's not right. It's right there, but I'm not getting a full read on it."

"Gloria?" Richard asked.

"Gloria," she whispered to herself. "Gloria, Gloria. Yes. That's right. That's this child's name. Someone crushed her skull like a grape."

Remi let out a strangled gasp next to him but did not remove her head from his chest to look at the spectacle before them.

"But if this Gloria is in Lucy's grave, where is Lucy?" Jamie asked.

Richard thought of the body of the girl found in the parlor with his family after the fire and Natalie's initial walkthrough of the property. How she'd declared that a child was buried in the wall. Could it be? Surely not.

Before he could say anything, Natalie's eyes glassed over, and her gaze traveled to a spot on the opposite side of the grave.

She carefully crawled forward and began to dig absently in the dirt until she pulled something loose. It appeared to be a piece of paper. She slipped it inside her jeans and then gestured for the others to help her out of the grave.

Mel and Baxter bent together to grasp her hands and pull her upward as she used her feet on the sides of the grave to push up until she was finally out.

She approached Richard and pulled the paper from her jeans, smoothing it out.

The others all gathered around, eager to see what it was.

The paper was slightly yellow, dirty, and torn from being in the grave, but it was still easily readable. It was a computer printout of a news article about a missing boy.

The familiar face of Donovan O'Ryan was to the right of the text which read:

**Lieutenant Robert O'Ryan and his wife Angela are urging anyone with knowledge of the whereabouts of their fifteen-year-old son, Donovan, to contact the sheriff's department immediately. It is believed the boy is in serious danger.**

**Donovan has been missing since Halloween night. A group of teenagers attempted to spend the night and have a Halloween party in an abandoned plantation home, Blackwood Manor, and tragedy ensued.**

**One teen in the group stormed into the sheriff's office, bloody, speaking of an attack at the mansion. When emergency services arrived, the bodies of four teenagers were found murdered. Donovan was not found.**

**Police say that further examination of the mansion showed evidence of someone living inside. The theory is that the teens disturbed the vagrant who had been living on site. There has been no word from Donovan, and his parents say that is unlike him.**

**Anyone with information as to Donovan's location should contact the sheriff's office immediately.**

"You said you knew Donovan?" Natalie asked gently.

He nodded. "That's him. Only he looked older when I knew him."

She then gestured towards something that he hadn't seen before. The date on the upper right-hand corner. It was dated the day before the fire that killed his family.

"This was printed out the day before…" she began, and then broke off in an effort to show sensitivity. "It would appear someone in your family learned Donovan's secret."

"Why was it in the grave though?" Rod asked, his usual sarcasm gone from his voice.

"The person who printed it was in that grave. They were probably the one to dig it up," she said gently and raised her hands to cup his face, tenderly urging him to look at her.

"I think they were investigating something else to do with the property and stumbled across that article. Whatever that something was is why they were in the grave. The article fell out of their pocket that night."

Richard crumbled the article in his fist, anger coursing through his veins.

"I still don't know *exactly* what happened," Natalie told him assuredly. "But we're getting closer. I can feel it.

# CHAPTER FIFTEEN

### Mel

Mel knew the stories and so much more. So she shouldn't have been shocked when she walked into her bedroom and found the portrait of the girl on her bed, sitting up against the bed frame. The piercing blue eyes seemed to pop off the canvas as it looked directly towards the door.

It was a painting. A painting of a child, no less. But still, a knot of tension balled up inside her stomach like a fist. Something wasn't right about that painting. She moved a foot to the left and the damn thing still appeared to be staring at her. She moved two feet to the right...it was still staring at her, and now appeared to be smirking as well. She knew she wasn't imagining it. The face had been expressionless before, and now it wasn't.

Mel backed up towards the open doorway, not taking her eyes off the painting, and called out to the others. She waited until she could hear their footsteps before stepping fully back into the room.

"Whoa," Rod let out a low whistle as everyone crowded in. "Lucy, I assume."

Natalie turned to Mel. "So, did you see?"

Mel shook her head. "She wasn't here five minutes ago. I went to the bathroom and when I came back, there she was."

"That seems to be her pattern," Richard agreed. "No one ever sees her move. She's just always...there."

Natalie approached the painting and put her hand on the frame and left it there for a moment. She then sat down on the bed and laid the frame flat, with the back facing up, and slowly began to remove the backing. Inside, there was a yellowing envelope. She gently took it out and tenderly removed the letter within before reading aloud:

*My Dearest John,*

*If you are receiving this letter, it is because I cannot bear the tragedy of our being any longer. War changes us, as you well know. It has changed Blackwood Manor as well. I do not care for the scars it has left on my heart and my body. The dangers did not go away with you. There was plenty to be had right here at home.*

*The servants left, one by one. The land was overtaken by dirty Yankees. They used Blackwood as their headquarters for a time. The thought still makes me sick. Those of us that were left here were forced to bend to their will, and all that implies.*

*There was an accident. Our Lucy is gone. I haven't told you yet. I don't know how to tell you. So, I shall do so here. I regret to say that it was at my own hand. It was not intentional, I promise. Please do not think that of me, my love. Still, it is a cross I cannot bear.*

*I have not entirely made up my mind. The only thing keeping me going is Percy. Our sweet boy. He is so sweet and giving and tells me every day that Lucy was not my fault.*

Ashley Bundy

*That it was an accident. Sometimes he makes me believe that everything has happened for a reason and will get better.*

*I cannot bear the thought of what may happen to him when I am gone, for he would be here alone. All the servants have gone. It is now just the two of us. If I should die, things would not be pleasant for him.*

*If I choose to bear my cross silently, you will never see this letter. I will keep it as a reminder to myself. I will keep it in Lucy's portrait as a reminder of what I have done. I can never forget.*

*All my love,*

*Your Margaret*

"Well, shit," Rod stated as she finished the letter. "She doesn't sound like a cold-hearted bitch."

"I always got the impression that she wasn't." Richard said. "Whenever people talked about her, they would say she was different in life. I don't know how they knew that, but apparently, there was enough hard evidence to believe it."

"She killed her child," Remi reminded them. "She admitted it. It's right there."

"Yes, but it does sound like it was an accident," Jamie said.

"She covered it up though," Remi protested. "If it was really and truly an accident why cover it up?"

"Unless it was the result of a bigger crime that was not an accident," Gus mused. "Think about it. She does something she shouldn't and doesn't want to admit to it, and her daughter got in the way somehow? We do have Gloria in Lucy's grave and no Lucy."

"So, what?" Rod asked. "You think she killed both girls? It seems like a stretch to me."

Mel's eyes were on Richard, whose eyes seemed to be trained on a single spot on the back wall. He appeared to be deep in thought.

"You okay, Richard?" she asked him.

He snapped his eyes off the spot and looked back toward her before nodding. "I was just thinking. I found Josie's diary in the cottage out back, but I haven't read it."

"Why not?" Natalie asked.

"I was advised not to by a friend of my parents. He said my mom became obsessed with it before she died. He didn't say it outright, but he strongly implied she disturbed something."

"Yeah, but he also said Josie and Margaret were secret lovers, right?" Jamie asked. "They probably only knew that because of the diary. There may be something about how the girls died in there."

Natalie nodded in agreement. "I agree. We need to know what's in that book. In the meantime, Gus and I were about to head out to the fields. I was getting strong vibes when we were investigating the cemetery, so I want to explore it further."

"Do you want us to come with you?" Remi asked.

"You can if you want, but it's not necessary. It was just a feeling. I didn't get any flashes, so I'm not sure if anything will come of it. In the spirit of staying thorough though…"

As everyone turned to leave the room Mel called after Richard and asked him to stay behind. Once the others filed out, she closed the bedroom door.

"What's up?" he asked, a puzzled look on his face.

Mel opened the top drawer in the dresser and pulled out a file. She'd turned part of the room into a makeshift office for her research. Richard had offered to let her use one of the other bedrooms—there was plenty of space—but she'd declined, wanting to keep her work as close to the vest as she could.

"I wanted to discuss this with you privately before bringing it to the attention of the others. I don't think it's common knowledge."

They both sat down on the bed as she opened the file. Inside were copies of sales receipts and deeds.

"What is all this?" he asked.

"Sales records. This here is a record of every time the property was sold. This one on the top is Claire. I went all the way back…" As if making her point, she flipped through document after document. "There were no documents dated before 1909. My best guess is it was understood before that the property would pass to the next generation. I thought I was at a dead end."

"Okay?" Richard asked, still confused.

"So, I decided to explore another angle," she flipped to the next page. "In 1909, Robert Blackwood sold the property to Daniel Thompson, a close family friend, and they continued to live on property for a while longer, although no longer owning it. Thompson owned the neighboring plantation, Heaven's Estate."

"That one's still operational I think," Richard said.

"Yes, it's thriving. So, I started to investigate the history of that property. Heaven's Estate is actually five years older than Blackwood Manor and it has stayed in the Thompson family the entire time. They have better organized documents.

"The original parcel of land was considerably larger and would have expanded over here. I did some calculations to make sure I wasn't off base, and I'm not. They owned this land before it was ever developed."

"So, let me make sure I'm understanding you," Richard said. "The Thompsons owned Blackwood Manor before 1909?"

"Yes. Before it was ever Blackwood Manor. Wade Thompson turned over a parcel of his land to Gerald Blackwood in 1808. Blackwood Manor finished construction the following year."

"Wait. He turned over part of the land?"

Mel nodded. "There is no record of an exchange of money, but he turned over this section legally. As you know, it's still a significant area. I'm not sure how accurate it is, but I found things in the archives that seemed to indicate he was obligated to. He lost a card game to Gerald Blackwood but didn't have the money to pay, so had to give him land."

Richard's eyes went wide. "The irony in that. Robert Blackwood selling to Daniel Thompson because of a gambling problem."

Mel grinned at him. "It's like we share a brain. Now, as if that wasn't weird enough, Heaven's Estate has its own history."

"Then why aren't people scared of that property?"

"It's not a ghostly history, per se. There are countless reports of neighbors reporting them to the sheriff due to missing or dead livestock. No evidence was ever compiled to suggest that the Thompsons were responsible, so no charges were ever filed, but the fact that the sheriff investigated many times is a major red flag in my book. Apparently, they used to be relatively shunned back in the day for not going to church. Essentially, they were considered godless heathens.

"Once certain views became more lax, their reputation seemed to improve. I couldn't find anything other than basic business dealings until two years ago. A descendant went missing."

Richard leaned forward. "There was a disappearance nearby not linked to Blackwood Manor? Recently?"

Mel nodded. "Kate Wilkes, the current owner, her grandson went missing two years ago. Joshua Harris, age twenty. There was a brief investigation, but no evidence was found to suggest foul play and it was concluded he left of his own free will. Which is fine. People move all the time. The fact that he left suddenly, without warning, without saying anything, and has not made any move to contact his family does have people in the community split on whether or not he was taken or left."

"Well, he is a grown man," Richard said. "He could have left for any number of reasons. I'd be a lot more concerned if it had been a child. So, quick question. Why did you want to discuss this privately?"

Mel sighed. "I know Natalie. This information makes the situation no longer about just you and your property. Now there are neighbors involved, and I think it should be completely up to you how to proceed. Natalie would take matters into her own hands and be going over, talking to them. She'd even sneak onto the property if she needed to. You needed a chance to, at the very least, prepare for that."

Richard nodded, soaking it all in.

"And Richard," Mel continued with caution. "You probably shouldn't let her touch you until you decide what you want to do. She'll know."

Richard moved toward the door and then turned back toward her. "Do you mind if I ask you a question?"

"Go ahead. Shoot."

"You don't strike me as the paranormal type."

She smirked at him. "That's not really a question."

"No, but—" he grabbed a chair and sat down to look at her. His eyes were glimmering. "There has to be a reason you do this. You didn't seem freaked out by the portrait at all."

"Oh, I am. I'm just good at staying calm."

"So, you don't have a reason for being in this field? I mean the others kind of make sense. Natalie is psychic. Gus has the technical side of things. Baxter will clearly have some sort of motivation to be dumping money into this endeavor—though I doubt he'd ever share. You're more of a question mark. I don't mean any offense by that."

She smiled. "You're not the first person to ask me that. I guess I just don't fit the mold. I doubt my story would fascinate you, but in the interest of being transparent, I'll tell you."

She ran her fingers through her short hair. "To make a long story short, I grew up in a haunted hotel."

"For real?" Mel loved how his eyes lit up. Nonbelievers were a drag to talk to—especially about this. But people who'd seen the other side kind of lived in a secret society. They loved each other's stories and wanted to peel back the layers like an onion.

She nodded. "For real. For ten years. After our mother died my dad moved us into a little apartment in the hotel. It was just him, my sister, and me. We got reduced rent in exchange for helping take care of the property. People came from all over to see it."

"So, you're kind of like me in a way. Growing up in a notorious haunted place. You get it."

"In some ways," Mel agreed and leaned back in her seat, allowing herself to be transported to another time. A time where she was young and innocent.

"I remember the first time I ever saw a ghost. It was the first night in the hotel. I had a hard time sleeping in a new place, so I went out to the living room to read a book. I heard clanging out in the hallway and went to check it out. This place had one of those old timey elevators with an iron gate, only it was out of order. There was a woman standing in front of it. I called to her, telling her it wasn't safe. She just smiled at me and turned to climb on."

"That's not so scary."

"No," Mel agreed. "Nothing threatening ever happened there, but I saw plenty. The people at the front desk said the lady's name was Lola, and she'd haunted the place for years. They believed she may have died in the elevator shaft, but they weren't sure. I became hooked. I wanted to know everything about her, about the hotel. I threw myself headfirst into books. I considered myself a detective. Turned out, I just have a knack for research."

"Oh," Richard's face was crestfallen.

"I told you it wasn't all that exciting," she said apologetically. "For what it's worth, I became obsessed with getting to the bottom of the history of haunted places. I ended up in Georgia because my research for Lola led me here."

His face brightened again. "In what way? Blackwood Manor?"

She smiled. "Not Blackwood Manor. Not everything is linked to this place, though I know it does feel that way sometimes. No. It turns out, Lola was born in Savannah. I came out here hunting answers about who she was and learned about Blackwood along the way."

Richard nodded. "Thanks, Mel. I know I must sound nosy."

"Don't worry about it, hon. It's not nosy to have questions about the people staying in your home. It's common sense. I'm honestly surprised more people don't ask. So, do you know what you're going to do about Heaven's Estate?"

He let out a long breath. "I guess I'm going to go talk to Kate Wilkes."

# CHAPTER SIXTEEN

### Natalie

*Natalie could see hands shooting up out of the ground, roots wrapped around dirty fingers. Agonizing screams filled the air, almost drowning the chanting coming from nearby.*

*A group of women in long skirts were gathered around a fire, hands joined and chanting a phrase that Natalie couldn't quite make out over the screaming. She could see one of them lifting a baby above the fire.*

*Instinct caused her to look away, but she could still hear the shrieks of the poor child burning up.*

Then the flash was gone, and Natalie was kneeling on the ground, her hand to the Earth, balling her fist around weeds.

"Natalie. Nat, you okay?" Gus was talking to her, and the trance broke completely as she looked up at him.

"I'm okay, but things are far worse than we thought."

"What do you mean?"

"Human sacrifice. This is either witchcraft or devil worship. I'm not sure which. I didn't see enough. Either way, we have a problem."

"You're saying someone did this to Blackwood Manor on purpose?"

"I'm saying it looked that way. It's what it felt like, anyway. Where's Mel? I need Mel," she pushed up to her feet and ran toward the house.

She pushed through the sliding glass door in the back and ran, calling out for her friend. When she reached the parlor, she stopped dead. There was an older man dressed like an old cowboy in there talking to Richard. He turned, and they locked eyes.

It was like time stood still for a moment, and only for a moment. She was a little girl again, feeling so much pain and heartbreak. He'd been the first man to break her heart, and she'd sworn she'd never allow another one to do so. She broke eye contact with him and asked Richard if he'd seen Mel.

"No, I think she went into town. Are you okay?"

"We'll talk about it later," she said and turned to go.

"Wait," the old cowboy said. "I think we need to talk."

"I have nothing to say to you," Natalie replied harshly.

"Wait," Richard said, glancing between them. "Do you two know each other?"

"In a manner of speaking," Natalie replied. "He's my father."

Two hours later, there was a knock on her bedroom door, and she asked who it was. Richard poked his head in, and she beckoned him inside.

He strode in and sat down at the foot of the bed and looked at her with pity. She hated that look. She'd gotten it many times throughout the years. She'd gotten that look when her sister Caroline died of leukemia, she'd gotten it when her parents divorced, and more times than she could count when people found out her father was not in her life. It was a look that said, "You poor dear. What a sad life you must lead." It sickened her.

"Don't look at me like that," she told him flatly.

He immediately wiped the look from his face. "Sorry. Are you okay?"

She shrugged her shoulders. "I wasn't expecting to see him, that's all. But I shouldn't have been too surprised. I knew he'd worked here before. It's not like it's going to change my life too much."

"Maybe you should talk to him," he said gently.

"What for? He walked out at the most difficult time of my life when I needed him the most. That sent a pretty clear message to me about how I was prioritized. Nothing he can say will change what happened."

"He told me he didn't walk out. That he lost custody."

"He lied," she reached for a cup of coffee on her bedside table. "Tensions were high after my sister died. Him and my mom were at each other's throats constantly. He got tired of the fighting and walked out. I saw it."

"How old were you?"

"Ten."

"You were young. Maybe you interpreted what you saw wrong."

"Richard," she said sharply. "Don't."

"I'm sorry," he put his hands up in surrender. "I'm here if you do change your mind and want to talk about it though."

"Thank you."

"So, before that happened, you seemed excited about something. What was that about?"

"Oh!"

In the excitement and surprise of seeing her father, she'd completely forgotten what happened outside. She quickly told Richard about her vision.

"So," he said once she finished. "You're thinking human sacrifice?"

"It's the only thing I can think of. The set up, the chanting, the baby. I've never heard rumors of that sort before. I'll have Mel do some digging to find out if the property is linked to witchcraft in any way."

# CHAPTER SEVENTEEN

*Don't let her touch you. Don't let her touch you.* Richard recalled his conversation with Mel. Was the woman high? He immediately chastised himself. Of course, she wasn't. He just didn't like the prospect of not being able to touch Natalie until he decided what to do with his new information.

He couldn't help but feel attracted to Natalie. She was beautiful and sexy as hell, and he felt tiny little bolts of electricity coursing throughout his entire body any time she touched his hand. He liked the sensation and didn't want to give it up. He also liked that Natalie was a pool of mystery. He wanted to know more; despite how much he'd learned. It wasn't a quality he was used to experiencing with women. It also seemed clear that she was into him too. The flirting, the cute, pouty little smirks. He couldn't wait until the investigation concluded, and he could ask her out.

He also couldn't help but feel conflicted since finding out Brad was Natalie's father. He'd heard both sides of the story and it honestly seemed to him like they both got the shit end of the stick. Brad was sticking to his assertion that his ex-wife was granted sole custody of Natalie and moved away. Natalie believed he walked out on them.

Richard didn't have reason to think either of them was lying, so he believed the truth was somewhere in between. He didn't want to pick sides and hoped they didn't put him in the middle. He was fiercely attracted to Natalie, and he was beginning to look at Brad as a father figure. This was the first time he could recall an older man showing any kind of concern for his well-being since his own father died.

The sooner he could get to the bottom of the situation with his neighbors, the sooner he could stop worrying about how to avoid Natalie and hopefully get her to at least talk to her father.

He pulled through the gate to Heaven's Estate and followed a perfectly clear, manicured path to the front of the house.

The contrast between Heaven's Estate and Blackwood Manor was remarkable. Heaven's Estate sported a beautiful brick exterior with a porch surrounded by intricate latticework. Gorgeous flowers wrapped the base around the porch and baby blue shutters adorned the windows. It was lively, joyous, and didn't look as if it had been built in the 1790s.

He strode up to the front door and knocked. He waited maybe two minutes before the door swung open and an elderly lady stood before him.

She was perhaps late 70s to early 80s, but she was trying to look much younger. Her hair was bleached blonde and piled high on her head. She was wearing bold blue eye shadow and heavy eyeliner. An extremely short, red skirt hugged her hips above the fishnet stockings on her legs.

"Yes?" she asked pleasantly.

"Hi, ma'am," he said as he extended his hand to shake. "I'm Richard Price. I own Blackwood Manor and wanted to introduce myself to neighbors."

The woman looked surprised. "Blackwood Manor? No one's lived at Blackwood Manor for ten years."

"Yes, ma'am. That was my family. I've inherited it now that I'm an adult."

Her eyes brightened, and she grasped his hand with both of hers tightly. "Oh! You're the boy! Emma's boy! I'm sorry,

I don't think I ever knew your name. If I did, I didn't remember."

"That's alright," he chuckled. "It was a long time ago."

"And I've gotten a bit old," she patted his hand. "Things aren't as clear as they used to be, I'm afraid. I'm Kate. Kate Wilkes."

"Oh, I recognize that name!" He said with recognition. "I remember Aunt Claire saying you welcomed her with a pie."

Kate smiled. "Yes. Real nice woman, that Claire. Did you know she returned the gesture when I had a heart attack? I wasn't home, but my daughter said she was lovely."

Richard smiled. "No, I didn't know that, but it sounds like Aunt Claire."

"Oh! Where are my manners?" Kate stepped back from the door and gestured him inside. "Come in! Come in!"

He followed her into a small sitting room off the entrance and sat on a cushy blue sofa.

"I was so sorry to hear about your family," Kate said with a sympathetic smile. "I know it's been a long time now, but I never got a chance to say so before."

"That's okay. I appreciate the thought."

"So, what can I do for you?"

"Well, I was going through some old property records, and I found something that indicated your family owned the property that Blackwood Manor was built on. I wasn't sure if I interpreted it right though because the Blackwoods didn't keep the best records. Things are spotty here and there."

"Really?" Kate furrowed her brow up in confusion. "I know we owned it for about twenty years in the early 1900s. Robert Blackwood sold it to my family. They were friends. He'd gotten himself into some money troubles, but they continued to live there. When they moved away, we officially sold. Is that what you mean?"

"No, I knew about that. I found something that made it look like Blackwood was originally part of Heaven's Estate."

"Oh," Kate let out a dejected sigh. "It's the first I've heard of it. I'm not saying it's impossible. I mean, it was hundreds of years ago. and I know the Thompson's and the Blackwoods had history, so it's very possible. I was just never told anything about it."

"I see," Richard sighed in frustration. "So how long have you lived here?"

"Oh, off and on my whole life," she laughed. "I moved out for a while in my rebellious, independent years, but came back when I inherited the land from my grandmother."

"Were you around Blackwood a lot while my family was there?"

"Popped in a few times, but I wouldn't say I spent a lot of time there."

Richard reached into his pocket and pulled out the article about Donovan that Natalie found in the grave. "Do you recall ever seeing this man around?"

Kate took the article and studied it for a moment before answering. "Yes, actually. I recognized him right away. When I had my heart attack, I recovered briefly at a nursing home and Claire came to see me. I remember telling her not to trust this man."

"Do you remember why?"

"Well, as this states, he went missing after a massacre at Blackwood Manor. His remains were never found. This article glosses over it, but it was strongly believed around here this boy was responsible. When I saw him at Blackwood Manor, I became concerned and warned Claire. The next thing I know, everyone in that house died, and this Donovan is missing again. So, if you see him, you'd do well to call the sheriff. Is he hanging around?"

"No, I just remembered him. When I found this, I was very confused."

"Yes, I can see that," she agreed. "I'm sure you're fine, but I'd keep an eye out just to be safe."

"I'll keep that in mind," Richard rose to his feet. "I'm sorry to have to rush off, but I have an appointment with a roofer in a few minutes. I appreciate you taking the time to talk to me."

"Oh, of course," she grasped his hand again and gave him a bright smile as she escorted him to the front door.

As Richard walked out to his car, he smiled with satisfaction. His mind was made up. He was going to give Natalie the new information. Kate Wilkes had just lied to him about Donovan, and he was determined to find out why.

# CHAPTER EIGHTEEN

Jamie

There were people out there who would call Jamie too sensitive. She was believed to be soft because she didn't talk much, and it was like moving mountains to get her to look into the eyes of someone she didn't know well. That was a façade though.

Part of having to grow up way too fast was shutting up and paying attention. It was the story of her life. Was she more likely to jump at a shadow in the dark? Probably. But was that really sensitive when, in your experience, the dark had teeth? Long, pointy, jagged teeth ready to rip you to pieces?

Jamie was strolling through the grounds behind Blackwood Manor, letting it all soak in. She didn't want to voice it out loud, but she found herself being just as mesmerized by Blackwood Manor as so many before her. The place may have been run down, but she was beautiful. There was something ethereal about being in the presence of this house. Jamie couldn't shake the feeling that she was being allowed to revel in the beauty and charm—clued in on the many mysteries that lay over the property line.

It was true that she'd been thoroughly creeped out at first, when the cab pulled up and the driver refused to get close. She'd been amazed at the sight of the porch staring out at them with the twisted grin formed by the columns and windows. The grin had seemed more and more ferocious as they'd hiked down the driveway.

Ashley Bundy

But as time went on, she'd felt more and more at peace. Strangely enough, she felt grounded and secure for the first time in her life. She wasn't too creeped out by the house despite seeing Lucy Blackwood. The occasional weird thing happened, but compared to her childhood and living on the streets, it was child's play. She was experiencing just enough to believe the house was haunted—the oil painting had a habit of turning up where it wasn't supposed to be so often it was no longer surprising, more shadows than she could count, but it was never enough to feel the urge to abandon everything she owned and run out in the middle of the night screaming.

She was brought out of her thoughts by a flash of blue hidden amongst the weeds at her feet. She knelt and pushed the weeds to the side to find a gorgeous blue stone.

She almost stood up and disregarded it, but her attention was pulled back like a magnet, and she picked it up.

The stone was small, about the size of her palm, and she was able to close her fist over it. It felt warm in her hand, and she brushed aside as much of the caked-on dirt as she could.

It was a sapphire blue, and one thing was absolutely certain—it didn't belong. A jewel in the rough. It didn't look like anything else she'd seen on the property—inside or out, and she wasn't completely sure what it was. It wasn't an actual jewel, though it felt like one.

As she held the stone, Jamie was overwhelmed with a warmth that started in her palm and trickled throughout her body. She felt powerful, joyful, and beautiful all at once. Like she could overcome anything.

She studied the stone closer and was overcome by the beauty. It needed proper respect. She wanted to wash it until it gleamed and began the stroll up to the house.

She'd never been able to have nice things. So, to an ordinary person this may just be a lovely stone—but to her it represented every nice thing that she'd ever been denied.

Suddenly, she no longer wanted to proudly display it. She was overcome by the strong desire to store it somewhere safe. It was hers and no one was going to take it from her.

"Don't move!" a voice yelled at her.

She jerked her head up to see Brad walking towards her briskly. His arms were over his head. She scowled at him. He couldn't have her stone.

"Don't panic," he said as he slowly approached.

"What?" she didn't have to wait long for an answer. There was a crunch in the brush nearby. She turned slowly to look.

It happened slowly, like a video being played frame by frame. Obscured by the tall weeds was the shadow of something large. The sticks crunched sickeningly under foot as it moved forward before finally emerging.

Time stood still for Jamie. There was a very large black bear not even six feet from her. Her heart thumped dangerously in her chest and sweat poured from every part of her body.

The bear was on all fours, but it still felt unnaturally large to her. On all fours, it was almost as tall as her shoulders. It was staring straight at her. She was close enough to see her reflection in its eyes and feel the warmth from its breath.

"Oh my God," she squeaked out. This was it. This was how she was going to die. She must have been a toilet brush in a past life.

"Do not move," Brad commanded, his voice strong and authoritative. "Don't panic."

She could tell from his voice that he was close, but her gut told her not to look away from the bear. Instinct told her it was just waiting for her to look away to pounce, so the standoff continued.

"What do I do?" she said, refusing to look away from the bear.

"Whatever you do, do not run," Brad told her. "Slowly wave your arms over your head and tell it to back off."

How was he talking so much, and the bear was still so focused on her? How was that possible? Still, she did what he said. She waved her arms in a slow, robotic like gesture, mimicking the way she'd seen Brad do when he'd first approached her.

"Oh my God, Jamie!" she heard Rod's panicked voice and thundering footsteps approaching.

"STOP!" Brad commanded. "You'll startle it. Keep going, Jamie. You can do it."

"Back off," she squeaked.

"You're the boss. Tell it!"

"Back off!" she shouted; her voice stronger this time.

The bear seemed aggravated. It let out a loud snort and took a couple of steps closer.

"Jamie, listen to me very carefully," Brad was telling her. "The cottage is a few feet behind you. It should be unlocked. Don't run. Don't turn your back. Walk back slowly."

Tears streamed down her face as she took a step back, continuing to wave her arms. Then she took another step. The bear took two steps forward.

"This isn't working," Rod was saying. "Do something!"

"Hey!" There was a loud shout coming from far to her left and the sound of banging. "Over here!"

The bear snorted again and jerked its head to look in the direction of the noise. Jamie took three giant steps backward before the bear snapped around to look at her again.

"Hey!" another voice yelled, followed by a whistle and more banging.

There was now noise coming from three different directions and the bear roared, looking from one direction to the next.

"NOW!" Brad shouted. "MOVE!"

Jamie felt a structure at her back, stuck her hand behind her, felt the knob, turned it, and dove backwards, slamming the door behind her.

She'd never been inside the cottage before, and she couldn't take in what she was looking at. She just ran to the nearest window and looked out.

Natalie and Richard were both circling from opposite directions with pots and pans that they were banging together. Rod was standing a few feet away from Brad, looking distressed. Baxter was all the way up at the house, leaning up against the door, observing everything.

Brad was waving his arms and yelling at the bear. It gave one final roar, and turned, running off in the other direction.

Everyone then ran for the cottage. Rod was inside first, and Jamie threw herself into his arms, finally allowing the hysterical crying she'd been holding inside to burst forth.

Everyone else started peppering her with questions, asking if she was hurt and if she was okay. It was a good minute before she was finally able to squeak out that she was fine.

Brad pulled his cell phone out. "It was headed in the direction of Heaven's Estate. I better call Kate and warn her." He disappeared down the hallway to make the call.

"What was that?" Rod thundered. He gave Richard an accusatory stare. "You never said anything about bears."

"I've never seen one before," Richard answered defensively.

Natalie shook her head. "Don't blame him. He's right. There hasn't been a sighting in this area since I was a little kid. I'm just glad I happened to look out the window and see it."

"What the hell was it doing here?"

"It wasn't an accident," Natalie agreed. "Enough of this. Ghosts are bad enough, but now we're dealing with wild animals. It's time to kick the investigation up a notch."

# CHAPTER NINETEEN

Baxter

Baxter stood under the spray in the shower, letting it pound down onto him. His skin was peppered in red from the heat, which he'd turned all the way up. He didn't feel the heat though. All he'd felt since arriving here, was dirty and disgusting. He had to wash the dirt away.

He ran his fingers through his hair and squeezed his eyes shut as he thought about what he'd seen. The girl from the video, who he knew was Lucy Blackwood, had been showing herself to him every day since he'd arrived. He hadn't told anyone.

He wasn't unaware of the irony of that fact. They were here for a paranormal investigation, but he was keeping his own experiences to himself. It didn't matter in the grand scheme of things. The goal was to get inside the manor, and he'd accomplished just that. It would only hinder his plans to tell the others.

Waking up and finding Lucy, half transformed into some devil creature, was jarring, but she'd made no moves to harm him. He knew why.

It started off with her simply staring down at him, then progressed to that damn menacing smile. Like she already knew how she was going to take him down. Then she'd started talking to him, whispering orders in his ear. He'd scoffed at first. He wasn't planning on taking orders from a child any time soon. But the things she was saying started to make more and more sense to him.

Ashley Bundy

When the water started to turn cold, he shut it off and climbed out. He felt as if there were eyes on him, and a chill ran up and down his flesh. He wrapped a towel around his waist and double checked the door to make sure it was closed. It was.

Then he turned to the sink, splashed water in his face, and reached to fill the basin. He glanced in the mirror at himself, and not liking what stared back out at him, then immediately looked down.

Once the basin was full, he went to work on shaving, attempting to look at nothing but the shaving cream.

He'd heard noises during his shower, something that hadn't surprised him. This uneasiness he felt standing here, with a blade to his face, however, was a completely different story.

He knew the stories, of course. There wasn't anyone in two hundred square miles that hadn't at least *heard* of Blackwood Manor, even if they had no interest in the paranormal. The place was simply synonymous with the term 'haunting.'

He'd grown up hearing about it constantly. His entire family was always talking about Blackwood Manor. The house, the land, the ghost stories, mysterious goings on linked to it for eons.

He'd developed a fascination from the time he was in diapers, not only with Blackwood Manor, but with ghosts in general.

He'd experienced something about five years back that made him doubt the paranormal. Everything he'd ever believed in was now a lie in his own mind, and he stepped back from investigating. Still, he hadn't been able to let go entirely.

Then he'd met his ally in a bar. The more they talked and exchanged stories, the more they realized they both would forever be tied to Blackwood Manor and would never live a normal life because of it.

It didn't take long for them to form a plan. Baxter had money. A lot of it. So, they devised a plan to join a paranormal group. They knew there was a possibility they'd never set foot in Blackwood Manor, that they likely wouldn't. But if there was any kind of chance, that would be it. One point had been stressed above all others. No one could know they knew each other before.

When Natalie said they would be investigating Blackwood Manor, it seemed surreal. He would have thought he'd have to hang around the paranormal scene a hell of a lot longer to stand a chance of getting close. It was too easy.

He heard a noise directly behind him and immediately tensed. He forced himself to take his eyes off the shaving cream and look behind him in the mirror.

Lucy Blackwood stood behind him. The blood stain on the front of her nightgown seemed to be spreading. She'd told him what happened. He felt for her, but he still couldn't stand to keep looking at her. The scaly blue appearance of her skin gave him the creeps, and it's not like it was a normal, everyday occurrence to have hooves and horns growing out of your body. She gave him that smile. The one that made his breath leave him and feel like there was a dagger in his heart each and every time.

She nodded at him once. "What are you waiting for?" she hissed.

He nodded back and relaxed his shoulders before continuing to shave. "Okay, okay. I heard you the first time."

# CHAPTER TWENTY

Remi

Remi sat in her car in the driveway, staring up at the house. She was trying to tamper down her anxiety before going inside; something that had become a cruel new ritual.

In many ways, she often wished she'd never come here. But it was important to Richard, and what was important to him was important to her. So, she would suck it up.

She constantly felt uneasy. Ever since that first night, she couldn't shake it. She heard voices, she saw shadows, and she couldn't shake the feeling that she was being constantly watched.

It wasn't the first time she'd felt this way in her life, but it was probably the most intense.

She hadn't initially been put off by the prospect of Blackwood Manor back in New York when she'd heard Richard talking about it. He'd said it was old, decrepit, and haunted. But at the time, she'd still considered it to be just a house. Could she really look at it that way now? Seeing what she'd seen? Learning what she'd learned?

Remi liked Richard immediately upon meeting him on the medical bus. She'd liked Rod and Jamie too but was especially drawn to Richard. He was going through so much but was still such a sweet and gentle soul.

Once, she saw him give his antibiotics to a mother with a baby. The woman had a nasty case of mastitis and needed antibiotics, but Richard had received the last. He immediately gave them up and said he'd come get his on the next run. He also gave the mother his last ten dollars for formula for the baby. Remi had never seen someone in such a deplorable situation as him be so selfless.

His clothes were in rough shape. They were ripped, torn, stained, and didn't properly fit, so Remi began bringing clothes and food when she knew they would be going through their area.

Eventually, they began hanging out and as she learned more about his life, the more compassion and respect she had for him. She'd been impressed with his vitality and optimism in the face of everything he'd gone through.

When he'd told the group he'd inherited Blackwood Manor and wanted to go back to get answers, she'd seen the pain in his eyes. He deserved answers, and she desperately wanted to help him get them.

But then she'd seen it. She'd never felt such an ominous level of discomfort like something was seriously wrong. She didn't want the paranormal investigation after her experience, but she couldn't help but hope that if she supported him through this that she and Richard may finally be able to take the next step forward.

Then she'd seen him with Natalie. He did nothing to hide the way he looked at her—when she was looking and when she wasn't. They'd been extremely cozy in the kitchen the other night—sharing cake, whispering softly, and holding hands. Remi felt just as humiliated as if she'd walked in on an act much more intimate.

Could she have been misreading the signs all along? She'd just known that Richard felt the same way about her. Her gut told her so, and her gut was rarely wrong. Jamie even told her that she and Rod thought the two of them would make a great couple. She'd believed he just needed to go slow. Maybe the reason he hadn't made a move was simply because he didn't feel anything like she'd thought.

She sighed and laid her head against the headrest while she looked back on that night.

Perhaps the most ironic thing about the entire situation was she actually liked Natalie. Not at first. When she'd first waltzed into the house and Richard chased after her like a puppy, Remi had decided that she was a cheap floozy.

Over time, though, Remi had grown to like her. She was nice, and spunky, and it was fun watching her pop off at Rod, something not many people did. Things would be so much easier if she could hate Natalie. But she couldn't.

Her thoughts were interrupted by a thump on the hood of her car. She jumped, snapping her eyes open and lifting her arms in a defensive gesture.

There was a dirty, mangy cat sitting on the hood, staring in at her. It was skinny with long, gray hair that was matted, and its eyes were wide.

"Oh!" Remi cried in surprise. She slowly opened her door and stepped out of the car, trying to not startle it. The cat stood defensively but didn't scamper away as she approached. It meowed but allowed her to pick it up. "You poor thing," she whispered gently and rubbed her ears.

Ignoring her fears, she walked into the house as she cradled the cat against her. She walked to the kitchen and gently placed it in the sink so she could carefully examine it for any injuries.

The cat did meow, and its hackles were up, but it let her examine it. Finding no injuries, Remi concluded that the cat was just a dirty stray. She reached for the Dawn dish soap and carefully lathered the cat up, putting the water on a slow trickle.

The cat was shaking, but it did not try to run as she carefully and slowly soaped it and used her fingers to work through the knots in its fur.

She heard a noise behind her but was careful not to get tense. She didn't want to scare the cat.

Footsteps approached her, and she used her peripheral vision to look next to her. She was relieved to see Richard standing there.

"What have we got here?" he asked.

"She was outside. Looking scared and lost. I couldn't tell if she was hurt, so I brought her in. She's not, thank God. Just scared and dirty."

"I can't believe a stray is letting you bathe her."

"I'd like to keep her, if that's okay." The words were out of her mouth before she even thought of it.

"Of course you can. I think we could use a pet around here. What do you want to name her?"

*Whiskers*. The name vibrated in her head. A woman's voice said it so confidently. Who was Remi to deny that voice? She repeated it to Richard, and he grinned at her.

"Whiskers?" He asked with an amused lilt to his voice.

She blushed despite herself and turned back to the cat. "It fits her."

"You're an extraordinary person, Remi," he said. She felt his hand on the small of her back as he peered into the sink at the cat.

She was annoyed at the tremor that ran down her spine. She hated that her body reacted this way to his touch, his nearness. The mixed signals had to stop. He was toying with her emotions. Could he not tell that he was killing her by saying these things when he would never be with her? She felt a sudden burst of anger and decided to let it out.

"No, I'm not," she answered. "If I were, I would have told you long ago you smell like a brewery."

She wasn't lying. The smell of vodka followed him around like a fog. She'd found a million reasons to excuse it. He was going through hell at home, he was returning to the site of an extensive family trauma. A drink every now and then was understandable. True as the words may be, she immediately felt guilty once they left her mouth.

She felt his hand tense on her back before it dropped away. She was expecting him to get defensive and snappy, but he didn't. Instead, he turned, placing his back against the counter, and hung his head.

"I know," he sighed. "I have a problem. I am trying. It's just being here. I have so many emotions, and I don't really know how to handle them. Half the time, I don't even realize the drink is there until I've already thrown it back."

Remi turned off the water and grabbed a towel to wrap the cat in. "Do you mean it's subconscious? Or that you aren't in control of your own body?"

"No, I'm in control," he answered carefully. "It's more like I do it on autopilot because it's there."

"Where's it coming from?"

"Well, you know I used to steal booze if I wanted to get drunk," he told her honestly. "That was on purpose, but it wasn't a lot. I haven't needed to since we've come back here. It's always in the cabinet. A couple of times, it's even been on the bedside table in my room. Usually, it's the cabinet though. Brad confronted me about this too. He took the bottle out of the damn house, but the next time I opened the cabinet, there it was. Getting rid of it doesn't stop it. So, sometimes I'll eat dinner, or a snack, and I'll notice after that the bottle is there half empty or I'll see an empty glass. It's like I don't realize it while I'm doing it. Only after."

Remi's blood felt cold. "And you keep saying you haven't experienced anything?"

He gave a small chuckle. "I guess you're right. I say that because I haven't seen anything. So it feels like everyone else is more in tune than me. But it's not normal. But I swear to you, Remi, I'm not trying to drink."

"You know how you said you're in control when this happens?"

He nodded.

"Hate to break it to you, but what you just described is a man out of control."

He hung his head, and she felt her desire to comfort him bubbling up inside again.

She gently toweled Whiskers dry while she tried to think of a plan. "Well, removing it didn't work but obviously we need to find a way to stop this from happening. We can see about getting you into AA."

Richard shook his head. "I'd be willing to, but would it make a difference if my body is acting separate from my mind?"

"It can't hurt to try."

He nodded and looked down at her. "You know, you're right. I'll never know if I don't give it a shot. It might not work but maybe it will."

"I'll go with you if you want."

"You'd do that?"

"Of course," she answered, and they exchanged an understanding look. "Which cabinet was it?"

He pointed one out and she strode over to it and opened it up. There were coffee mugs and plates but no bottles of alcohol.

"Are you sure?" she asked him. "There's nothing in here."

"What?" he strode over and peered in. "That doesn't make sense. It's *always* there." He closed the cabinet and reopened it. Now there was a full bottle of vodka in the front.

"What the hell?" Remi snatched the bottle out and poured it down the sink. "That's not normal."

Richard's face was crestfallen. She hated seeing him look defeated.

"When Brad took the bottle away from you the first time, did he take it out of the cabinet or did you?"

"He did. I pointed it out, but he opened it up and pulled it out."

An understanding took hold of her, clenching around her stomach like a fist. "So, the house is learning."

He furrowed his brow in confusion. "What do you mean?"

"Well, think about it. It made alcohol appear to you before and didn't hide itself from Brad. He removed the bottle so now it doesn't appear for anyone but you."

He shook his head. "That doesn't even make sense."

"Why did it not appear for me but *immediately* appeared for you?"

"Did what appear for you?" Natalie said as she walked into the kitchen.

Remi was immediately annoyed at her appearance. He was opening up to her, and of course, his new boo thing had to interrupt. At the same time, though, this could help to prove her point though.

Rather than answer Natalie's question, Remi gestured towards the cabinet. "Could you open that, please?"

"Are your hands broken?" Natalie asked her.

Remi narrowed her eyes. "No. I'm trying to make a point to him."

Natalie gave a dramatic sigh and walked over to the cabinet and opened it. There was no bottle of alcohol. "What am I supposed to be seeing here?"

Remi stared Richard down, waiting for him to acknowledge it, but he didn't say anything.

"Hello?" Natalie snapped.

Remi turned to her. "Richard's been drinking alcohol that appears to him and no one else."

"Remi!" he snapped out in shock. "I told you that in private."

"What?" Natalie said and went to stare him down as well. "Is that true?"

He didn't answer her, so she turned to Remi. "What's the story?"

"He told me there's always a full bottle in that cabinet when he opens it. It wasn't there when I opened it or when you did. That's weird enough, but the first person he told was Brad. It was there when Brad opened the cabinet, but he removed it. I think the house is learning. Richard told me it not being there for me was a coincidence."

"Son of a bitch," Richard muttered under his breath.

Natalie tensed at the mention of Brad's name, but she remained calm. "If that's true, it's very concerning."

She turned to Richard. "Open the cabinet, Richard."

"Look, I really don't think it meant—"

"Open it," her voice was sharp, and her gaze cut into him like a knife.

Ashley Bundy

Remi sent up a silent prayer, thankful that Natalie wasn't looking at *her* like that.

He reached over and angrily snapped the cabinet open. There was the bottle in the front.

Natalie grabbed the bottle and held it in her hand for a moment before looking up. "This is a major problem. It wants you compliant because you're a threat."

He looked at her for a moment. "The house wants me compliant?"

She shook her head. "Not the house. Something *in* the house does."

# CHAPTER TWENTY-ONE

### Remi

Remi's eyes snapped open, and she looked over at her clock. 3:07. Of course. She was waking up around this time almost every day. Some mornings there was no known cause, other times there were. This time she'd heard crying.

It was a sorrowful wail that she felt in her bones. Her own eyes welled up. How she hated to feel people's pain like this. She'd felt other people's pain all her life. She'd never been able to fully understand why. She knew when people were angry, but what truly affected her was sadness.

It was like feeling their pain and sadness spiraled her own mental health, and she would find herself thinking of unspeakable things. Sometimes, those thoughts would only be present for a matter of seconds, but it was always enough to scare her.

She heard a meow coming from the foot of the bed, and she looked down to find Whiskers staring at her. Her eyes were wide and the hair on her body was standing on end.

"I know," Remi whispered. "I hear it too."

She threw the bedcovers off and scooped the cat up in her arms before walking out into the hallway. A chill ran down her body as she immediately noticed that the crying stopped.

"Great," she whispered. "It's coming from our room."

Whiskers meowed, and Remi tenderly kissed her head. "Shake it off."

Ashley Bundy

She decided to go down to the kitchen to make a cup of hot cocoa for herself and a saucer of milk for Whiskers. She glanced to the end of the hallway and the entrance to the servant's staircase. She immediately chose to go the long way. Even though it had been so many years since Richard was attacked there, Remi hadn't been able to bring herself to go that way.

Dread began to squeeze in her gut when she entered the dining room. She could hear voices coming from the kitchen. They were low, and the light was off.

Remi took a deep breath and forced herself to walk quickly to the kitchen doorway and flip the light switch. Her lungs burned at the sight before her.

A young man and a girl turned to look at her. The man had nubs for horns on the top of his forehead and looked just as startled as Remi felt. The girl was a light skinned Black girl with burns, and she smirked in her direction.

The two appeared to have been mid-embrace when she turned on the light. Her lungs burned because she'd forgotten to breathe.

The cat let out an angry meow and swiped at her with its paw. She didn't let go though. Besides Richard, this cat was the only thing in this house to give her any kind of comfort at all.

"Hey," the guy said as he raised his arms up to show he was unarmed. "Easy now."

"Richard!" she called out with a shaky voice.

"No, no, no," his voice was firm and gentle all at once. "We're not going to hurt you." If it hadn't been for the horns on his forehead and the unsettling smirk of the girl behind him, Remi may have actually been calm. But she couldn't unsee those things.

*Run. Now.* The two words thundered in her head insistently, and she unfroze, running back toward the front of the house screaming at the top of her lungs.

### Gus

Gus rolled over in his bed and tried to silently decompress his annoyance. It was so exhausting pretending to be this happy, go lucky, excited guy all the damn time. Mostly, he was annoyed and disgusted. At least it would all be over soon.

He didn't particularly care about the paranormal, but he'd be damned if he'd admit that to anyone. He'd only learned enough to be passable. He'd only joined the group to ultimately fuel his overall cause. Just this last investigation, and he would never have to spend time on this ridiculous bullshit ever again. Blackwood Manor had been his goal all along, and he was finally here. It wasn't like he'd never tried other methods. He'd come to the property on three separate occasions. Once he'd tried to come in through the window in the parlor, once through the kitchen door, and once he'd even climbed the drainpipe to try to get in upstairs. He'd been unsuccessful each time. The window wouldn't break, the door was locked tight, and he could have sworn something tossed his ass right off the roof. Luckily, he'd landed in a bush and been unharmed. He didn't get it. Other people broke in all the time, but he was unable to. It was like he needed an invitation. The paranormal group was the easiest way to get one.

He couldn't stand Natalie. He found her cocky and arrogant, and he wasn't sure how much of her "powers" he believed. Instinct wanted to call her a quack, but the only thing putting him off entirely from that point of view was the fact that she wasn't making any money doing this, so she was a complete mystery to him.

Today was particularly annoying. Natalie dragged everyone in the house down to the damn kitchen to open a cabinet and see if a bottle of vodka appeared to anyone. It didn't appear to anyone but that Richard guy. She'd then set a rule in place that Richard could no longer open that cabinet and in order to make sure he didn't, he was banned from the kitchen. Everyone else was to bring him his meals. Like an infant.

He was also having a hard time going off to investigate things. Every time he thought he had a free moment to sneak off, he'd run into someone and get sucked into something, forcing him to abort the mission. There were too many people in this damn house.

He'd been listening carefully, and he hadn't heard any noises for almost half an hour, so he felt that it was now safe to do what he needed to do.

He threw the covers off him and got out of bed. As he walked out into the hallway, the floorboards creaked under his feet. He stopped and silently cursed before moving forward again more slowly. He made his way to the stairs and toward the cellar.

He began feeling along the walls looking for loose bricks. He didn't find any and grunted in frustration before hearing a noise in the middle of the room.

He jerked around and saw a pretty Black girl about thirteen. Despite being obviously burned she was beautiful. Her electric blue eyes pulled him like a magnet. She was standing next to the dumbwaiter door. The group had marked that door to be explored later. Natalie said it was unstable.

The girl rolled the door open and climbed inside. He was drawn forward and could hear her moving deep within as he followed her.

He didn't even realize until he was deep into the shaft that he never grabbed a flashlight. There was a light emitting from the girl that was lighting the way.

Just as he realized that fact, the light surrounding her went out. He continued walking several feet in the direction the girl had been headed. Eventually, he realized he couldn't even hear the girl moving anymore. There was zero light. He was lost.

PART TWO

# CHAPTER TWENTY-TWO

Richard shot out of his bed before he was fully awake. The sounds of Remi's screams tore through him as he wrenched his bedroom door open. Not again. This couldn't be happening again.

Other doors opened as the others came out of their rooms rubbing their eyes and brandishing weapons. Rod held a lamp over his head.

Instinctively, Richard turned toward Remi's room, but Jamie grabbed his arm and pushed him toward the stairs. He flew down them, and Remi ran right into his arms. She was crying hysterically. "Someone's in the kitchen," she told them. "A young boy and girl."

Without a word, everyone made their way to the kitchen. There was no one there. Remi told them that she'd seen the pair at the kitchen island.

Baxter checked all the corners of the room and cursed when he noticed that there were no cameras in here. "There should be cameras in every room," he growled. The others all ignored him as they looked for any potential clues as to who the couple was.

No one was in the pantry and the back door was locked up tight. Collectively, they all moved from one room to the next, looking for any intruders, but they didn't find any. Eventually, it was decided that whoever it had been was gone. They were furious they didn't have any camera footage of what Remi saw but agreed it was best for everyone to go back to bed so they could operate fresh the next day. In all the chaos, not one person noticed that Gus had not joined their search.

Richard followed the calls coming from Gus's room the following morning. The others were already gathered in the room, and it didn't take Richard long to realize that Gus wasn't there.

Mel knelt in front of the bed over some documents that were spread over the duvet.

"What's going on?" he asked.

Mel turned, and she looked relieved to see him. "Good. You're here. I saw Lucy in the hallway and followed her. She led me to these papers and disappeared."

"What are the papers?" Jamie asked.

"You better take a look at this," Mel said as she handed one to Richard.

It was a missing person's poster for a young man. Richard immediately realized it was Kate's grandson from Heaven's Estate. Attached was a copy of his birth certificate. The picture on the poster bore a strong resemblance to Gus.

"Holy shit, Dude!" Rod exclaimed. "Is that Gus? That's Gus, isn't it?"

"What the hell?" Jamie said. "Why would he come back to Blackwood instead of his own plantation?"

Natalie looked down at a lockbox at the foot of the bed that was flipped open. "Did you break that open?" she asked Mel.

Mel shook her head no. "Everything was laid out on the bed when I came in."

Natalie placed her hands on the lockbox and appeared to be concentrating hard. Before she could say anything, everyone's attention was broken by Rod.

He was now standing at the opposite end of the room looking at the computer monitors that Gus had set up, fiddling with the controls.

"Whoa, Rod," Mel strode toward him. "That stuff can be temperamental. It's best not to mess with it if you don't know what you're doing."

Rod continued doing what he was doing. "I'm no expert, but no stranger either. My old lady ran a gas station for a while when I was younger, and she would take me to work with her. The cameras were similar, so I think it's the same basic idea."

Jamie approached him and put a hand on his shoulder. "But babe. Why are you messing with it though?"

"We don't want him to come back and find us going through his shit," he said. "It doesn't look like he's in the house now."

He ran it back and was examining frame by frame. "Here!" he exclaimed, pointing toward a camera set up in the cellar that picked him up crawling into the dumbwaiter shaft.

"He's in the tunnels," Natalie said with an eerie calm to her voice. "What's the time stamp on that?"

"3:10 in the morning," Rod answered.

"That's when Remi started screaming," Jamie exclaimed. "I remember because I was facing the clock when I woke up."

Rod switched to the camera that was aimed at the stairs from the first floor. "Here's where we all meet Remi, and there we go to the kitchen. Gus came down right after we were out of view and rounded toward the cellar."

"It's after eleven now," Natalie said. "He wasn't captured coming back out?"

Rod went back through the frames slowly, making sure he didn't miss anything. He made sure to check the camera in the cellar and the one in Richard's bedroom. "No, not from the entrances we know about."

"Then he's still in there," Natalie whispered. "Something's wrong. We need to search for him. Damn it, they're unstable. We need contractors."

"Natalie," Richard interjected gently. "I know you don't want to hear it, but…"

She nodded. "Call my father. See if he knows of anyone to bring with him. It'll take more than one person."

Two hours later, everyone was assembled in the cellar, getting ready to enter the tunnels beyond the dumbwaiter shaft.

Brad brought four other men with him that he'd worked with previously.

"Okay," Brad took authority. "Remember, we have a young man lost in there for at least ten hours. Be thorough and careful. We have reason to believe there is a stability issue inside."

He gave each of his men a headlamp and a heavy-duty flashlight. They also all carried tools in case they were needed.

"We should all pair up," Natalie added.

"That's not happening," Brad interjected. "You all are kids and unskilled. We know what we're doing. We can move faster and more safely without you."

"This is non-negotiable," Natalie put her hands on her hips and glared at her father. "If you don't take us with you, we go in after you."

"Natalie Jean Morse," he growled out.

"Don't go middle naming me," she snapped back. "And for your information, I haven't gone by Morse for years. It's Morgan now. You know damn well you need me."

He glared at her. "Fine. But just you. And you go with me."

"Wait a minute," Richard interrupted. "This is my house. I think I have a right to know what's back there."

"If he goes, we go," Rod chipped in. "We're not going to be the only ones sitting here on our ass not knowing if you're all buried alive in there."

"You all are not qualified!" Brad growled.

"We all go with someone who is," Remi suggested. "That way, we aren't wandering on our own."

Brad threw up his hands, exasperated. "Fine. Natalie goes with me. Richard, you go with Paul."

"I want Remi to come with me," Richard cut in. She beamed at him.

"Fine," Brad nodded. "Baxter can go with Phil. He's our fastest guy."

Baxter did not respond verbally, only nodded his head in acknowledgment.

"I'm assuming Jamie and Rod will want to stay together. So, you two go with David. And Mel can go with Steve."

Everyone teamed up with their prospective leaders while Brad handed out whistles. "If you find Gus, give two sharp blasts on your whistles. We'll all know to come back here then. If you get hurt, three long blasts, wait thirty seconds, and another three. Do this until the rest of the group joins you. If you get lost or separated, stay where you are and continuously blow your whistle until we get to you. Do you all understand?"

Everyone nodded in agreement and then they all began to climb into the tunnel.

# CHAPTER TWENTY-THREE

Brad and Natalie

*"Is it possible to start your life completely over three times?"* Brad pondered to himself as he strolled through the tunnels with Natalie.

He'd been riding an out-of-control see saw on the ride of life for as long as he could remember. It was enough to give a person whiplash.

The first time his life changed was going to prison for defending a helpless child who happened to be Black. He wouldn't take it back, even knowing the outcome. The behavior of those boys was deplorable, and he'd always felt society had a job to keep each other in check. Otherwise, that outrageous behavior would become an untethered balloon.

No, he wouldn't take it back. But there was no denying it changed his life. When he got out, he was treated differently, like the scum on the bottom of every person's shoe he came across. Well, almost every person. He still had a decent rapport with enough people to keep him from hardening like he'd seen so many of his fellow prison mates do. There were good people in his life that he felt were amazing relationships. He'd always been extremely close with his grandmother, Sadie, and she'd loved him fiercely despite the prison record. Kate Wilkes had been a present figure in his life from childhood, and he'd always had the utmost respect for her. Their bond only strengthened after his prison sentence. Claire just might have been the best friend he'd ever had. And of course, there was Sylvie. He'd met her after prison.

Ashley Bundy

He'd joined a church, trying to integrate himself back into society, though he'd never been particularly religious. That's where he'd met his Sylvie. She didn't judge him. If anything, she respected him and fell for him hard because of his actions. She'd told him so many times that there was nothing sexier than a man who would always do the right thing, even if it meant a negative outcome for himself.

He strongly believed that if it weren't for that prison sentence, he never would have met his wife or had his two beautiful daughters. So, no, he wouldn't take it back. It catapulted him into the best years of his life.

However, the second time his life completely changed, it had been a stark drop toward rock bottom. In such a short time, he'd lost a group of amazing friends in a horrifying way, and he'd blamed himself. His sweet Caroline died, and he'd blamed himself. He'd spiraled, bringing his issues home, eventually losing everything.

Now, as he walked behind his daughter in an awkward silence, he asked himself how likely it would be that his life could change for a third time. The question thundered in his head like a desperate prayer. Could he get her back? He'd do anything for the possibility of making up for lost time. At the present, it didn't seem like the odds were too high, but he couldn't help but have hope that he could prove himself to her somehow.

He didn't know how to talk to her anymore. So much had happened.

The air in here was stale and damp and, were it not for the headlamp and flashlight, it would be too dark to see a foot in front of his face.

He'd been amazed ten years ago when Claire was in here. The fact that there were so many tunnels had been a surprise. It was always assumed there was a narrow shaft that led the dumbwaiter from one floor to the next. Behind it, though, there was a massive maze of tunnels.

He and Natalie were working together on this relatively well, but it was all business. At least for her. She was using her gift to lead them along, pressing her hands to the walls, leading first one way, and then another. If they needed to crawl over rock, they assisted each other. But that was where the cooperation died. They weren't speaking unless it was her saying, "This way."

He desperately wanted to talk to her, to hold her hand for longer than it took to help her up over a rock. He'd never thought he'd see her again, and he'd accepted that fact. So, the day she'd run into the parlor to talk to Richard, it was like seeing a ghost. She'd grown up so beautifully.

She clearly despised him and that hurt worse than a dagger to the heart. He had half a mind to talk to Sylvie and find out what the hell she'd been telling her all these years, but he no longer had a contact number for her. He'd asked that Mel girl to get him information and keep it confidential, but she hadn't gotten back to him yet.

She'd inherited her great-grandmother's gift. Kind of. But it worked differently. He both hated that she would have to deal with that curse for the rest of her life, but also couldn't help but be proud as he watched her operate. He loved that she had such control already.

He'd suspected that when she was a child, of course. She always seemed to know things she shouldn't but was never very specific about how she would know. Abilities did run in the family, but he wasn't sure of the extent of hers. He'd been out of the picture before he could find out.

He cleared his throat and attempted to talk. "Natalie…"

Ashley Bundy

She cut him off with a sharp, "We have a mission. This is neither the time nor the place."

"There's no reason we can't talk until we find him."

"We could miss hearing him call out," she answered.

"That's bullshit," his voice remained gentle. "With an echo, we'll hear just fine, and you'll still feel anyway," he gestured towards her hand running along the wall.

Natalie sighed. "There's nothing to talk about. You're a stranger now."

"Yeah but," he stopped and gently took her arm to pull her back, "that wasn't what I wanted. You know that don't you?"

She shrugged his arm off. "What I know is I lost my sister and my father in the same month. I know I'm sickened by the pity I get from people when they learn about my situation. I heard from Grandma until she died. But not you."

"I walked out that day, yes," Brad insisted. "But not forever. I needed to cool off. I came back."

Natalie scoffed.

"I did," he told her. "But you and your mother weren't there.

"Don't you shit talk my mother," she said fiercely through gritted teeth. "She struggled to raise me alone because you couldn't even be bothered to pay child support. She sometimes didn't eat for a week because she could only afford food for one of us. She's the only reason I even made it."

"I have nothing against your mother, baby," he said gently. "I loved her then, and I love her now. She clearly did a good job with you. You've turned out amazing. You're beautiful and smart, and you care about people."

He reached out to place his hands on her cheeks, but she stepped away from him in disgust. He put his hands down but implored her to see reason anyway. "You have a gift, Natalie. Use it. Can't you tell I'm not lying?"

She looked at him. "But I know for a fact my mother didn't. And because of that I still can't fully trust you."

She shook her head and gave him a hard stare. "We need to keep moving."

# CHAPTER TWENTY-FOUR

### Richard and Remi

Richard and Remi had been following Brad's buddy Paul for quite some time. Richard sensed Remi shaking beside him, so he reached over to squeeze her hand.

She automatically leaned into him, and he pulled her close, throwing an arm around her shoulders. She was freezing cold.

"It feels like it's been going on for hours," she said nervously.

"This isn't on the blueprints," Richard admitted.

"It wouldn't be, would it?" Paul chuckled. "The public blueprints on this house weren't drawn up until the 1920s. There's no telling how many secret passages this place has."

"But why?" Remi asked. "Why would they need all these tunnels underneath the house?"

"That's a ten-million-dollar question, isn't it?" Paul answered.

Richard felt a lump in his throat and forced himself to swallow. He thought of Aunt Claire, wandering down here alone in the dark. How had she made it out? It was nothing short of a miracle.

Paul threw up an arm to stop them in their tracks. "Hold up. Let me see your light."

Richard held up the flashlight to brighten the walkway in front of Paul.

"Oh my God!" Remi cried out, throwing her hands up to clutch at her cheeks.

In front of Paul was a body on the ground.

"Gus!" Remi screamed.

Richard reached for his whistle, but Paul gestured for him to stop. "It's not Gus."

"What? Of course, it is!" Remi cried.

"No," Paul took the flashlight and shone it directly on the body. It was a man, taller than Gus and skeletal. "From the look of his clothing, he's been here at least ten years."

He knelt down and began going through the man's pockets until he found his wallet. "Richard, Remi, meet Brock Donahue. Nice to meet you, Brock."

Richard's blood was cold. Brock Donahue. Aunt Claire's abusive ex-husband. The man who was wanted for killing people who helped her. So, he'd ended up here after all. How did he end up in the tunnels? And how had he died?

"We might as well keep moving," Paul said. "There's nothing we can do for him now. We'll mark the spot so we can find it again and call someone once we find Gus and get out of here.

"Mark it how?" Richard asked. "Should we use the whistle and gather the others?"

Paul shook his head. "It would just distract from the main objective. Finding Gus."

They looked among themselves and their belongings.

Paul gestured toward the scarf that was wrapped around Remi's neck. "May I?" He removed it and walked to the mouth of the tunnel that they'd entered and wrapped it around a beam.

Inwardly, the gesture pissed Richard off. How presumptuous to remove her clothing.

"This way, when we come back and get to the fork, we know this is the way we came."

Ashley Bundy

Remi nodded. "I guess that's okay. As long as we come back for him."

Paul agreed. "We will. Of course. But our priority has to be the man who is alive and possibly injured."

They continued their journey.

# CHAPTER TWENTY-FIVE

### Mel

It felt a little strange for Mel to be traveling down a narrow, rocky tunnel alone with a stranger in near darkness. She would have preferred to be with one of the groups but understood the more groups they had, the better the chance they had of finding Gus.

This wasn't the way she'd expected her day to go when she woke up this morning. She'd felt the house was unnaturally still that morning...almost like an ordinary home, but she wouldn't have guessed this.

She'd been shocked to discover all those papers spread over Gus's bed like an inventory of gold waiting to be explored.

From the time they'd first formed the group, Mel liked Gus. He was a little strange, sure. But he was a sweet enough kid.

Now, knowing he was the missing kid from that neighboring plantation, she was baffled. What did it mean? Where had he been? Why did he come to Blackwood Manor instead of going home? Why was he messing around in the cellar in the middle of the night and *why* had he climbed into the dumbwaiter? Especially considering Natalie told them it wasn't safe.

"So," she said, trying to break the uncomfortable silence. If she was going to be stuck in here with this guy for a while, it made sense to get to know one another. "How long have you known Brad?"

He looked at her briefly before continuing. "We used to live together. In a more difficult time."

"Oh, you were cell mates?"

He looked surprised. "You know about that?"

"I'm the group's researcher. I pretty much know everything about everyone. Except you, since this is the first time I've seen you."

"Hmm," he grunted out. "I got out about a year after Brad. I was having a hard time getting work, so he helped me get licenses and such. I work over in Macon, but Brad called in a favor for me to help him with this here search."

"It's my understanding that half the crew that was working on the place under the last owner were ex-cons," Mel said.

"Does that statement have a point?"

"No," she laughed nervously. "I was just wondering if you were on the crew back then. I know Brad was. So, I just figured maybe you were as well."

"No," he shook his head. "Brad did ask me, but I didn't like the vibes that came off this place. Just driving by this place made me nauseous. Didn't want to think about working here all day every day."

"But you're here now," she pointed out.

"It's a rescue mission," he said simply. "A one and done. We find this boy and then I'm gone. Plus, I can't explain it, but it doesn't feel as oppressive as before. It's not gone. But it's less."

"That's interesting," she stated. "No one else has said that."

"So, Miss Mel, the researcher, what's your story?"

"Not much to tell," she answered. "I grew up in a haunted hotel and that fueled an interest in the paranormal.

But I also developed an interest in the places, not just the activity itself. I have a theory that the history of the property is just as important to the why as the spirits. Maybe even more."

"That's cool," he nodded in approval. "It's a new way of looking at it that most people don't think of. So, have you learned a lot about Blackwood Manor?"

"Oh, it's a treasure trove of information," she laughed. "And I'm still not done. Natalie has me looking into the possibility of witchcraft."

Steve stopped. "Say what now?"

"Apparently, she had a vision that led her to believe witchcraft may have been performed here back in the day. She wanted me to investigate it. I'm not finding anything to support that as of right now, but I'm still looking."

"That's fucked up," he said.

"Actually, I think it clears a lot of things up if it's true. Especially how certain people's entire personalities changed while living on the property."

He looked ahead and then stopped in his tracks as he stared ahead. "Maybe you're a witch. You talked this into existence."

"What are you talking about?" she asked, but then she saw. They'd come to an alcove in the wall that led to a small room.

There was a dull, red glow emitting from it. They approached it, and Mel called out Gus's name, in case he'd taken refuge inside and lit a candle.

There were candles placed in a circle, a pentagram drawn in dirt in the center and skulls placed all around.

"This is fucked up," Steve stated. "How the hell are these candles *lit?* Someone's been here recently."

Ashley Bundy

Mel moved her flashlight up to reveal a skeleton in the wall.

"Hell no!" Steve exclaimed. "I'm out! If you're smart, you'll do the same."

He turned and began to rush down the corridor. "Steve, wait!" she called as she rushed after him.

# CHAPTER TWENTY-SIX

Baxter

*That little prick,* Baxter thought to himself as he followed his guide, Phil, down the narrow corridor in the tunnel.

What had Gus possibly been thinking coming down here in the middle of the night and not even bothering to turn off the camera? He knew they were there. *He put them up!* This was such a stupid move. Then, of course, he'd had to go and climb into the fucking dumbwaiter like a dumb ass. They were wasting so much time by climbing around down here in the dark.

Gus probably wasn't even down here anymore. After all, it had been like twelve hours by this point. But he couldn't complain about it without giving himself away. There was no choice but to go along with it.

When Gus reappeared, he was going to get a thrashing. This was not part of the plan. Why have a plan if they weren't going to stick to it? And now the group knew who Gus was. They *could not* learn who Baxter really was.

"Whoa, check this out," Phil said suddenly as he sprinted to kneel over someone ahead of them on the ground.

"Is it him?" Baxter asked coldly.

"No," Phil answered, too distracted to notice Baxter's tone. "He's been here awhile." He examined him more closely. "It's a kid!"

Ashley Bundy

He turned to face Baxter who swung out to hit him hard in the face. Baxter stared down at Phil, who'd crumpled to the ground like a sack of potatoes.

# CHAPTER TWENTY-SEVEN

Rod and Jamie

Rod held Jamie's hand and squeezed it. Her breath was growing ragged beside him the further into the tunnel they went. She was claustrophobic, so this was no small task for her.

Rod grew increasingly amazed by Jamie by the day. He knew she was scared, but she kept it mostly internal. He could tell because he knew her telltale signs, but the average person would most likely think she was cool, calm, and collected.

Her claustrophobia stemmed from her father and stepmom continuously locking her in a closet as a child. Something he was pretty sure she'd only shared with him. She wouldn't take elevators, always opting for stairs instead. They slept with a light in their room that shone stars on the ceiling. If anyone asked, they said it was pretty, an answer that was basically accepted. There wasn't any need to say that Jamie needed a nightlight because she was scared of the dark.

Some people may think her childish if they were to learn that fact, but Rod completely understood. When you had a shitty childhood, being raised in shitty circumstances, it could shape your future.

Rod had his own vices. He had an extremely unhealthy relationship with food. Having been basically starved as a child, he'd been forced to steal what he could from gas stations. Some days, he'd get lucky and score a nasty hot dog that had been marinating under heat lamps all day. Most of the time, though, it would be a bag of chips and a candy bar.

That was how he'd met Richard. They'd shown up to the same gas station on a day where the clerks were more present than normal. It may have been an inventory day; they never really knew. But they'd teamed up.

Richard caused a distraction, drawing the clerks away, and Rod went through with a bag and grabbed all kinds of food. They'd met up on the corner and split the loot. The friendship became instantaneous. Partly because they just got along, and partly because there was an unspoken understanding that the other knew the hell they lived in every day. They were no longer alone.

Likewise, when Rod met Jamie, she was sitting on a street corner with a sign begging for food. He'd witnessed a man pull up next to her and dump a drink out the window onto her head.

He'd gone over to her and offered her the only clean shirt in his bag and helped her dry off the best she could with the limited supplies they had. He'd watched her cry and listened as she talked about how after a lifetime of abuse, her father finally dumped her and taken off for good and how she didn't know what to do and she was so hungry. He'd taken her under his wing. She reminded him so much of himself, but she had a strength and positivity that he'd never possessed himself. He'd always have bitter anger for his circumstances and swore one day his family would rue the day they put him in such a deplorable situation. She saw the best in every situation and was always ready to roll up her sleeves and jump into anything head on, no matter how scared she was.

"You okay, babe?" he asked as he gently nudged her arm with his elbow.

She nodded and gave him a reassuring squeeze back. "I'm fine. At least we have lights. I think I would feel better if we hadn't split up into so many groups. You know how you always want to yell at the screen when people split up in horror movies."

"I know," he agreed. "But it was really the only way. There were so many different routes that if we'd stayed one large group, it would take days."

"I just hope no one gets lost."

"Don't worry," their guide David smiled at her. "All of these guys are very good at what they do. Your friends are safe with them. And even if they do somehow get separated, we all have whistles. They won't be lost for long."

She smiled back and Rod gave David a fist bump of appreciation.

They continued in silence for a few more minutes.

Rod began to hear a light, muttering noise and raised a hand to grab David's arm. "Do you hear that?"

"What?" David asked.

"That," they held their breath a moment and began to follow the quiet sound around a bend that wasn't on their direct route.

They came cross a man sitting on the ground with his knees to his chest and rocking back and forth. There was a bundle at his feet.

As they came closer, they could see that it was Gus. His arms were wrapped around his knees as he rocked and muttered under his breath. They couldn't make out what he was saying, and he didn't seem to notice that they were there.

"Gus," Rod said, kneeling in front of him. "Hey, man. Everyone is really worried."

Gus continued to rock and mutter, not acknowledging Rod.

Rod shined the flashlight in his eyes, and his pupils did react to the light, but he didn't blink or jerk his head away.

Rod reached over and slapped him in the face with all his might.

Gus jerked to the side and threw up his arms in a defensive gesture and started yelling.

"Gus! Gus it's me! It's Rod!"

"No!" Gus's eyes were wild, and he continued aimlessly throwing his arms around. "Not real! You're not real!"

"Sorry, dude," David muttered before hitting him in the head and making him slump forward.

"Did you just—" Jamie asked quietly.

"He's not dead," David assured her. "Just knocked out. He was too hysterical to get out of here safely."

Before she could answer, whistle blasts began and seemed to come from multiple directions all around them. They didn't know where to turn. They were everywhere.

# CHAPTER TWENTY-EIGHT

The whistles were echoing against the tunnel walls, making it impossible to tell what direction they were coming from.

Brad whirled around, trying to determine which direction seemed louder. He also tried to listen for a pattern, but it sounded like whistles were overlapping, and he couldn't tell if multiple people were blowing their whistles, or the echo was just worse than he'd anticipated.

Natalie placed both hands against the tunnel walls that seemed to be thundering beneath her palms.

"Can you tell where it's coming from? Or the code?" he asked her.

"Multiple," she answered. Her brow furrowed with frustration. "Someone has found Gus, but someone else is lost and there's another. I think someone is hurt, but I can't tell which is coming from what direction."

"Should we go back to the house?" he asked her.

She shook her head. "If someone's lost, we'd have to come back in anyway."

She'd barely finished her sentence when they heard thundering footsteps in the distance and stopped talking to watch as a flashlight beam came into their view.

"We're down here!" Natalie shouted, and the flashlight beam changed directions and began coming toward them.

Natalie shined her flashlight down at the ground so as not to blind the person coming toward them. As the person ran closer, Natalie could see it was Mel.

Ashley Bundy

She stopped before them, dropped her whistle from her lips and bent at the waist. She had her hands on her knees as she struggled to regain her breath.

She was no longer blowing her whistle, but whistle sounds continued to echo around them, reinforcing Natalie's theory that multiple people were using their whistle simultaneously.

"Are you okay?" Brad asked, taking her arm, and forcing her to look up at him so he could stare into her face. She was slightly flushed and out of breath from running but seemed unharmed. "Where's Steve?"

"He left me!" she gasped. "We found this weird room with candles and skulls, and he got spooked and left. I tried to follow him, but he was too fast for me. So, I started blowing my whistle. I know we were supposed to stay where we were if lost, but there were so many echoes from others blowing theirs, too, I figured I might not be heard, so I tried following the sounds. I figured I'd come across someone eventually."

Brad nodded his approval. "That was quick thinking. If it weren't for the echoes, I'd be scolding you. But it's very possible we couldn't have isolated your sound so good job."

They continued to glance around as more frantic whistling happened all around them.

"Did you see anyone else?" Natalie asked.

Mel shook her head. "But I think we were relatively close to someone not too long ago. I heard footsteps on the other side of the wall before we found that room."

Natalie put her hands on either side of Mel's face and closed her eyes, trying to pick up on Mel's vibrations rather than the whistles.

She then began to move in the direction that Mel came from with Brad and Mel following her. Occasionally she would stop to touch Mel again, and then she'd be back on her way.

This went on for a while before they reached the room. The candles were lit, and the light was flickering against the walls, giving it a reddish tint. Skulls were scattered throughout the room and there was an obvious skeleton embedded in the wall.

"Was it like this when you found it?" Brad asked.

"Yes," she answered. "Steve freaked out and ran off."

Natalie then put her hands to the wall opposite the room and began to follow it down another corridor. Brad and Mel were careful to stay close to her.

One of the whistle noises became more distinguished the closer they moved, and they soon came on another light.

"Thank God!" Baxter rushed up to them. There was blood running down his face from a gash near his eye.

"Baxter!" Mel exclaimed. "What happened to you?"

"We were ambushed!" he said, his voice fast and loud. "We found this body and while he was looking to see if it was Gus, something attacked us."

"What was it?" Brad asked. "A ghost?"

"I don't know. I didn't see it," Baxter answered. "Something hit me in the head, and everything went dark. When I came to, Phil was down."

"Where?" Natalie asked.

Baxter pointed down the corridor, and they followed him.

There were two bodies piled on top of one another. The one on top was Phil, head lamp still strapped on. His eyes were blank, and he was covered in blood.

Brad knelt to feel for a pulse. He then looked up at the others. "He's dead."

"Oh!" Mel cried out, raising her balled fists to her mouth, her eyes wide with terror.

"What about the other one?" Natalie asked, her voice choked. "Is it Gus?"

Brad gently pushed Phil's body off the other to examine it. "No, this one's been here awhile. He patted it down, looking for a wallet. When he found it, he opened it to check for the ID. When he did, he went quiet for a moment, staring at the ID before finally speaking. "Looks like we finally found out what happened to Donovan O'Ryan."

"What are we going to do?" Mel cried. "There are tons of bodies down here, we don't know where the others are. Our people are being attacked!"

"Tons might be a slight exaggeration," Natalie said gently.

"There are skeletons in the wall! In what world is that normal?"

Around them there was another whistle, though more subdued of a sound and the pattern was distinguishable.

"Someone found Gus," Natalie said, echoing his own thoughts.

"Question is, is he alive?" Brad said.

Collectively, the four of them began to follow the whistle.

Rod and Jamie both blew their whistles simultaneously. They used the same rhythm and pattern but decided to blow both to hopefully be heard over the echoes.

They let out collective sighs of relief and dropped the whistles as the footsteps came nearer. Natalie, Brad, Baxter, and Mel were coming towards them.

Natalie knelt to the ground and put her hand to Gus's forehead.

"I had to knock him out," David said. "He was hysterical and not making a lot of sense."

"He's okay," Natalie said, looking up at the others. "But something scared him pretty bad. We need to get him out of here."

"We can't," Jamie said, shaking her head. "Richard and Remi's group aren't here."

They stayed silent, listening carefully for a moment. There were no whistles, no sound of footsteps, no noise in general.

"I have no clue where they are," Natalie said "but we can't wait. We have to get him out of here and Baxter needs medical care as well."

"But—" Jamie protested.

"Look, we need to get the injured out of here," Brad said, authority in his voice. "We found some very concerning stuff down here. We can come back for them."

"I agree, babe," Rod said. "The vibes in here are darker now. We need to get anyone out of here that can't defend themselves."

Brad and David hoisted Gus's unconscious body up between the two of them and began to drag him. Rod led the way with the flashlight out front and Natalie grabbed the bag that was at his feet.

Three hours later Blackwood Manor was once again the source of much chaos and gossip. The lawn was full of police cruisers and ambulances.

Once the group made their way out of the tunnels, they'd called the police to report the bodies and request an ambulance for Gus and Baxter.

There were barricades at the base of the driveway preventing the press from coming up on the property, but reporters were taking pictures and shooting footage from as close as they were able to get.

The local police had requested assistance from neighboring police forces and bodies kept being extracted from the house.

Brad and Rod offered to go back into the tunnels with the police to show them where they were, but the offer was declined. They were told it was now a crime scene, so they wouldn't be allowed in the tunnels.

Richard, Remi, Paul, and Steve still had not exited the building, which caused a good deal of stress for the rest of the group.

Baxter and Gus were both sent to the hospital and Natalie rode with them to keep an eye on their progress and find out what the prognosis was.

Growing tired of watching bodies being wheeled out of the house, Brad began to circle the perimeter of the property, making sure no one was trying to sneak in through any weak points. He did pass people on borders who were talking among themselves, spurring on the endless gossip that would forever plague Blackwood Manor.

"What is it with this place?" one woman was whispering to her friend behind her hand. "Every time there is a major fiasco in these parts, it's *always* Blackwood Manor."

"There's Brad Morse," another one was saying, not bothering to lower her voice. "He's a con, you know. And he worked here when that last group of people were killed. Doesn't shock me there are bodies popping up where he is. The police need to put two and two together and lock him up."

Brad continued to breeze by, pretending not to hear them. The miserable old hens.

"Bradley! Bradley!" The shout came from a tree near the edge of the property. He turned to see Kate Wilkes standing there.

He made his way over to her, and she grasped his hand. "Is it true what they're saying?"

He nodded. "I don't know a number. Looks like they're still pulling people out. But yeah. Tunnels under the house were full of bodies, and we have people still down there somewhere."

Her eyes brimmed with tears. "And what about? Well...there are rumors that one of them was Joshua?"

He held her hand tightly. "I don't want to make you any false promises, Kate. The reason we were in the tunnels in the first place is because the kids found paperwork that seemed to suggest that one of the paranormal team is Joshua and the cameras showed him going inside. I don't know if it's true though because we never got a chance to question him about what they found. He is alive but was sent to the hospital. Something happened to him in there, but we don't know what."

Ashley Bundy

"He's alive?" she asked the only question that she seemed to grasp from what he'd said.

"If it's even him. I don't know."

She dropped his hand and began to sprint as fast as her legs would carry her back across her own property.

Brad was just about to go after her when Rod called out to him.

"Brad!!"

He turned to face Rod, who was standing nearer the house.

"Remi!" he yelled, pointing in the direction of the front door.

Brad sprinted up to the front of the house and joined Rod at the steps to see Remi speaking with one of the officers.

A blanket was wrapped over her shoulders and her hair was wet.

"Remi!" Rod called as they darted up the steps. Rod wrapped his arms around her and pulled her into his chest. "I'm so glad you're okay. We were so worried."

"I'm okay," she chuckled, pushing gently against his chest to loosen his grip on her. "We just got a little too deep in the tunnels and couldn't hear the whistle blasts."

"Where are the others?" Brad asked.

"Richard is in the cellar talking to one of the officers and Paul is in one of the ambulances. He got a scratch on his leg, and they're checking him out."

"What about Steve?" Brad asked.

She shook her head. "I haven't seen him. He's missing?"

"Yeah. For a while."

"What about Mel?"

"She's okay. I'm not sure where she is though. They got separated."

Knowing how easily spooked Remi could be, Brad decided not to tell her about the room they'd found until he had a chance to talk to Richard about it.

They waited around another two hours, answering police questions before heading to the motel where two rooms were being provided for them.

The house was currently a crime scene, so they wouldn't be allowed to stay there for a few days. Exhausted, the group made their way to the motel to relax their tired bones. They did their best to avoid the media circus but knew the reprieve was only temporary. It was just beginning.

# CHAPTER TWENTY-NINE

### Natalie

Natalie sat flipping through a magazine, completely patient, as the time passed. Media tried to get a peek at the people that been admitted, but the hospital staff did a good job of keeping them out. Pictures had been avoided before the ambulances took off and names hadn't been revealed, thankfully.

Natalie spent the first couple of hours casually strolling the floor that Gus and Baxter had been admitted on. The staff knew she was with them, as she'd arrived in the ambulance with them, but she wanted to keep her defenses up.

Security was added to the floor on the off chance any reporters did figure it out, and Natalie heard staff mentioning through radios that there were a number of attempts to gain entry, including one woman claiming one of the men was her missing grandson and demanding to see him.

Now she sat at Gus's bedside and set aside the magazine she'd just finished and reached for another one.

Gus began to stir in the bed next to her.

He moaned as he opened his eyes and squinted at the light. There was a gash over his eye and a busted lip, and an x-ray revealed broken ribs.

"Hey," she said softly, and his eyes roamed over to her. They were wide, though she was unable to determine whether it was with fear or confusion.

"Natalie?" he asked. His voice was raspy, but he seemed relatively calm. That was something at least.

"Welcome back," she answered pleasantly. "You've been out of it awhile."

"What happened?"

"We were hoping you could tell us. What do you remember?"

This was all just a test, of course. She'd touched him while he was asleep and had a pretty clear picture of what happened. She was hoping that he wouldn't lie to her though, meaning he could be trusted.

Instead of answering, he just asked, "Where am I?"

"Hospital," she answered as pleasantly as if she were answering a question about the weather.

His eyebrows furrowed in confusion and then his eyes widened as understanding hit him.

"Oh," he said simply. "Then I guess that means you know about the tunnels."

"Oh, yes," her voice had a pleasant lilt to it. "It took us a while to find you."

"I got lost," his voice shook with embarrassment.

"Easy enough to do. When we left, there were still people in there."

"I followed a girl. It looked like she was trying to lead me somewhere. Then she disappeared, and I couldn't find my way out. Guess it was pretty stupid to go in without a light, huh?"

"Pretty stupid to be fucking around in the cellar alone in the middle of the night," her voice shifted and was now harsh.

His cheeks flushed, and he averted his eyes. "I guess you want to know about that."

She sat forward in her seat, fixing him with a calculating look. "You and I both know I already know about that. What I don't know is why."

He didn't answer, only continued looking down at his lap like a child being scolded.

"I'm not unwilling to work with you. But if you want my help, you better start spilling your guts, Gus. Or should I call you Joshua?"

He looked up and took a deep breath before beginning to speak.

## Richard

Richard sat in an armchair that night in the fleabag motel the police arranged. The day had been incredibly hard and despite standing in the shower with the hot water pounding on his aching muscles as hot as he could tolerate, he was still a ball of tension.

"You okay, dude?"

Richard looked up to see Rod standing in the open doorway and nodded his head.

They'd been issued two adjoining rooms. Rod and Jamie in one, Richard and Remi in the other. It was agreed that Natalie and Mel were just going to stay in their own homes until they were cleared to go back into the house.

Remi looked up from where she lay lounging on the bed reading a book and silently rose to her feet and went to the other room to join Jamie.

Rod closed the door behind her and moved further into the room. "What a day, huh?"

"This is just so much bigger than I thought," Richard shrugged. "I mean, I knew there were tunnels but not that they were that extensive. And the bodies…"

"That's not your fault, man," Rod sank down on the bed opposite his friend.

"I don't know how Aunt Claire got out of there on her own."

"She must have had someone guiding her," Rod said gently. "Someone wanted her to get out."

"Yeah," Richard sighed. "That's what I thought too."

"So, if someone guided her out, do you think someone guided Gus in?"

"Probably. I mean, he was being secretive, nosing around where he had no business being. Pissed someone off."

"I'm wondering if he was close to finding whatever it was he was clearly looking for."

Richard grunted. "What the hell was he looking for anyway?"

"Has Natalie talked to him yet?"

"I don't know. She hasn't answered my calls in a few hours."

"Are you sure we can trust her?"

Richard rolled his eyes. "Jesus, Rod. This shit again?"

"Hear me out," Rod's usual sarcasm was absent from his voice and his tone was calm. "Medium shit aside, we don't know these people. He came with her. She knows him.

They've worked together for who knows how long. How do we know she wasn't in on whatever he was looking into?"

"I just don't think Natalie would do that."

"Why? Because you have the hots for her?"

Richard blushed but set his mouth in a thin line. "That has nothing to do with it."

"Bullshit. Stop thinking with your dick. If you want to get laid, there is a perfectly good girl within reach that actually has potential to become something."

"For your information, I'm not getting laid," Richard snapped. "And I'm not even trying. Yes, I find her physically attractive but as long as we're working together, I'm keeping it professional. I happen to think she's a good person."

"I'm telling you, dude. Something is off about that girl."

"She's Brad's daughter."

"So what? They're estranged. Their running into each other at the house was a complete surprise to them both. That doesn't automatically mean she doesn't have an agenda."

"Drop it, Rod."

"Fine," Rod snapped before rising to his feet. "But don't come crying to me when it all goes south."

Richard was fuming inside as Rod made his way to join the girls in the other room. He hated how crass his friend could be at times, but part of his fury stemmed from the fact that Rod's instincts were usually right.

He scored good points and Richard hated that. The simple fact was that he *didn't* know these people. Natalie brought Gus and the others into the fold, and they were a pretty weird bunch.

Gus was nosing around in the cellar in the dead of night before entering the death tunnels and getting everyone lost for the better part of a day. Baxter was basically an horror movie reject, and Mel was socially awkward.

Was Rod actually right? Were his feelings for Natalie skewing his judgment? Did the four of them have some secret mission between them? Was the "paranormal" team just a front to gain access to the property?

Annoyed, he reached for his phone and attempted to call her again. He let it ring until the voicemail picked up and then hung up, not bothering to leave a message. There was no point. He'd already left her several.

Just as he attempted to set the phone back down on the table, it began to ring, and he rushed to answer it.

"Hello? May I speak to Richard Price, please?"

"This is him."

"Hi, Mr. Price. My name is Diane Lloyd from Smith Pines Hospital. You left a message with our receptionist regarding Jessie Landry?"

Richard sat forward in his seat. He'd almost given up hope of getting to talk to Jessie.

"Yes. Yes, I did."

"I'm sorry for the delay getting back to you. Jessie often has restrictions on visitors, so I'm guessing we weren't notified until she was given clearance to receive them again."

"That's okay. So, am I able to come see her?"

"Yes. Visiting hours are typically from ten am until six pm, but the doctor cuts off visitors for her at two o'clock. Shall I put you down for tomorrow?"

"Yes, please."

Richard profusely thanked the woman and hung up. Finally, things were going right. Something about that seance mentally broke Jessie Landry, and he strongly suspected that there was more to it than Alex's account of events. Was this the mental piece that he needed to finally get to the bottom of everything?

He prayed that Natalie got back to him that night because he wanted her to go with him. He felt that even if he couldn't get much out of Jessie verbally, Natalie would be able to pick something up off her.

He quickly shot a group chat message to the others that he was going to bed because he had an early appointment the next day, then set an alarm and climbed into bed.

# CHAPTER THIRTY

Remi

While Richard slept soundly in the next room, Remi was reviewing the camera footage for the third time.

The bag that was found with Gus contained the cameras from the seance that Richard had been looking for since he first found out about them.

Remi wasn't sure if Richard was told about the cameras; she was almost positive that if he knew they'd been found he would be obsessing over them, but she was glad she was getting the chance to go over them first.

She wasn't an idiot. She knew that Richard kept secrets from her and tried to downplay the house to keep her calm, and she felt that she had the right to know what she was living in. She'd been surprised that the cameras were still in such good shape.

Her blood chilled again each time she reviewed the footage. The clarity was unnaturally clear. Honestly, it looked like a well-lit set from a horror film, and she could feel the terror of each person.

It looked like such a fun night at the start but then quickly devolved into a sinister nightmare. The lights going out, the doors on the second-floor slamming shut, and that creature flying down the hall towards the girls, beginning to attack them.

Even on camera, the thing was vile. It was half woman and half something else. Blue, scaly skin, horns on the top of its head and hooves peeking out beneath the hem of a white skirt.

Another ghost appeared and began to fight the thing, protecting the girls. This one was of similar height and wore an almost identical dress, a maid's uniform. She was near skeletal, flesh hanging off her bones and no face, and Remi could almost smell rot, even through the camera. Still, there was a comforting presence about the woman. She possessed a certain motherly energy.

There was something about the footage that kept nagging the back of Remi's brain that she couldn't quite put her finger on, and that was why she kept re-watching it.

She recognized relatively quickly that one of the girls in the footage was the same girl she'd seen in the kitchen. But she was different. She thought back to that night and the way the girl smirked at her, how unsettled that made her feel. That was not the expression on her face in the footage. That wasn't what was bothering her.

She ran the footage back again and began to move it forward frame by frame, carefully scrutinizing as she went.

Once the fight between the two spirits began, she started noticing subtle nuances that were near impossible to see at normal speed.

"Oh my God!" she exclaimed.

"What?" Jamie asked as she and Rod came to crowd around her to look at the screen.

"I barely noticed this watching normally," Remi began, "but I knew something was bothering me about it. So, I decided to do a frame by frame and look at this."

She pointed at the wall between the two spirits and zoomed in. In the shadows, appearing to be part of the wall, was a face with an amused grin.

"Holy shit!" Rod exclaimed. "Is that a face?"

"Is it a wall or another ghost?" Jamie asked.

"This image is clear as a bell and to me it looks like part of the wall.," Remi answered.

"I agree," Rod nodded. "And the wall doesn't actually look like that."

"And this," Remi went forward a couple of frames, tapping the screen. "See, the face is gone. But look at Bailey. Her eyes are completely black."

"Oh my God. They are," Jamie whispered. "I just got chills."

"Didn't Richard say things got weird with her right after this?" Rod asked.

"He did," Remi agreed. She went forward another couple of frames and pointed out another nuance. "Look at the creature's dress next to the other one."

Both white dresses bore very similar patterns. Simple white with a bunching at the hem. Upon closer inspection, the creature's dress was duller. When Remi zoomed in on the image, the dress was slightly transparent. Not so much so that it was obvious, just enough that the table just behind her was lightly visible. However, the face, hands, and hooves were completely solid.

"Is it just me, or can you see the table?" Rod asked.

"I see it," Jamie said.

"I do too," added Remi.

"It's like the dress is a mirage."

"It's willfully altering its appearance," Remi declared.

"That's not good," Rod's voice shook. "I think I'll go wake up Richard."

He rushed to go into the adjoining room.

"You're a fucking genius, Remi," Jamie's voice was full of awe.

Remi just looked at her friend, unable to respond. It was hard to be proud of the compliment in that moment when she didn't know what this discovery was going to mean for them when they got home.

Remi sighed and tapped her fingernails against the table. She glanced down at the computer screen again, and couldn't help but feel jealous.

Here they were piecing together a mystery from ten-year-old footage, and she couldn't even use the cameras that were currently in the house to find Whiskers.

When the police told them they'd have to leave, and gave them a time limit on gathering their things, she'd tried hard to find the cat. Eventually, Sherriff O'Reilly told her they were out of time, but he would keep an eye on Whiskers' food and water. She longed to view the footage and make sure everything was alright, but the main hub was inside the house, and the only phone the footage was linked to belonged to Gus. She really hoped he got out of the hospital soon.

# CHAPTER THIRTY-ONE

Jamie

When Jamie got out of the shower the next morning, she stared at her reflection in the mirror and let out a frustrated sigh.

The stress of the previous day had taken a toll on her. She was even more pale than normal and longed for her make-up, but in the chaos of everything, she'd left it at the house.

Her eyes travelled to the scar that cut through her right eyebrow, standing out like a sore thumb, and her stomach clenched at the sight of it. Just as it always did.

Her shitty stepmother had a long list of punishments that she got some warped sense of satisfaction out of. Different things that she would torture Jamie with. The icepick was one of her favorites.

The door to the adjoining room opened, and Jamie instinctively swung around, brandishing the hair dryer like a club. Remi pushed back against the doorjamb, her eyes wide with shock.

"Damn it," Jamie breathed out, lowering the hair dryer, and pressing a hand to her abdomen in an attempt to still her nerves. "I'm sorry, Remi. You scared the shit out of me."

"I did knock."

"I was lost in thought."

"I bet." Remi's eyes were focused on the scar and Jamie felt her cheeks flush. She turned to place the hair dryer back on the counter and began to braid her hair in the opposite direction, in a style to pull attention away from it, but hair wasn't one of her strengths. She never let anyone see her without makeup. Not even Rod. She was able to greatly subdue the scar with eyebrow product.

"Hey, you didn't happen to bring any makeup with you, did you? Some eyeliner? Or maybe eyebrow tint?"

"Sorry," Remi's voice dripped with pity, and Jamie felt a ball that was a mix of fury and embarrassment twist up in her gut. She liked Remi, but sometimes the girl was so unaware of her own privilege that it could be infuriating.

She pushed the ball down, forcing herself to let it go. She didn't want to yell at a perfectly good friend for simply being concerned. The guys would get it. Remi wouldn't understand that it was insulting. She just never experienced that kind of horror, and Jamie was glad she hadn't.

"So, I guess you're wondering about this, huh?" Jamie gestured toward her face and took a seat on the bed.

"Not if you don't want to tell me," Remi answered, sitting opposite her. The pity was gone from her voice now, and Jamie smiled. This was the good thing about Remi. She didn't force you to talk about your problems, but she was always there if you needed her to be.

"My stepmother liked to play games."

"Games?"

Jamie nodded her head. "The icepick was one of her favorites. You see, when she was trying to force me to do something awful, she'd pin my legs down and sit behind me, holding me in this big bear hug with an icepick to my temple. She'd threaten to drive it in if I didn't do exactly what she said."

"My God," Remi exclaimed. "What a bitch."

"No shit," Jamie gave a halfhearted smile before continuing. "She would push it in a little too. Not enough to cause any real damage, but enough to draw blood. It would spook me into doing what she wanted. Anyway, this one time she'd been drinking before, and she slipped. Actually pushed it through. Luckily, her aim was off from the drinking, so it was only my eyebrow."

Remi's skin appeared cool, pale, and clammy, and her eyes were wide, mouth a round "O" of surprise.

"Why am I telling you this?" Jamie nervously chuckled, and she averted her gaze to the bedspread where she began to pull at a loose thread.

"Kind of sounds like you need to talk about it," Remi said gently.

"Well, anyway, I passed out. I woke up locked in my closet, covered in the wet stickiness of blood, and I could hear them arguing just outside the door about what they were going to do with me. It didn't take me long to realize that they thought she'd killed me and were casually trying to figure out what to do with my body. You want to talk about your life flashing before your eyes?" She chuckled again and her voice broke off.

"What is it?" Remi asked.

"Ever since we went into those tunnels, I've felt just like that. When we were inside, I didn't think too much about it. I just thought it was my claustrophobia. But getting out did nothing to give me relief. Isn't that weird, Remi? Ever since we got out, I feel like that little girl, sitting in her closet listening to her parents plan her body disposal. It's like I'm being stalked by death. Literally. I mean, even the bear, I was eye to eye with a fucking bear, and I didn't know what to do. It should have torn me to shreds."

They stared into each other's eyes for a moment, letting the weight of Jamie's words fully sink in. Remi was just opening her mouth to speak but was cut off by a single, loud thump on the door.

They shared an apprehensive look before staring at the door. The walls of the motel were thin, and they hadn't heard any footsteps approaching or leaving. Also, the noise wasn't a typical knock, as if there were a guest. It was a single, loud bang.

While they sat there contemplating what to do, there was a muted, meow from the other side of the door.

Remi furrowed her eyebrows in confusion and slowly rose to her feet to approach the door. She opened it. There was no one on the other side.

There was a tiny meow again, and Remi looked down. There was a cat sitting just in front of the door.

"Whiskers?" Remi said incredulously.

"Whiskers?" Jamie asked. "Are you sure?"

"Yeah," Remi bent down to pick up the cat and closely examine it. "This is definitely her."

They exchanged glances, and Jamie fought back against the chill on her skin. When the police told them they'd have to vacate the house for a few days, Remi spent her limited time searching for Whiskers, but hadn't been able to find her.

Jamie's heart was pounding dangerously in her chest. "Remi? That's weird. We're not at Blackwood right now."

Remi nodded. "I know." She pulled the cat to her chest and gave it a gentle squeeze.

"Maybe she got your scent."

"Maybe. But she didn't knock on the door."

Jamie didn't reply. All she could do was look back at her friend, cradling the cat in her arms. For once, she wasn't ashamed to be trembling in front of someone else. Because Remi was trembling too.

She hadn't been able to put her finger on it, but something about this cat had always given her the creeps. She didn't have an issue with cats per se…but this one had a way of staring at her that made her think it would rip out her throat if it ever got the chance. She'd been secretly glad when Remi hadn't been able to find it. Now here it was—somewhere it had no business being.

She didn't want to speak aloud the big question that was floating around in her brain. If the cat was here, what else followed them from Blackwood Manor?

# CHAPTER THIRTY-TWO

When Richard pulled to a stop in the parking lot of Jessie Landry's psych hospital, he felt a sharp tightening in the pit of his stomach and felt overcome with sadness.

He sat for a moment to let it in. He knew this was the same hospital that Bailey was committed to shortly before her untimely death. He'd never come to see her when she was here though.

He wondered for a moment if this was how his mother had felt when she'd come to see Bailey. This sadness, and this reluctance.

He looked down to check his phone, already knowing there was nothing for him to look at. He'd lost count of just how many calls and texts he'd sent to Natalie, but he knew exactly how many responses he had. A big fat zero.

He scowled in annoyance and began to take in long, cleansing breaths. He'd wanted Natalie to come with him to talk to Jessie. He didn't know what to expect, what her mental capacity would be, but he'd hoped that Natalie would be able to get something off her even if only gibberish came out of her mouth. But he hadn't heard a word from her since she'd left for the hospital with Gus and Baxter the day before.

Finally, he told himself it was time to face the music and got out of the car, stuffing his phone into his pocket as he approached the building.

Whatever he'd expected from the outside, a simple brick building lined with simple green hedges, had been wrong.

Once Richard passed through the sliding glass doors, he was greeted by a homey lobby.

The walls were a pleasant mint green, adorned with vivid artwork, and lined with fluffy white couches. There were end tables with magazines fanned out, welcoming the next reader readily.

"Can I help you, dear?"

He turned toward the voice and found himself looking at a smiling elderly woman seated behind the reception desk.

"Yes," he smiled back and swiftly approached her. "My name is Richard Price. I have an appointment to see Jessie Landry."

"Okay. Let me take a little look see here." She typed on her computer for a moment and then looked back up at Richard. "Give me just one moment to see if they are ready for you."

She rose from her desk and disappeared behind a door almost completely blocked from view.

Richard began to scan the artwork on the walls, and his heart tugged as he realized they must have been created by the patients of the hospital. Many were childlike in nature and boasting vivid finger paint colors. Each one had the creator's signature on the bottom of the page. He began to quickly scan the pieces, looking for familiar names.

"Excuse me, dear?"

Richard silently swore, upset that he didn't find the artwork he'd been looking for, and turned back to the beaming receptionist.

She placed a plastic bin on the counter. "I'll need you to surrender the following: keys, phone, shoelaces, belt, and any pocketknife or jewelry you may have."

He hurriedly began handing over the requested items. "Is she dangerous?"

"It's just standard procedure, dear."

Once he'd double and triple checked his body, she led him to another door on the opposite side of the room and scanned an access badge to allow him in.

"The nurse will be in with Jessie momentarily," she said sweetly, and before he could reply, she'd stepped back out of the room, and he heard the click of the door behind him.

Suddenly, he felt very closed in. He surveyed the room. It was a rec room with a very different feel from the lobby. It was messy with older mismatched furniture. A bookcase with board games lined one wall and patients sat throughout with visitors.

Being in the room with the door locked behind him made Richard feel extremely uneasy, like he'd been tricked into locking himself away.

"It's just a precaution," a voice said from behind him.

Richard turned to see a security guard stationed just on the other side of the door.

"Excuse me?" he asked.

"The door," the guard answered. "About a decade ago one of the patients just walked out with a visitor and ended up dying that night. So now the doors stay locked for their own safety."

"Oh. I see." Richard felt an embarrassed flush begin to warm his cheeks. He didn't want to say that he knew exactly who was responsible for this policy change.

A door opened on the opposite side of the room and Richard turned towards the noise. A nurse entered the room with a young woman wearing a blue robe trailing behind her.

"Richard Price?" the nurse inquired, and he nodded. She gestured towards a couch near a window. When he approached, she was sitting Jessie down. "I'm just going to be over there if you need me." With that she quickly slinked away.

Jessie looked very different from what he remembered. Her curly hair was messy and unkempt, and her face was lined with dark circles under her eyes.

"Jessie? Hi, you probably don't remember me. I'm Richard Price. Bailey was my sister."

Jessie's eyes cleared, and she looked at him more directly. "Richie? No way. You're eight."

He chuckled. "I'm eighteen."

"Ten years? Has it really been that long?"

"Well, you know what they say. Time flies when you're having fun."

She gave a bit of a maniacal laugh. "Fun. Yeah. That's what this has been. Well, anyway, Richie. How the hell are you?"

"I'm good, but I was hoping you could help me with something. I'm not sure if you knew or not but Bailey died a long time ago."

"I heard," she gave him a sympathetic smile. "I was so sorry to hear about the family."

"Thank you. So, I inherited Blackwood Manor, so I recently moved back to take ownership, and it's been stirring up a lot of old memories and raising questions about what happened. I know that you, Bailey, and Alex had a seance not too long before it happened, and I was wondering if you could tell me what happened?"

"Haven't you heard? I'm crazy?" There was a chill to her voice.

Ashley Bundy

"I don't think you're crazy," he said gently. "I just want to know what happened to my family. I was so young back then and I only had a vague idea of what was going on. I'm trying to get information from everyone I can so I can figure it out."

Her face softened, and she reached out to take his hand. "I guess I can understand that. I only went to Blackwood Manor one time. For the seance. It was so crazy and completely changed the conjecture of my life. I don't really understand what happened myself."

"Can you at least tell me what you remember? I may be able to piece it together with something else."

"Well, Blackwood Manor was somewhat of a legend when we were kids. Kids would dare each other to go on the property and take something, or even to just spend an hour inside. When your aunt bought the place, it was a dream come true for us. The three of us were obsessed with the supernatural. Ghosts, witches, you name it. I don't know how she did it, but Bailey got permission for us to do a seance on the property and it was even more cool because we would be alone."

"So, was it messed up right away?"

"No. I mean, I did hear a voice in my head telling me to leave, but I thought it was just my subconscious that was nervous because of all the rumors so I ignored it," she snorted. "Figures. The one time I ignore the voices in my head, I shouldn't have."

"What do you mean? You hear voices a lot?"

She nodded. "Every day. Despite the meds they give me. Funny thing, though, it started at Blackwood Manor. At first, everyone was cool about it. We'd been through a shock, and they all thought it was my way of coping. After a while, though, I was diagnosed paranoid schizophrenic."

"So, you hear voices. Like telling you what to do? Do you ever see anything?"

Jessie shook her head and put her hand to her mouth to begin chewing on her cuticle. "I haven't seen anything, but I hear the dead. Always telling me to go back to Blackwood Manor."

"But while you were there, you were told to leave?"

She nodded.

"Okay. So, you ignored the voice telling you to leave. Then what happened?"

"Bailey gave us a summary of the little bit she did know, and we set up cameras where we knew there were sightings. Things didn't go to hell until we broke out the Ouija board."

"Okay. What did Bailey tell you exactly?"

"That these messages were appearing all over the place saying, 'help Gloria,' and that they'd found a letter written by Margaret Blackwood stating that she'd accidentally killed her daughter Lucy."

*The letter from the portrait? It must be.* "Did you see the letter?"

"No, but I fully believe it existed. Bailey said your mom and aunt found it and one of them told her about it. I don't see why they'd lie about it."

"Okay. So how did everything go to hell when you did the Ouija board?"

She hesitated before asking, "Did you see the cameras?"

"Yeah, but it's not very clear. I think I'd do better from an eye-to-eye account."

"Well, I've told this story before, and I ended up in here."

Ashley Bundy

"After everything I've gone through, I can promise that I will believe you."

She sighed. "She started asking the board questions about how many spirits there were and who Gloria was. The lights went out and noises were coming from upstairs, so we went to check it out.

"All the doors up and down the hallway were slamming. Then this woman creature appeared. She looked half woman, half devil or something."

"Was she solid or transparent?"

"Both actually. When she first appeared, she looked like a really sinister woman, but after she attacked us, she was kind of transparent. She seemed to be focused on me for some reason. Threw me into the wall, was levitating me in the air at one point. Then this other spirit appeared and started fighting her. It felt like she was trying to protect us. Alex and I made a run for it, but we didn't realize Bailey wasn't with us until we were already outside."

"Is there else anything you can tell me? Like anything unusual?"

She hesitated before continuing. "I thought I saw a face in the wall, watching the fight play out. It was smirking like it was amused."

"Where was the face?"

"Let's see. I was on the ground by that point so it would have been about here," she put her hand up to just above the armrest of the couch. "About child height."

"And what about Bailey? Can you remember anything at all about her after that night? Was her behavior or demeanor any different?"

"In what way?" she furrowed her eyebrows in confusion. "I mean, we were all a little different after that night. Kind of hard not to be when you experience that kind of trauma."

"Well, she seemed different at home. She became moody, started dressing different, and she attacked Callie."

"Attacked her?"

Richard quickly told her about the attack on Callie, which led to an attack on Aunt Claire.

"I never saw her get physical with anyone," she answered after he'd told her the story. "But she was different. Like I said, we all were, so I didn't question anything. She'd mouth off in class, not paying attention, not doing her work. She said a few things that seemed a little heartless, but I never saw her put her hands on anyone."

Richard didn't know whether to be happy or disappointed at that news and it must have shown on his face because she spoke up again.

"Well, there is one thing. I'm not sure if it means anything though."

"What is it?" he desperately asked her.

"She started freehand drawing. She was good too. We'd be having a conversation and look down and there would be an absolutely stunning piece of artwork in front of her. She wasn't even looking at the page, and they looked professional. She never could do that before."

"Was there anything special about the drawings?"

"Blackwood Manor was always in them. I asked her why she would draw that awful place, and she just said she couldn't remember doing it."

"You wouldn't still have any of those pictures, would you?"

She shook her head. "There were a ton of them though. They've got to be in the house."

"I went through her room and there weren't any drawings in there."

"I'm sorry," the nurse reapproached them. "The doctor wants to keep her visits short. She gets upset otherwise. Come on, Jessie. Time to go."

The nurse stuck out her hand, which Jessie took and allowed herself to be led towards the door they'd entered through before turning around. "Pay attention to pictures. Don't ignore them. Secrets can lie in the most obvious places."

*What was that about?* He thought to himself. Then, as if a magnet were leading him, he looked up towards the wall next to the bookshelf of games. It was adorned with more of the weird artwork that was in the lobby, though there wasn't as much of it. He walked over and began to scan the signatures. It didn't take long for him to find a picture with the signature, *Bailey Price.*

It was an expertly done drawing of Blackwood Manor. His blood ran cold at the unbelievable likeness of it. The picture stood out because there wasn't much color in it. The face of Blackwood was eerily similar, and though restorations had come a long way at the time Bailey was in the hospital, she'd drawn it broken down and overgrown.

On the front porch, leaning against one of the massive columns was Bailey herself, with the blue of her eyes and blue bolts of electricity coming out of her fingertips were the only color in the drawing.

Richard reached into his pocket for his phone before remembering that it was confiscated before he'd come back.

"Excuse me, sir," the security guard's voice floated to him. "Are you waiting for another patient?"

"No, I'm not," Richard answered him.

"Then I'm afraid I'm going to have to ask you to vacate the area," he gave three short raps on the door, which Richard quickly realized was a code.

The receptionist opened the door and smiled at him as he exited back into the lobby.

## CHAPTER THIRTY-THREE

Richard's stomach was gripped with anxiety as he stood on the porch of Blackwood Manor with Rod, Remi, and Jamie. The sheriff called that morning to state that they were free to go back. It surprised Richard. The only thing he could figure was it was because it was obvious that all the bodies had been there for years. It was his understanding that the medical examiner would be identifying them for a while.

When he'd gotten the news, he'd quietly informed the group, and they'd all pensively packed up their few belongings and made their way back with little conversation. He'd texted Natalie to inform her of the sheriff's decision, and she'd simply messaged back, *Okay*. Okay. That was what she had to say after ghosting him.

He stamped out his annoyance at the message and unlocked the door, leading the others inside. His anxiety grew as they stepped in the door. The house looked like a bomb had gone off. Papers littered the floor, and objects lay around shattered.

"Oh my God," Remi whispered and ran into the parlor.

"What?" Richard ran after her, alarmed, and immediately felt relief when he saw that the room was largely untouched. It was the only room that had been redone in its entirety so far, and the thought of all the hard work being undone would make him sick to his stomach. Other than a few objects being upended, the room was in good condition.

"Guys, do you remember seeing this before?" Jamie asked tentatively.

Richard turned towards the sound of her voice and immediately saw what she was referring to. There was an old-fashioned music box sitting on the credenza. It was made of a heavy, dark stained wood and the top was opened with a ballerina of fine glass standing proudly.

He'd never seen it before—especially not here in the parlor. The mere presence of it unnerved him. There was an energy that seemed to radiate off it like heat. The wide top sitting open seemed to be mocking them as menacingly as the house itself would.

"When's Natalie coming back?" Remi asked with a shaking voice. Richard put a comforting arm around her shoulders and gave her a gentle squeeze. He knew she was as freaked out as he was to be asking for Natalie.

"I don't know," he answered honestly. "I texted her and told her we were coming back and all she said was 'Okay.'"

His annoyance shot back up as he was reminded of it. Until that message, he could pretend she didn't know he was trying to reach her somehow, but that was proof she knew and was actively ignoring him.

"Awfully convenient, isn't it?" Rod asked, though his normal tone was not dripping with his usual sarcasm.

Normally, he would admonish his friend's attitude toward Natalie, but in this moment, he was inclined to agree. Why ignore him if she wasn't hiding something? He could have used her help when he went to see Jessie Landry and she should have been leading the charge when they came back to the house.

He was about to speak when there was a loud, otherworldly roar, a bang, and a crash from the back of the house. Remi screamed, and Richard gave her a squeeze.

Ashley Bundy

Collectively, the group moved towards the direction of the noise—the kitchen. Every cabinet was flung open, and the floor was littered with broken dishes. It looked as though a bomb had gone off—shattering every dish in the house all at once.

"I'll get a broom," Remi whispered, and scurried out of the room as quickly as she could.

Richard couldn't blame her. He knew she wasn't built for this level of activity.

"What does this mean?" Jamie asked.

"It's obvious, isn't it?" he answered. "The house is waking up."

He strode over to the cabinet under the sink and was relieved to see that trash bags were still stored there. He reached for one and felt an uncontrollable fear as he saw the blue bolts of electricity radiating out of his fingertips in tiny pulses. He hurriedly stuck his hand in his pocket, as though concealing something dirty, and grabbed a trash bag with his other hand.

# CHAPTER THIRTY-FOUR

Natalie

Natalie frowned at her phone as she sat at the kitchen table in her apartment. It had been a full two minutes since the message from Richard came in. *She's waking up.* The message stared out at her like a sore thumb against the blue light of the screen.

She wasn't ready for this. What did the message even mean? They hadn't been back at the house long. It was just that morning that Richard told her they were going back.

She'd been purposefully vague when she'd answered him with 'okay.' She'd thought she'd have more time to collect herself and deal with the new information she'd learned, but it seemed like that option was quickly disappearing.

"Everything okay?"

Natalie looked across the table at Mel, who was watching her over the top of her laptop closely. She sighed and nodded. "They're back at the house. Apparently, it's waking up. We'll have to go back."

"Do you think it's smart to go with the boys?"

Natalie nodded. She'd confided the secret to Mel because she knew she could trust her to keep her mouth shut. Plus, she'd known she'd need assistance verifying the information she'd learned. "I think it would look worse if we didn't. They'll think we're being deceptive. They probably do already."

Mel agreed. "Honestly, they'd be completely naïve if they weren't questioning it at all." She didn't wait for a response, just turned back to her laptop.

Natalie looked down at her phone and chewed her lip as she tried to carefully plan out what she was going to say. Finally, her thumbs flew across the screen. *"Okay. Give me time to compile the team. Is tomorrow morning okay?"*

She let out the breath she'd been holding, hoping he'd agree to that. She didn't technically need until morning. Mel was right here, she'd talked religiously to Gus since the hospital, and she knew Baxter would be eager to return. Mentally, though, she'd be better prepared.

The next morning, when Natalie stepped out of the van at Blackwood Manor, she was fighting to stamp down the nerves in her stomach. There were many things making her feel that way.

She walked to the rear of the van to help the others with the equipment and tried to ignore the darkness radiating off the property. It was more suffocating than ever before.

As they walked up to the porch, the front door opened, and Richard stepped out. He seemed as different as the property itself. His eyes were dark and brooding, and he was standing in a defensive stance, his arms crossed in front of him. She sensed hate in him without even needing to touch him. It pooled off him.

The others walked around him easily, seemingly unaware of the change in his demeanor, but he blocked her way forward.

"I've been trying to reach you," he said. His voice was level and calm, but the tone was biting...it couldn't have felt more like he was slapping her in the face if he'd actually done just that.

"I know." She blushed. "I didn't realize it right away. But there is a reason, I promise."

"Can we just get this over with?" He dramatically swept his arm to the side to allow her to go first, but it was not a gentlemanly gesture. He was being sarcastic. He was pissed. This wasn't going to be fun.

She walked into the house and was unsurprised to find it destroyed. Everyone was congregating in the parlor, which seemed to be the least affected. At least from the rooms she could see. Gus was setting up at the coffee table bin front of the sofa, beads of sweat furrowed on his forehead from the exertion, looked extremely pale, and was noticeably avoiding the glances of the others in the room. Jamie and Mel sat in chairs opposite the sofa, chatting amongst themselves like no time had passed. Her father stood awkwardly in the corner. His eyes softened when he saw her, but he didn't speak. She sighed at the sight of him. It broke her heart in half every time, but she'd come to understand that he was part of the package being here.

Baxter stood at the window, surveying the room with a silent authority that he hadn't earned. Rod sat on the floor at Jamie's feet. Richard and Remi walked behind her into the room, and he walked as far away from her as he could before he began to speak.

Ashley Bundy

"Okay, so a lot happened with the tunnels and since. We've all been split up and not everyone is in the loop on certain things. I think it's important that we all regroup. For those of you who don't know, I went to see Jessie Landry."

"What?" Natalie asked before she could stop herself. "I thought she was on visitor lock down or something."

"Well, she was, but her restrictions got lifted. Which you would know if you hadn't ignored my calls," he snapped.

There was an awkward silence from everyone in the group. Natalie didn't clap back like she normally would if someone gave her that kind of attitude. His feelings were valid. He continued.

"It was a very insightful conversation. She confirmed my sister had a serious personality shift following the seance and even some of the stuff that Remi so shrewdly found on the cameras."

"Which things?" Rod asked.

Quickly, Richard gave them a rundown of the conversation he'd had with Jessie.

"She sounds nuts to me," Baxter sneered. "She is in the nuthouse."

Richard glared at him. "Because what happened at Blackwood Manor affected her, and she didn't bother to hide it. I can assure you when I talked to her, she came across very lucid and intelligent. Anyway, I felt like she was giving me a code before the nurse took her away. So, I took another look at more of the patient artwork. It's a good thing I did because I found one that was drawn by Bailey."

"What was it of?" Natalie asked.

"A picture of Blackwood Manor. It was very good actually, but the weird thing was, Bailey was never much of an artist. Jessie also mentioned that Bailey developed a strange talent for freehand drawing. She started drawing amazing pictures that featured Blackwood Manor…but she couldn't remember doing it."

"Did you take a picture of the drawing in the hospital?" Natalie stuck out her hand for him to give her his phone.

"No. They confiscated my phone at the desk. But I studied it good."

"Okay, can you describe it?"

"It was a crazy accurate drawing of Blackwood Manor, all overgrown and broken down. There was no color in it at all except for Bailey's eyes and these blue bolts of electricity coming out of her fingers."

Brad's spine straightened, and he crossed his arms in front of his chest.

"Where was Bailey in the picture?"

"She was standing on the porch leaning against one of the columns."

"That could be significant." Natalie bit her lip and then turned to her father. "Your body language changed when he described the picture. Why?"

Brad shrugged his shoulders. "I don't know if it means anything."

"Well, maybe share with the entire group and then we can all decide together."

He cleared his throat. "Golden warriors."

"What?"

"Your grandmother never talked to you about it? Well, I heard about golden warriors a lot. That was the name she gave to people that had special abilities to vanquish a bad haunting. This person alone could put a stop to anything negative happening and sometimes even cleanse an area."

Richard straightened up. "How come we never heard about this?"

"Well, according to my grandmother, it was a rare phenomenon. The person would never know about their powers before they were forced to use them. They'd come out in a moment of great need, but there were characteristics that would make a person more likely to be one. There was a theory that Bailey may have been the golden warrior for Blackwood Manor."

"How did that theory come around?" Richard asked him.

"I don't remember a lot," Brad said honestly. "There was one day I'd been at the hospital with Caroline all day. She hadn't been doing good. I got a call from your mom asking me to meet her at the nursing home because she wanted to talk to my grandma. When I got there, Bailey was with her. I do remember she said something about blue electricity. It freaked her out enough to break Bailey out of that psych hospital. I don't really remember anything else about it though."

"Maybe we ought to touch on another pretty important point," Rod cut in. "What the hell has been going on with the three of you?" He looked at Natalie, Gus, and Baxter in turn. "Gus is fucking around in the cellar in the middle of the night, ends up lost in the tunnels, we find countless bodies, then you guys disappear to the hospital, and we get radio silence over here? Want to explain that?" He stared pointedly at Gus.

Gus flushed and looked down at the table in front of him. Natalie waited for him to speak, but she knew him well enough to know he was scared. It wasn't something he could take back once he'd said it, and he didn't want to say unless he could do it just right.

"Okay guys look," Natalie cut in and looked around the room. "There are a lot of trust issues in this room right now, and it's completely understandable. But we won't get to the bottom of it if we can't talk to each other. I'd like to make a proposal. We put everything out on the table. Right here, right now. In this room. We throw out our concerns, talk about the things we're keeping secret, and everyone has to agree to let go of judgment going forward. Okay? No judgment."

Everyone exchanged looks and muttered their agreement.

"Okay, Gus. It's okay now. Go ahead and tell them what you told me at the hospital."

Gus looked up and took in a large gulp of air. "My name isn't Gus. It's Joshua. I'm the missing grandson from Heaven's Estate."

They all looked at him with expressionless faces.

"And?" Remi pressed him to go on.

"Wow," he shook his head and let out a breath. "I thought you'd be more surprised."

"How do you think we knew you were in the tunnels, shithead?" Rod growled. "We went through the shit in your room."

"Rod," Natalie snapped. "No judgement, remember?"

"So, you're a Thompson?" Remi asked slowly, steering the conversation back to safe territory.

He nodded. "I grew up hearing all the same stories about Blackwood Manor that everyone else did. Then a few years ago my grandmother started getting sick, so I moved in to help her for a while. I was taking care of a lot for her, including the accounts and a lot of stuff simply wasn't making any sense.

"One night, I got a weird feeling in my gut. To this day, I can't describe what it was or understand where it came from, but I felt like something was wrong. I went to check on my grandma, but she wasn't in her bed. I started checking the whole house, and no one was there but me.

"I eventually found them around back. My grandma, mom, and brother were all gathered around a campfire, and they slit the throat of a baby goat. They were doing a lot of chanting in a language I didn't recognize. I felt sick. I don't know if they knew I saw them, and I don't care. I went inside, packed a bag, and left."

"Wait a minute. That still doesn't explain why you used a fake name," Jamie chimed in.

"Well, there were a few reasons. The first is what I learned after I left. It wasn't meant to be this big, elaborate thing at first. I was in shock...still couldn't believe what I'd seen. Originally, I holed up in a hotel, trying to process it. Then I took a phone call. It was from my brother. We'd always been tight. I'd ignored calls from my mother and grandmother, but my brother—that hit different. I wanted to believe that I hadn't seen him doing what I thought I had. I wanted him to convince me it wasn't true. That's not what I got."

"What did he say?" Jamie asked gently.

"I pick up the phone and he just says, 'you know.' His voice wasn't accusing, mean, or spiteful. He sounded pained. He tells me they know I knew because of cameras. Apparently, somewhere in the family legacy, there is a rule that only the first-born to each generation can be aware. If anyone other than the first-born discovers the truth, they are to be slaughtered. So, I couldn't come home, you see. They'd kill me if I did. They'd kill him if they knew he warned me—so it was a big risk."

"Okay," Richard let out a breath. "That's one reason to change your name. What was the other?"

Gus didn't answer but shot a look at Baxter on the other side of the room.

"Do you want to give your side, or do you want us to just keep going?" Natalie barked at him.

He narrowed his eyes at her, then turned his gaze on Gus, dark and unrelenting. He said nothing, but the message in those eyes was clear.

Natalie wasn't about to let him off the hook so easily. He didn't want to give his side of the story, fine, but the truth would come out. She turned to Gus and put a hand on his shoulder, rubbing gently. She nodded her head at him. "Go ahead, Gus."

Gus cleared his throat and looked back down at the table again. "I wandered aimlessly for a while. Not knowing what to do. Then I met a man in a bar."

"Shut your mouth," Baxter growled.

"This man told me he was part of the Blackwood line. That he was the rightful owner, and he needed to find a way back in. He'd tried to get in several times on his own, but he kept finding himself back at the property line. As though he was unwelcome. Once we figured out that we were both descendants of the Blackwoods and the Thompsons, we devised a plan. The man was Baxter."

"You little shit!" Baxter flew across the room and made a lunge for Gus. Rod and Brad shot in front of him to hold him back. He swung a fist at Rod, but Brad grabbed it and twisted his arm behind his back. "We had a deal, damn you!"

Ashley Bundy

"I didn't sign up for people dying," Gus snapped back and finally looked up to glare into Baxter's eyes. "That's not what I'm about. There were bodies down there. A lot of them. Do you not get that?"

"It's Blackwood Manor!" Baxter screamed. "Of course, there are bodies! It comes with the territory. You just fucking ruined everything. What did I tell you would happen if you told anyone?"

"Alright. That's it, Buster. I'm sick of your attitude," Brad began to shove him towards the door, never releasing his arm.

"It's Baxter!"

"Who cares?"

Natalie wrenched the door open, and Brad shoved him out. He spun back toward the door and ran at it as it slammed in his face. He beat hist fists against the door and clawed at it. "Watch your fucking backs!" he screamed at the top of his lungs.

Natalie moved back into the parlor to place a comforting hand on Gus's shoulder and gave it a firm squeeze. "Go on."

"Baxter had a lot of family money. He said he could help me get a new identity and protect me if I helped him. He said there was something valuable at Blackwood Manor, but he never told me what it was. He floated the idea of starting a paranormal group. He'd fund it, and I would learn all about the equipment. We knew we'd have to do other investigations to keep credibility, but Blackwood Manor was always the goal. He said it was only a matter of time before someone wanted a paranormal investigation and if we were invited in, we'd be able to freely look for his property. He also said if I found it, he'd give me twenty percent of the value. I desperately needed that."

"And sneaking around in the cellar?" Rod sneered.

"No judgment, Rod. Remember?" Natalie chided him.

Rod rolled his eyes but kept his mouth shut after seeing the sharp look from Richard.

"Well, that kind of is why I was down there," Gus answered. His voice was lighter as if he was relieved to finally have everything out in the open. "Baxter told me that there was a hidden cubbyhole in the cellar, and he asked me to look for it."

"Why didn't he just look for it himself?" Jamie asked.

"That's an excellent question, but it never occurred to me at the time. But I never found whatever he was looking for. A girl appeared and led me into the tunnels."

"What did she look like?"

"She was young. Maybe twelve or thirteen. Light-skinned Black girl with bright blue eyes."

"That's Bailey," Richard's eyes were wide with concern. "Why would she be leading you into the death tunnels?"

"So, is that why you've been avoiding Richard?" Rod asked Natalie.

"It had a lot to do with it," she confessed. "I touched both Gus and Baxter at the hospital, and I saw it in them. Not the full extent, but their real names. I wanted Gus to have an opportunity to come clean on his own. I figured that Baxter wouldn't."

"I appreciate that. Being able to explain it in my own way, I mean," Gus smiled at her.

"Of course," she smiled back and then looked back up at the rest of the group. "In the interest of getting everything out in the open, I think it's only fair to explain my own motivations. I really do want to help you, Richard. I do. But that wasn't my only draw to Blackwood Manor. I knew my dad worked here when I was little. I knew something bad happened. My family fell apart after my sister died. It wasn't even a month before my dad left. It always stung that he fought so hard for her but dismissed me so easily. I guess I thought by coming here myself, I'd be able to piece together the truth of why."

"Is that what you thought?" Brad asked, shock and pain evident on his face. "Honey, I didn't leave. Those times were tough. I can admit that. Between losing my friends and losing your sister, I developed a drinking problem, and your mom was pissed at me about a lot. She didn't like I worked for Claire right up until the very end, and she didn't like that I was drinking. She divorced me, and I don't blame her. She got custody of you. I didn't have a legal right to you anymore."

"Were your fingers broken?" she snapped. "Couldn't have picked up the phone in all that time? You might not have had a legal right to visitation or having me under your roof, but you could've dialed a damn phone or written a letter."

"I did!"

"You didn't."

"No judgement, Natalie," Rod sneered. Everyone gave him a dumbfounded look, and he flushed and looked down at the floor. "Sorry."

"I don't understand why you think I never called or wrote. I mean the letters—that makes sense, I guess. You never responded. Your mom could have kept them from you. But we did talk on the phone in the beginning," Brad continued as if Rod never spoke.

Natalie let out a laugh she knew sounded somewhere between a maniacal chuckle and serial killer. "We never spoke on the phone."

"Yes, we did. In the beginning. After you guys moved. A handful of times. They started off as normal conversations. Then gradually tapered off. You'd have excuses to get off the phone faster and faster. After a couple of months, your mom always said you were either asleep or you weren't home."

"The last thing I *ever* heard you say," Natalie growled out slowly, "was *'I can't take this anymore'* right before you busted out the damn door."

The look that Brad gave her was pained and she couldn't take it, so she turned around to look at Richard. "So, you see, my motivator wasn't money, it was just a drive to figure out why I lost my family...same as you."

"Alright." Richard didn't look completely melted but he was softer. "I guess I can understand that. Just don't ignore me anymore, alright? If I'm trying to reach you, there's a reason. I could've used your help when I went to see Jessie."

She nodded her agreement. "It seems you found out a lot, though."

"I got lucky."

"I'll find some way to go into the hospital myself and see what I can dig up."

## CHAPTER THIRTY-FIVE

Baxter thanked the Uber driver that let him out at the gas station around the corner from the rundown apartment building that Gus was living in. Normally, he wouldn't bother. He considered people that did such menial work beneath him, and therefore not worthy of his time. But he knew his request was strange, and the guy didn't ask questions when told to forget Baxter was there.

The gas station was in a shady part of town—half run down itself, with a board where the plate-glass window should be. Add to that, it was currently one in the morning and Baxter knew it was obvious that he did not belong in this part of town. Everything from his three-piece suit to his expensive Italian shoes screamed he was uptown.

He'd made sure to tip very high on the app in hopes that his driver would conveniently forget about him. He had a busy night planned, and he didn't want any questions.

He was starting with Gus, that spineless, traitorous piece of shit. He hadn't expected to be double crossed by him—he rarely even made eye contact. Baxter was in complete control from the moment they'd met in that bar.

He should have known better than to put so much faith in such a sniveling creature—but until now, he'd been easily controlled. And Gus *was* a Thompson. He hadn't believed his luck on discovering that.

Years of failed attempts at trying to gain access to Blackwood Manor had been extremely frustrating. Then he'd stumbled across a Thompson, practically giving him back door access.

And he'd paid for the piece of shit to start over. He'd literally funded his change of identity and the deposit on his shitty apartment so he wouldn't be on the streets. And he'd betrayed him that easily and thwarted the mission. The nerve!

Baxter was no idiot. He knew what the others said about him and the way they mocked him. He'd overheard that Rod asshole shit talking him on more than one occasion. Yes, he wasn't social. This type of thing was exactly why. He didn't trust anyone. Eventually, they would all stab you in the back. He'd seen it too many times.

You'd think that if you took personal risk and completely bought someone a new identity to protect them from their crazy family, they'd show a little more gratitude than that. His one and only request was that no one could know who they really were. At least until they found the haven stone.

Despite his natural distrust of people, he thought this particular secret was safe with Gus. After all, he had just as much reason to keep his mouth shut, if not more.

He knelt behind a car in the lot across from Gus's building to survey the area. The lot wasn't well lit but there was an old woman walking her dog, and he couldn't afford to be seen, so he opted to wait in his hiding spot until she went back inside.

He kept looking back on the scene at the house. Gus melted so easily, and it just didn't make sense. Why? Why had he given up with so little prompting?

*Natalie.* He sneered at the thought of her. She must have had something on Gus. Something worse than his true identity. Something so vile that he thought it was better to just come clean about their secret. It was the only thing that made sense. Natalie went to the hospital with them, and she'd spent a considerable amount of time with Gus. She must have threatened him in some way.

Not that it mattered. Gus could divulge his own secrets all damn day for all Baxter cared. But he had no right to divulge *his* and ruin all his plans. For that he would have to pay. He would take care of Natalie separately.

He watched the old woman usher her dog into a unit on the lower level and the light in her window turn out. Good. She was going to bed. He waited a couple of minutes for good measure, gave the surrounding area a quick sweep with his eyes, and then emerged from his hiding place.

He strode across the deserted parking lot as quickly and quietly as a cat and climbed the stairs to the second floor, coming to a stop in front of Gus's door.

He reached into his back pocket and slipped a key from his wallet. Gus didn't know he had a key but hey, Baxter paid for him to get this hole, he had a right to a key.

He slipped the key into the lock and walked right into the apartment.

Baxter glanced around and sneered at the surroundings. He'd only been inside once before. It was right before Gus moved in. They'd signed the lease and the two of them had done a quick walkthrough when it was empty to assess for damage. He'd thought it was a hole then, but if anything, it seemed even worse now.

The living room was cramped with a ripped plaid sofa, a scratched coffee table, and a floor rug that smelled like dog piss.

Enough of this. The sooner he took care of business, the sooner he could leave. He reached into the inner pocket of his suit and pulled out his gun, making sure that the silencer was attached.

He heard a door crack open and a small voice called out, "Mama?"

He furrowed his brow in confusion, not having time to react before a figure arrived in the door frame. It was a kid. A little boy about two years old standing there rubbing his eyes and wearing a t-shirt and a sagging diaper.

The kid's eyes went wide when he saw Baxter and his bottom lip began to quiver. Baxter only had about a split second to react. Gus didn't have a kid. He'd been bullshitted once again.

# CHAPTER THIRTY-SIX

The following night, the group was gathered in the parlor making plans on how to move forward with the investigation. They were all huddled around the sofa with laptops surrounding them and with papers spread all around, exploring different angles.

"Holy shit. Hey guys, check this out!" Gus interrupted and strode over to the TV to turn up the volume. They all looked up at the view.

The screen was filled with images of one of the older rundown apartment complexes from the projects.

"Local authorities say the call came in around six o'clock this morning," the newscaster was saying. "Anna Ramos went to wake up her two sons for breakfast and two-year-old Benito was not in his bed. After a quick scan of the apartment and his favorite hiding places, she called the police."

A picture of chubby-cheeked little boy with bright eyes and a crooked smile filled the screen.

"The bizarre thing about this case is there is zero evidence," the footage went to a press release of Sheriff O'Reilly talking. "The boy was not in the apartment and the door and windows were all locked. He was put to bed along with his brother at nine last night and was gone at six this morning. There is no sign of an intruder, and Benito could not reach the lock on the door himself, so it is not believed that he wandered off. The boys' father is no longer in the picture, and no one heard anything."

The footage changed to an overhead view of the complex along with commentary from the newscaster. "A thorough search of the community finally unearthed a small piece of CCTV footage from a business across the street."

The footage switched to an extremely dark and grainy image of the parking lot. "The footage shows an individual walking into the parking lot on foot. They then proceed to lurk behind vehicles for several minutes before approaching the building. This camera angle never showed the person exiting. The police now believe this person is responsible for the kidnapping of Benito Ramos."

The footage flipped to an elderly woman hugging a small dog tight to her chest. She was visibly shaking. "This is so scary. Nobody heard or saw anything. No one. The police say that video clip they got was right after one in the morning and I was walking my baby at one. That nice family lives right above me. This person was probably out here at the time watching me, and I didn't have a clue! Or they managed to walk right past me. That's terrifying! I don't know what our community is coming to. That family is so nice, and that little boy is adorable and well behaved—always smiling. This is evil, is what it is."

The picture of Benito filled the screen once again with descriptors on the right side of the screen. "If you have any information on Benito's whereabouts, or the person in the CCTV footage please notify police immediately."

"That's my old apartment building," Gus said under his breath.

"How long were you there?" Richard asked.

"About a month. But I was weirded out. Not only is it a bad area but I've never trusted Baxter. He paid for my deposit to get in there and I started getting serious vibes that he thought he owned the place because of that. Once I saved up a couple of paychecks, I moved to a different complex and didn't tell him."

"You don't think that person was Baxter, do you?" Jamie asked. She was pale and worry lines filled her face.

"It's impossible to tell." Mel shook her head. "That footage was so grainy it was hard to make out anything. I couldn't even tell if it was a man or a woman."

"Man. Definitely a man," Rod said. "Way too big to be a woman. The shoulders were broad. But I couldn't say it was Baxter."

"Wait a minute now," Remi said. "We're not considering one very important thing. Why would Baxter kidnap some random kid on the bad side of town?"

"Well," Richard said gently. "If that's Gus's old complex and even his old building, it very well could have been his apartment. Gus just said he didn't tell Baxter he moved. He may have gone there looking for Gus and the kid saw him."

"Maybe but he wouldn't hurt that kid," Remi said.

There was a moment of silence, but they were all thinking the same thing. They remembered how irate Baxter was when Gus told everyone who the two of them were. He'd been unhinged.

"We should go to the police," Mel said.

"And tell them what, exactly?" Rod asked. "We don't have any proof. All we'd be saying is we had a falling out with our financial backer, who has no reason to be on that side of town. And Gus used to live there. It's not much to go on. The police department is fed up with us enough as it is."

"I'll reach out to the mother tomorrow," Natalie said. "Maybe she'll let me walk through the apartment, and I can see if I pick anything up. I may be able to see something whether Baxter was involved or not."

They all agreed to those terms and to settle the investigation for the night. Everyone headed upstairs except for Natalie and Richard. She held back to talk to him.

Since returning to Blackwood Manor, she'd noticed that Richard was actively hiding his right hand. He always either had it tucked into his pocket, or his arms strategically crossed in front of him to where his arms were tucked out of sight.

"Are you injured?" she asked him once they were alone.

He stared at her before shaking his head. "No, why would you think that?"

Even now, his hand was buried in the pocket of his hoodie. She gestured toward it. "You're always hiding your hand. It's incredibly obvious. You keep doing things with your left hand, badly, because it's not your dominant hand."

His eyes narrowed at her slightly, but he didn't answer. She strode forward, grabbed his arm, and jerked his hand out of his pocket.

His eyes flashed with fury, and he jumped up from his seat, pushing her shoulders hard. This wasn't Richard. That was obvious.

She stuck her palms out straight in front of her. A white light shot from her palms and hit him square in the chest. He flew backwards into the wall.

He shook his head back and forth a few times, and his eyes cleared. They both looked down at the blue crackles that were now emitting from the fingertips on both hands.

Shit. This was what she'd been afraid of. She hadn't wanted to display her own power either. Not on the property. The spirits here knowing exactly what they were capable of put targets directly on their backs. It had been the only way to knock the possession out of him before it entirely took hold. She'd been forced to play her hand too early. She shook her head in disappointment at him. He'd been hiding his powers from the living when he should have been worried about the dead.

She approached him and looked him directly in the eyes. "I know what you are. I know what you're hiding and the mental struggle it must be causing you. But so help me God, if you put your hands on me again, I will tear you limb to limb. Now you know I can do it."

With that, she turned and glided from the room.

That night, Richard sat in the parlor watching the video frame by frame for the details Remi found. He hadn't seen it initially but once she pointed it out to him, he couldn't unsee it. It made sense with the info that he'd gotten from Jessie and now he was staring at the screen until his eyes began to water, wondering if there was anything else hidden in the frames that they'd missed. His mind also wandered to his earlier encounter with Natalie.

When she'd pulled his arm out of his hoodie he'd been overcome with rage. It bubbled up inside him and flooded his body. He'd moved outside of his own volition. He was horrified he'd put his hands on her, but she'd held her own. He was dying to ask her about the how she'd pulled him out of it. All he could remember was a white light. He didn't dare approach her right now.

"Are you still going over that?" Remi asked.

He looked up to see her as she walked into the parlor wearing nothing but a white, fluffy robe.

He looked away quickly, hoping she wouldn't catch the flush he felt creeping into his cheeks. "Yeah. I keep feeling like we're missing something."

She strode over and sat next to him, beginning to apply lotion to her legs. "Well, I went over it myself and I'm pretty sure we already found everything in the footage."

He stared hard at the computer screen, hoping it was a good cover, but he kept catching himself watching her out of his peripheral vision. Legs were a weakness for him, and they always had been. So, seeing her sitting so close to him, running her hands up and down the length of them was hard to ignore.

"Maybe it's not in the footage. I just can't get over the feeling that we're missing something. Something big." He snapped the lid of his laptop closed and ran his fingers through his hair.

"You look stressed."

He chuckled. "Probably because I am. I don't think I'm ever going to get relief from this tension."

"You should go to Natalie." She gave him a sly smile that didn't quite reach her eyes.

"Why?"

"Well, you know. Get you some stress relief."

He felt like a large hand took hold of his gut and twisted. Why would she think that?

"I'm not sleeping with Natalie."

"You aren't?"

"No. I mean she's attractive and everything. But I don't think it would be very professional, do you?"

"No, I guess it wouldn't. But you do like her? You know... like that?"

"Sure. I mean maybe once the investigation is done. She's hot."

She looked back down at her legs and the expression on her face appeared to have dropped. This was one of those moments where he was having a hard time getting a read on her. It was one of the things he liked about Remi. Her reactions weren't always what he would expect. At the same time, it frustrated him.

"What?" he asked. "You've never experienced that? Meeting somebody hot and wanting to jump their bones?"

"No, I haven't." She smiled at him. "I can appreciate a good-looking man. Don't get me wrong. But for me, the rush comes from knowing someone inside out."

"Come on. Seriously."

"Seriously. I like knowing everything about the other person and what makes them tick, long before I ever explore a physical relationship."

She rose to her feet and stood over him, placing his knees between her legs. She didn't lower herself onto his lap, but she kind of hovered over him, placing her hands on the back of his chair. "What they like, what they don't like. What excites them. What scares them. It makes their pulse race, and I can practically smell it."

His heart caught in his throat as she had her breasts almost entirely in his face, covered only by the fabric of the robe. "Whatcha doing there, Remi?"

She lowered herself to his lap and wrapped her arms around his neck. "Knowing what turns them on and using it to my full advantage. For me that's the real rush." She leaned in and gently pulled his earlobe between her teeth.

She smiled at him, then gave him a gentle pat on the shoulder before rising from his lap and moving to sit back on the sofa.

He grabbed her by the waist and spun her around, pulling her back into his lap to kiss her feverishly on the mouth. He shoved his tongue into her mouth with none of the gentleness he normally reserved for her.

She ground against his erection and moaned into his mouth, driving him wild.

He grabbed the sash of her robe and yanked it, causing the robe to fall down her shoulders and exposing her breasts. He bent her backward and took one nipple into his mouth and teased it, then the other one, going in slow circles before pulling it between his teeth.

He stood, holding her legs firmly around his waist and lowered her to the sofa.

The next morning Richard woke up gloriously naked, with nothing covering him but the silkiness of Remi's skin. He gently pushed her leg off him and rose from the bed, quietly putting his clothes on.

He left the room and made his way down the stairs and into the kitchen where the delicious scent of coffee was wafting from.

Rod stood at the island with a mug and gave him a smirk with a raised eyebrow.

Ashley Bundy

Richard plopped down onto a barstool and blurted it out.
"I slept with Remi."
"I know."
"You know? You were listening? That's fucked, man."
"Were we listening?" Rod chuckled. "Pretty sure the whole house was listening. Don't want people to know what you're up to, maybe don't squeal. Or make her squeal. Not sure who was squealing, but it was very entertaining."

Richard narrowed his eyes and pursed his lips.
"Well, anyway. Congrats. It's about fucking time."
"I don't know."
"You don't know?"
"I think it was a mistake."
Rod rolled his eyes. "Oh, stop with the 'she's practically my sister' speech already. You done fucked her. You can't claim that anymore."
"That's kind of my point," Richard exclaimed. "We're friends. Close friends. There is a sibling like bond so now that it's done it feels wrong. I feel like I fucked my sister, and I feel disgusting."
"Well, if you were that disgusted, why did you do it?"
"She seduced me."
Rod chuckled. "Remi? Seduced you?"
"What the hell are you laughing for? She did."
"This is Remi we're talking about. She's a goody goody."
Richard stared him down.
"Okay," Rod relented. "So how did she seduce you?"
"It's kind of a blur," Richard admitted. "She was straddling me in a tiny robe with her boobs in my face talking about turn ons. For the life of me, though, I can't remember how we got there."

Rod threw his head back in a throaty laugh. "Good for her. If she'd waited forever on you, she'd be old and gray before she got any."

Richard was about to bite out a retort but was cut off by his phone ringing. He dug it out of his pocket to answer it.

"Hello?"

"Hi. Is this Richard Price?"

"Yes, it is."

"This is Bates Photography. I'm calling to let you know your pictures are ready."

"My pictures?"

"The ones your assistant dropped off," The man's tone was slow and calculated, as though he were talking to a small child. "They're ready."

"Oh right!" Richard relented. "I just didn't think it would be so soon. Thanks. We'll be right in."

He hung up the phone and gave Rod a puzzled look.

"What was that about?" Rod asked.

"That was a photography studio. Apparently, the pictures my assistant dropped off are ready."

Rod furrowed his eyebrows. "What pictures?"

"Got me. But I damn sure want to find out."

He opened a search and looked up the address for Bates Photography.

# CHAPTER THIRTY-SEVEN

Gus threw a look over his shoulder and let out a sigh of relief. He'd started suspecting someone was following him a couple of hours ago and spent that time trying to shake the tail.

At first, he wasn't sure—he'd been jumpy ever since the tunnels. He'd seen someone out of the corner of his eye when he'd been at the laundry mat. It was a quick movement, like a flash of black, but nothing was there when he turned to look. But then he'd experienced the same thing when he'd gone for a walk in the local park. It was the same movement in his peripheral—the same flash of black. Only that time, when he'd looked, he'd seen a person disappearing behind a tree. He hadn't seen who they were, but it thoroughly creeped him out.

It occurred to Gus then that he'd been living a relatively routine lifestyle recently. It wouldn't be hard for someone to figure it out if they wanted to. He had an assumed identity for a reason. He didn't want anyone to know where he was. So, he'd try to throw whoever it was off his trail.

He'd driven to the local outlet mall because it seemed like a good place to disappear into a crowd of people. There were stores and restaurants every few feet—stuff everywhere and, at this time of day, the crowds were unavoidable.

He'd shot first into one store, power walking as he careened down random aisles. His legs screamed from burning, pulled muscles.

Now, in the middle of Target's maternity section, he no longer saw the person dressed in black, and hadn't throughout two stores now, but he'd pushed himself to keep going just in case he was missing them.

He stopped walking and bent at the waist, placing one hand on each thigh, and pulling in deep, stinging breaths.

"Sir, are you okay?"

He looked up to see a pretty woman with concern on her face peering at him. She pushed a buggy with a car seat inside it and had a very pregnant belly.

He nodded. "Yeah. Thanks. Sorry. I'm a bit out of shape I guess. My wife got away from me. I figured she'd be over here. We're expecting. In March. Guess I sprinted for nothing."

The woman didn't look convinced, but she didn't say anything else and just nodded and pushed her buggy away from him.

*"Don't stand out. You can't stand out,"* he chastised himself.

He no longer felt like he was being stabbed in the chest by simply breathing, but he knew he'd need to give his tired legs a break or he'd never make it back to his car.

He limped up to the cafe in the front of the store and put in his coffee order, along with a cookie. He wasn't normally a big coffee drinker, but ordering one gave him the right to take up one of the little tables and give his legs a break without looking like a weirdo.

He chose a seat slightly behind a column, which gave him a wide view out the window with a lower possibility of being seen. While he was positive that he'd lost whoever had been following him, he couldn't afford to take any chances on his shaky legs.

Ashley Bundy

He sipped his coffee slowly, allowing the heat to refreshen his body, forcing the cold out, and tried to think about who the person in black may have been.

To an outsider, he would seem extremely paranoid. Truth of the matter was though, there were too many people it could be, and none of the options gave him any sense of comfort.

The most obvious person to jump to mind would be Baxter. Baxter was not a good man, and Gus regretted the day he'd run into him in that stupid bar. It was hard to believe he was ever that desperate. He was a violent, cruel person and the others had no idea what he was capable of. Ever since seeing the news report the night before, Gus had a sick feeling in his gut and was worried about that little boy. He cringed as he remembered Baxter's face back at the house when he'd lunged for him.

Baxter hadn't cared that the room was full of people. He wanted Gus's blood. A person with inhibitions that low had absolutely nothing to lose, and that terrified Gus more than anything else could have. His eyes were wild, and spit shot from his lips he'd been yelling so hard.

No, Baxter would be anyone's first choice. But he was a bigger man, and the person in black seemed somewhat smaller.

There was another possibility, though he didn't want to think about it. It could be someone in his family. After everything went down in the tunnels, his cover had been blown. There was a possibility that the people at Blackwood Manor were not the only ones who knew his identity. Even if they were, it was only a matter of time before Baxter let it get out.

He'd been told at the hospital that they had to go through extreme measures with security. There were plenty of people trying to get in to see him. He'd even been told one woman was demanding to be let in because he was her missing grandson. Sure, it could have been an overzealous reporter getting creative. But that would be a hell of a coincidence. Chances were, it really was his grandma.

He sighed and ran his fingers through his hair. A family member. He should be jumping for joy at the thought of a reunion. He should have run up to the person in black, thrown his arms around them in a tight bear hug and proclaimed how much he missed them. Because he *did* miss his family. But now he could never come out of hiding, attend get togethers, or have any kind of a family life. He knew too much.

Damn. Why did he let his curiosity get the better of him? Why had he ever questioned anything he'd found in the account books or anything else in the records?

It wasn't his house. It wasn't his business. As the old saying went, "Curiosity killed the cat." Gus was the cat.

No, he'd had to go and be nosy and look what happened. He'd witnessed that horrible scene in the back, an image that still plagued his thoughts every single day. Now his family wanted him dead. It would have been so much better if he'd never known. He could have gone on being blissfully happy. But he'd seen it, and he couldn't ignore it. That wasn't his way.

Gus threw back the rest of his coffee and began to walk back toward his car. His legs were still aching but at least it wasn't that burning pain that stopped him back there in Target. He just walked slow and absentmindedly rubbed his palms against his thighs as he went.

Ashley Bundy

As he approached his car, the air left his lungs and his mouth went dry. Someone had done a number on his car. It looked like someone took a baseball bat to it.

There was a crowd gathered around the car, as well as a police cruiser. An officer was talking to a woman off to the side.

Glass from the headlights littered the ground. The windshield was busted in, there were huge dents everywhere and the tires were slashed.

"Excuse me!" he called out once he was fully on the scene. "This is my car. What happened?"

The woman talking to the officer turned away from him and approached Gus. "Oh, you poor thing. What is wrong with people these days? The world that we're living in—"

"Did you see this happen?" He cut her off.

"Well, yes," she sighed, as though annoyed he hadn't let her continue her compassionate rant. "I was loading up my car when I heard the noise. I turn around, and he was smashing it with a bat."

So, he'd been right.

"I walked over and asked him what they thought they were doing, and he ignored me, pulled out a knife and went for the tires. I screamed at him to stop it. He jumped up and stomped toward me, telling me, *'mind your own business bitch. Or you're next.'* It was quite rude."

"What did they look like?"

"It was a man. He was around five foot eight or nine, and lanky. He was wearing all black. It was hard to make out his facial expressions because he was wearing a hoodie with the hood up so his face was mostly in shadow."

Too small to be Baxter.

"What happened next?"

"Another man ran up between us to protect me with a gun pulled and the guy left."

The officer interrupted. "Sorry to jump in guys, but I'm going to need you to come to the station to file reports. Sir, you can ride with me and ma'am, you can follow us."

"Okay," Gus said and headed for the cruiser. What a day.

"You're welcome," the woman said sarcastically before heading for her own car.

As Gus buckled his seat belt, he wondered just how things could possibly get any worse.

# CHAPTER THIRTY-EIGHT

Brad sat on the sofa in his worn-down apartment staring helplessly at his phone.

He'd gotten off the phone with Mel not even five minutes before. There it was. The information he'd asked for but not expected to get. Scrawled on a piece of paper on the coffee table was his ex-wife's number.

Now that he had it, his mind kept swirling with the different scenarios and possibilities that could present themselves now. The situation was already so difficult, and he wasn't sure what the right answer was.

Natalie had a very skewed view of everything that happened, and he desperately wanted to know how she'd come to those conclusions. The only way he could think of to understand and have a shot in hell at repairing his relationship with her was to talk to Sylvie and find out.

But at the same time, he could see that backfiring on him. Natalie was fiercely loyal to her mother, and he was proud of that. Sylvie had done a damn good job of raising their girl and doing it alone. But if Natalie felt in any way that he was accusing her mother of anything nefarious they'd be taking ten giant steps back.

So, he sat, and he stared. At the phone number. At the phone. Wondering how his life became so fucked up in the first place.

He pushed himself up from the sofa and strolled to his kitchen and opened the cabinet to stare inside. There was the bottle of vodka he'd taken away from Blackwood Manor.

It sat there in front of the coffee mugs, beaming at him like a monster threatening to take him down. He wasn't surprised to see it. This wasn't the magically rejuvenating cabinet following him home for a taste of punishment. Despite telling Richard he'd get rid of it, he hadn't. He'd brought it home and stuffed it in the cabinet. He wasn't sure why. It just felt important at the time.

What did surprise him was the way the empty bottle refilled to the brim while his eyes were on it. His mouth instantly watered, and his body immediately ached for just one little taste.

In shock, Brad slammed the cabinet door and threw his body away as though he'd been burned.

*No. This wasn't supposed to happen this way.*

He marched back out into the living room and snatched the phone number off the coffee table and punched it into his phone before he could lose his nerve.

His heart thundered in his chest as the line rang once, twice, three times.

He was just about to lose his nerve and hang up when she answered.

That brisk, "Hello," on the other end of the line stirred up a hundred emotions all at once. Admiration for the woman who loved him at his worst, when no one else would even give him the time of day, as well as a hatred for the way she'd turned on him.

"Hello," she said again, this time sounding slightly agitated.

"Sylvie. It's Brad."

He heard the softest sound coming from her end that sounded slightly like the smallest intake of breath. There was a slight hesitation before she spoke again.

Ashley Bundy

"Brad. Wow. It's been awhile, hasn't it?"

"It has."

"So, how have you been?"

"I've been doing real good," he answered her, glad she was being cordial. Hopefully, this wouldn't end up being a nasty fight. He was sick of those. "Sober. How are you?"

"Oh, Brad. That's so good to hear. I'm doing great. Delaney and I started a fundraiser through the church. All the proceeds go towards helping children with cancer. It's done wonders helping me heal."

Delaney was Sylvie's sister and was never Brad's number one fan. She hated the fact that he had a record, despite the reason, and never shirked from an opportunity to look down on him for it.

If pushed to name something, Brad would say he was probably the only point of contention to ever appear between the two. Because normally, whatever Delaney said flew. She snapped her fingers, and Sylvie drew to attention. She said jump and Sylvie would ask, "How high?" She had the ability to lead Sylvie around like a puppy—something Brad always detested about her. Some Christian lady. He could only imagine what poison she'd been spreading the last several years.

But he didn't say anything because he didn't want to spoil Sylvie's good mood. After all, in the grand scheme of things, it didn't matter.

"That's great. Congrats! Listen, Sylvie. I really need to talk to you about something."

"Of course. What is it?"

"How often do you talk to Natalie?"

There was a brief pause before she answered. "Not as much as I would like to, honestly."

"Did something happen?"

"Not really. We did have a bit of a disagreement and agreed to take some time apart to cool down, but it wasn't anything particularly nasty. Why?"

"Well, she's back here. I didn't know if you knew that."

"That's what our disagreement was about. After she graduated, she told me she wanted to move back, and I thought it was a bad idea. There are just so many bad memories involved with that place. It was never home to me. And after we lost Caroline, it was even less so. But I didn't forbid her or anything of the sort. I just asked her why she would want to put herself through that, and she said she needed answers and believed she'd never get them if she didn't go back."

"Well, if you didn't tell her she couldn't come, what did you fight about?"

"She wanted me to go too, and I just couldn't do it. I told her she's an adult now, and I wouldn't stop her, though I did not agree with her decision. She could do what she wants, but I would never set foot in Georgia again. She thought it was selfish of me. And maybe it was. I don't pretend to be a saint. But it simply wouldn't be good for my sanity. We agreed to step back from each other for a while and try to see the other's point of view. We didn't want to wreck our relationship."

"I see."

"I am surprised you even know she's there though. I'm not trying to be hurtful, Brad, but I might as well be honest. I suggested she look you up if she were to go back there. But she vehemently refused. She didn't seem to have much interest."

"See, now I'm surprised to hear you say that."

"Well, she hasn't seen you since she was a little girl."

"No, I don't mean that part." He was having a harder time keeping the heat out of his voice. "I'm surprised to hear you say you suggested it."

"Why wouldn't I?"

"Due to some current confusion." He forced himself to even out his tone more and remember his overall objective. He couldn't afford to piss her off.

"Natalie didn't look me up, but we've kind of been thrust into each other's inner circles anyway."

"How so?"

"We ran into each other at Blackwood Manor."

"Blackwood Ma—what the hell is Natalie doing at Blackwood Manor?"

"Investigating it."

"Son of a—"

"I know. Believe me. I know."

"What are *you* doing at Blackwood Manor?"

"Richard inherited it, and he's moved in. I've been helping him out with some repairs and stuff. I kind of feel like I owe it to him. Believe me, I was shocked when she walked into the room. She was the last person I expected to see there."

"I don't even know what to say. I don't like it. But I'm not sure how I'm supposed to be able to help you."

"Natalie is extremely hostile towards me."

"Well, again, she hasn't seen you since she was a small child. She was very hurt the way you disappeared from her life."

"I know. And if she were merely indifferent, I would understand. But she's openly hostile and some of the things she says—they just don't make any sense."

"Like what?"

"Like that I walked out, for one."

"Brad, you did. That is what happened. We were fighting, and you walked out the door."

"Yeah, for the night!" he growled out. "She makes it sound like I dropped off the face of the planet, never to be heard from again. We both know I came back the next morning to an empty house and a note saying you were at Delaney's. It was *you* who never came home, Sylvie. I mean she says I never called and never wrote, which is just a flat out lie. What were you telling her?"

"Umm, excuse me," he knew the tone well. It was her annoyed, 'don't even start with me,' tone. "I haven't been *telling* her anything. She was there, and she wasn't three years old. She was old enough to draw her own conclusions based on what she was witnessing. I'm sorry if she doesn't view you the way you want her to, but that is literally due to your own deplorable behavior at the time."

"Okay, fine. But what about saying there were no phone calls or letters when there was both? I've tried explaining to her I couldn't see her as much as I would have liked to because you had sole custody. Her response is always, 'were your fingers broken?' I'm understanding, but I'm beginning to lose my patience on that, considering I did all those things. I did everything I was supposed to do."

"Well, I must say you have a very different memory of it than everyone else involved."

"What the hell is that supposed to mean? You know damn good and well I called her because I spoke to you first."

"For the first two weeks maybe. When we're looking at the grand scheme of years, a couple of weeks doesn't hold much merit."

## Ashley Bundy

"Two weeks, my ass. For one, even if that was the truth, which it's *not*, she doesn't even acknowledge that. She says she never saw or heard from me again after I walked out the door that night. Second, yes, I admit I did eventually give up. But I tried a hell of a lot longer than two weeks. I had normal talks with Natalie at first. Then it started getting stranger. She would be quiet and despondent to the point that the conversation was basically one sided. Then she'd be in a rush to get off the phone. Eventually, she wouldn't come to the phone at all. You'd always say she was either asleep—ridiculously suspicious at five in the afternoon—or at a sleepover with a friend. I can't tell you how much that hurt me.

"People in my life would tell me it was suspicious she wouldn't talk to me. That she was short with me the few times I did manage to get her on the phone. Everyone said it sounded like a classic case of parental alienation. But I would say, 'no. Things might not have worked between me and Sylvie, but she wouldn't do that to me. Sylvie isn't like that."

"I never bad mouthed you at all," she hissed. "I didn't lie to her if she asked me questions, but I never put you down. I happen to think you're a good man, Brad, and that never changed. You had a problem you needed to work on, and I was honest about that, but I never felt you deserved to be bashed. You gave up. You did that. And she formed her opinions on you from feeling abandoned."

"I called her for God's sake! I don't even see you denying it."

"You did. For a few weeks, like I said. Then maybe a random call here and there with no sense of regularity, and half the time when those calls came in, you sounded drunk.

Do you know that our thirteen-year-old daughter told me at one point that she felt like she was an afterthought? That you only wanted to talk to her when you were drunk?"

"It's the only time I wasn't ashamed," he admitted. "For the longest time, I hated myself for losing everything. Even though now I don't think I was solely to blame. I thought so at the time. I didn't know how to talk to her. The point is, I still did it. *I did it, Sylvie.* I might have needed a little liquid courage, but I'm not getting credit for it at all. And besides, the calls are not the only issue here. What about the letters?"

"What letters?"

"Oh, please. The letters I sent. I sent her letters every single week for two years. When I didn't get a reply, I gave up on letters and sent her a card on her birthday and Christmas for the next few years. I did not receive one reply. *Not one.*"

"Maybe you had the wrong address."

"No. You gave it to me yourself. And I verified with you on three separate occasions to make sure I hadn't copied it down wrong. And besides, if the address was wrong, they would have been returned. I didn't get a single piece of returned mail until her birthday two years ago."

"Well, I don't know what to tell you, Brad. I never saw any mail."

"Not a single piece in all that time?"

"Not one. Maybe she got them after all and just chose not to reply."

"She says she didn't, and I don't see her accusing me of being no contact if she'd seen them. Come on, Sylvie. I may be a simple man, but I'm not stupid."

"What do you mean?"

Ashley Bundy

"Can't we just put the past behind us? I don't know why you did it, and I promise I won't hold it over your head anymore. Just tell Natalie I tried so we can start to repair our relationship and I'll forget the whole thing."

"Brad, I've had about enough of this! I told you I never saw any damn letters, and I saw pathetic attempts at phone calls. I never bad mouthed you to Natalie. If anything, I talked you up more than you probably deserved. I will not call my daughter and lie to her just to clear your conscience. If you want a relationship with Natalie, you're going to have to put in the work and earn it. I won't give you a get out of jail free card with her. I thought you knew me better than that. Do not call me again."

There was a click, and the line went dead. Brad let out a scream of frustration and threw his phone down onto the couch. He put his head in his hands and screamed again, plopping down on the couch.

He shouldn't have lost his temper. He knew he shouldn't have lost his temper, but he'd gone and done it anyway. Now what was he going to do?

Now, for the first time in a long while, he contemplated walking right back into that kitchen and pouring himself a nice, tall glass of vodka.

As if by fate, bursting in to stop him from making a terrible mistake, the phone rang.

He took a deep breath and answered it.

# CHAPTER THIRTY-NINE

Natalie felt dirty. She didn't like what she was doing, but it was necessary if she wanted to get back into Richard's good graces.

She was walking into the employee lounge of Smith Pines Psychiatric Hospital. She'd called to make an appointment to see Jessie Landry but was told that, once again, her visitors were being restricted. It was important to Richard that she talk to Jessie and see if she could get anything off her. If it was important to Richard, it was important to Natalie.

So, she'd used her fake ID to get a job at the hospital. She didn't like it—it felt like she was going too far for an investigation—but she'd refused to take a job in patient care without being qualified. So, she was a maid. At least she would have an employee badge and access to all the rooms.

She stared into the mirror over the seat in the lounge and frowned at her reflection. The uniform was a crisp white skirt that hung to the knee, white knee socks, a white scrub top, and the ugliest flat, black nonslip shoes she'd ever seen in her life. She barely even recognized herself.

"Hey there!" Natalie turned at the voice that joined her in the room to see Brittany grinning like a wild woman and approaching her.

Brittany oversaw housekeeping. Natalie's interview was with her, and now they were about to do a walkthrough. Brittany was only a few years older than Natalie, but she was unnaturally chipper and bubbly and was already beginning to work Natalie's last nerve. She sent up a silent prayer that she'd find a way to talk to Jessie soon.

"Look at you! Looking all official and everything. You clean up real good!"

Natalie gave a half chuckle—her attempt to cover her true emotion, wanting to kick that backhanded compliment straight in the shin.

"So, here we go," Brittany held out a stack of bandages.

"What's that?"

"For your tattoos."

Natalie must have given her a blank-faced stare because she began to elaborate.

"Management insists that all tattoos be covered. It's not very professional, you see."

"No one said anything to me when I interviewed."

"Well," Brittany pasted on a fake ass grin and batted her eyelashes a few times. "No one thought it necessary to spell out. If you read the handbook, it is explicitly stated there may be no visible tattoos. Common sense would surely tell you if you didn't cover them yourself, we would have you cover them."

Yeah. Natalie was going to have issues with this woman.

"Of course, if you don't want to cover them, we completely understand. Not every job is agreeable for every person."

Natalie pasted on her own fake smile and reached out for the bandages. "No, no. It's fine." She took them and turned back toward the mirror to begin applying them. "I was just surprised. Seems a bit discriminatory is all. I mean, the patients in here have problems. I doubt they care what we look like."

"Well, you're right there," Brittany laughed. "Most of our patients are off in their own little worlds, locked away in their own brains. It's not so much for them as it is for their loved ones. We need to provide as professional and as clean of an image as possible for them to feel safe leaving their loved ones under our care. And tattoos kind of have a jailbird look about them, don't they? Especially snakes."

Natalie blew a heavy breath out of her mouth and mentally counted to ten. It wouldn't do her mission any good if she got fired before ever leaving the employee lounge because she punched this bitch in the face.

She studied her reflection and felt her soul leave her body. The bandages were white, square Tegaderm bandages. She looked like a zombie, literally wrapped in white from head to toe. Yeah. She was going to need to find Jessie Landry. Today.

Brittany started off with a tour of the building. The employee lounge was on the first floor, directly behind reception. She led her down a hallway and into a room that looked like a rec renter. There were couches sitting around, games, and a wall with artwork hanging on it. This must have been the room where Richard visited with Jessie.

"This is our recreational area," Brittany told her. "When our patients have visitors, this is typically where they will be together. Visitors never go to the patients' rooms. If this area is full and the weather is nice, sometimes patients who are better behaved will be allowed to visit in the back garden. This room will be cleaned twice a day—once on each shift. Always when it is not being occupied. We clean it before the start of visiting hours. So, after we complete our tour, it will be the first place you'll clean. You'll empty the trash, sweep the floors, and pick up any discarded recreational items and put them back in their proper homes."

"Why do we need to clean this room twice a day?"

"What?"

"Why clean it twice a day?" Natalie repeated. "I mean, if we clean it in the morning before the start of visiting hours and it's not used after visiting hours are over, then it seems to me to be a waste of time. No one comes in after the evening clean, and then clean again in the morning. Why clean a room that is not being used?"

Brittany giggled again. "Well, dear. Someone is ambitious, aren't they? I never said we don't use the room in the evenings. I said it is the room used for visitation, which is correct. But even outside of visiting hours, it is still a recreational space. Many patients spend free time here in the evenings—under careful supervision. You know, it may serve your job better to simply do as you're told instead of questioning practices you know nothing about."

Natalie grinned. "Of course."

*It's not nice to hit. It's not nice to hit.*

"Now, as I was saying before I was interrupted. We clean this room twice daily. The evening shift has a smaller window to clean—it will be in the thirty minutes that patients are being served dinner. Many come in here to unwind afterward. Now come along, we have a lot of ground to cover if we are going to stay on schedule."

They toured the entire building in an hour and a half. Natalie's feet were already killing her from these ridiculous shoes, and she hadn't even started working yet. She prayed again that she found Jessie Landry soon.

The first floor consisted of the rec room, the cafeteria, director's offices, the employee lounge, supply room, and therapy rooms. The second and third floors had patients' rooms. The second floor was half patient rooms, lower security patients, drug lock up, as well as procedure rooms. The third floor was entirely patient rooms, separated by security risk. There was a ward that was completely gated off for the more dangerous patients.

Just going off the information she had of Jessie being a problem patient and frequently having her visitor hours taken away from her, Natalie was estimating that she would be somewhere on the third floor. But would she be under lock up or not? That was the part she had a hard time deducing. As far as she knew, Jessie was not dangerous or violent. But she did act out. It was hard to imagine her being locked up with violent crimes, but she seemed to be in trouble too much to be in lower security.

Even with a maid's job, accessing her would prove to be difficult. The third floor was locked down tighter than Fort Knox. Security around every corner, a whole new check-in desk. She wasn't sure yet how she would pull it off, but she needed to.

Now, it was eight in the morning and time to officially begin cleaning. She swiped her employee badge and entered the empty rec room.

Ashley Bundy

She was glad that she was being allowed to do it alone. She would have free rein until it was time to move upstairs, where she would be taught a specific protocol.

She walked the room, running her hands over the furniture and various objects. She was overwhelmed with sights and sensations. Of course, she was. So many had been here, suffering with mental illness, tragedy, and yes, abuse.

She approached the wall of patient artwork and carefully studied it, scanning each name carefully until she came to the one signed Bailey Price.

It was just as Richard described it. A scarily accurate drawing of Blackwood Manor, completely devoid of color except for the blue of Bailey's eyes and the sparks protruding from her fingertips.

Natalie placed her hands on the drawing and closed her eyes. Almost instantly, she felt her stomach pull forward and her feet leave the ground. She was twirling through a black fog and then she was a spectator to a colorless Blackwood Manor.

She was surrounded by fog, a web of black and white leaving her barely able to see a foot in front of her face. She was watching Bailey kneel before one of the columns clutching a small, blue stone and a panel was opening in the column.

"What are you doing?" The voice pulled her out of the vision.

Natalie snapped her eyes open and jerked back, turning toward the voice. A muscular man in a security uniform stood before the door leading to the reception area with a sour look on his face and his arms crossed over his chest.

"What are you doing?" he repeated, his tone harsher.

"The picture fell off the wall. I was putting it back," Natalie answered, praying she was thinking fast enough.

"Not what it looks like."

Natalie shrugged her shoulders. "I don't know what it looks like to you. That's what happened."

"Look, the patients will be here any minute. Maybe you should finish up with your actual job."

Natalie nodded and turned to grab a trash bag.

As she went about the room placing garbage in the trash bag and sweeping up the floor, she was unable to do any more actual investigating. The security guard was watching her like a hawk. She was seething on the inside.

She exited the room on the employee side and mentally fumed as she took the route for the first floor that she'd been instructed to take. Therapy rooms first. These rooms were set up more like offices. She emptied the trash and vacuumed the carpet. She ran her hands over the desks and chairs that she assumed the patients sat in, hoping something involving Jessie would jump out at her, but it didn't. There was too much of a jumble as bits and pieces from hundreds of conversations flooded her all at once.

She then went to the cafeteria. All she had to do there was mop the floor and remove the trash from breakfast and throw it in the dumpster out back. When she was coming back in Brittany caught up to her and told her to go ahead and take her lunch even though it was early. The girl that would be training her in the patient rooms was on hers, and Brittany didn't want the schedule to be thrown off while they waited on Natalie.

Natalie walked into the employee lounge and retrieved her lunch from the refrigerator. There was one other girl sitting at one of the tables. She was dressed identical to Natalie and gave her a warm smile.

"Hi, you must be the new hire. I've never seen you around before."

"Yeah, it's my first day," Natalie confirmed.

"I'm Reena. I'll be training you on the patient floors today."

Natalie felt a surge of excitement flood through her. She would be spending the rest of the day with Reena and thankfully, the woman was friendly. She could be a good source of information if Natalie played her cards right.

"Vickie," she responded, using the name that appeared on her fake documentation. It aged her up a few years and showed she had experience working at medical facilities previously when she didn't.

"Please, join me." Reena gestured toward the seat opposite her, and Natalie gladly took it.

"So, how are you liking it so far?"

"It's okay," Natalie said honestly. "Nothing too tough yet. But I haven't been off the first floor except for the tour. Brittany is a little intimidating."

Reena gave her a sympathetic smile. "I can see how you might think that but don't let her be. Brittany is on a power trip since she was promoted to department head a few months ago. She likes to act like she has more power than she does, especially with newbies who don't know any better. She pushes her own beliefs a lot."

Natalie's hand flew to her neck. "So, I don't have to cover my tattoos? The bandage has been itching the hell out of me."

"Unfortunately, that one is a real rule. But she can be way too nasty about it because she personally thinks they're tacky. You may be allergic to the adhesive. I have one too on my ankle. They made a big deal about it during my interview, which I find hilarious because you can't even see it through the tights. Brittany didn't even know it was there until last month. I had somewhere to be right after work, so I changed into street clothes at the end of my shift, and she saw it then. You should have seen her face. She was hopping mad, but she couldn't say anything because I always kept it adequately covered. That was a fun day."

Natalie laughed. "I had the exact opposite experience. No one said anything during my interview at all, but she blindsided me at the start of my shift shoving bandages at me and talking about being unprofessional and looking like a jailbird."

"Ooh, lucky you. She was giving you her best in the first few minutes of your very first shift. She must really like you. So, what is it? Your tattoo?"

"Well, the most prominent one is a snake. It wraps around my throat and disappears down my shirt. It's supposed to be the snake that tempted Eve to eat the apple. No one ever gets it, so maybe that was a mistake, but I still like it. And I have another one on my upper forearm. It's my sister's face. She died of leukemia at six years old."

"Oh, I'm so sorry to hear that."

"It's okay. She was in so much pain toward the end that it was almost a relief."

Reena nodded in understanding.

"So, what's your tattoo about?"

"It's a canary. No special significance or anything. I just like canaries."

Natalie laughed. "Nothing wrong with that."

## Ashley Bundy

"Is the tattoo thing the only thing that's bothering you, honey? You seem a little apprehensive."

*Time to lay it on thick.*

"Just nervous, I guess. I've worked in nursing homes and regular doctor's offices before but never a psych hospital. You hear such horror stories. I'm ashamed to admit it, but the idea of dealing with patients with these kinds of problems scares me a little. I guess I can't help picturing a faceless, knife wielding stalker. Does that make me a bad person?"

"I don't think so. It's natural to be nervous when you don't know what to expect. But let me set your mind at ease. We don't have anything quite on the level of horror movie villains."

"But during the tour, when Brittany took me up to the third floor, she said that one area was gated off for violent patients. And it looked so dark and dreary up there I couldn't help picturing horror movies."

Reena nodded. "Yes, and no. We only have two patients that have killed someone. They are in the gated area and honestly, you will never encounter them. They don't even have their visitation in the rec room if anyone comes to see them. There is a separate room on the third floor specifically for them. The others in that ward are a danger to themselves and on twenty-four/seven suicide watch. Plus, it's my understanding that those two won't even be with us that long. Word of mouth is we're working on getting them transferred out."

"Really?"

Reena nodded. "Yeah, but I don't know much about it. They've been here awhile. But apparently there's all kinds of red tape that needs be sorted through before anything can actually be done. But yeah. The directors don't want them here. For the most part, our facility is on the lower end of what you expect from a psych hospital. Sure, we have a small handful that attacked others—before they were properly medicated. Now, they are functioning just fine, and I can't help but wonder why they are still here. A few are here due to suicide attempts. Most of them, though, just struggle with various mental illnesses and need assistance navigating them. There really isn't anything for you to fear."

"Well, that's good to know," Natalie said, being sure to give an appropriate relieved smile.

"Just keep in mind when the patients are upset, it will almost never be with you. You aren't their doctor or nurse. You aren't security trying to intimidate them into settling down. A lot of them love us. Leave them an extra blanket or let them keep a personal care item—as long as it's safe—and they'll be your friend for life. Really, the only issue we'll have with patients if one of them has an accident. Sometimes they'll make a mess if they're having a meltdown, but it's never personal."

*Was that why Jessie Landry was always losing visitation privileges?*

"So," Reena said. "You ready to hit those patient rooms?"

The second floor was a breeze. Reena went over the routine for the patients on the second floor quickly. Sheets, towels, mop the floor. Rinse and repeat. But Natalie was thrilled to see they were assigned patient rooms that they would regularly tend to. She snuck a quick peek and saw one of her rooms did, in fact, belong to Jessie Landry. She was located on the third floor. It took a colossal level of restraint to not speed through her second-floor rooms to get there faster.

Reena did two rooms with her before they split off to take care of their own sections. Natalie introduced herself to the patients as she cleaned the rooms and kept up pleasant chatter, but she did her best to not touch anyone. The last thing she needed at the moment was to take on anyone else's issues. No distractions. That was crucial. She thoroughly paced herself and could barely contain her excitement when she met Reena by the elevator.

"Third floor is slightly different," Reena told her as she hit the call button. "They are the higher security patients. We don't go in the gated area."

Natalie's heart sank. She knew Jessie was on this floor, but was she in the gated area?

"We're escorted by security into the other rooms."

"I thought they weren't dangerous."

"Typically, they aren't. But you never know when an episode may arise."

As they took the elevator up, Natalie mentally tried to figure out how she was supposed to talk to Jessie with security looking over her shoulder.

Jessie's room was the second one Natalie came to. The security guard that was escorting her was named Chuck, and thankfully he seemed a bit thick headed. While cleaning her first room, he merely stood in the doorway and scrolled on his phone, and she was correct to assume he would do the same at Jessie's room.

She took a deep breath as she turned the doorknob and stepped into the room. She was surprised to see the woman standing in the middle of the room, staring at the door as though she'd been expecting her. She wore a blue bathrobe and turned up the corner of her mouth in a sneer. Instantly, Natalie felt uneasy, automatically assuming Jessie really was crazy.

"Hi, Jessie. I'm your new maid, Vickie."

"No, you're not." There was an almost musical lilt to her voice. "But that's okay. I know why you're here." She extended her hand.

Natalie stared at it for a minute, thrown by the unexpected turn of this interaction. She was also thrown off by Jessie's eyes. They turned from their dull hazel to a deep, electric blue as she looked into them. Realization dawned on her. She wasn't sure how she knew but she was one hundred percent certain.

"Bailey?" she whispered.

"Go on. Take it. The big lug won't even notice."

Natalie took her hand and was jolted into a wild ride.

She felt like her feet left the ground, and she twisted through fog and smoke. She was familiar with. What was new was the landing.

Normally when she travelled through the fog, she was travelling through a person's memories faster than the speed of light. Now, when her feet hit the ground once more, she found herself in literal fog, in a black and white version of Blackwood Manor.

Standing before her was not Jessie Landry, it was the girl from the drawing, and from Richard's descriptions, Bailey.

Bailey hummed to herself and sat down on the porch of Blackwood Manor. Natalie stared in amazement for a moment and sat beside her.

"We're at Blackwood Manor," she began slowly, "but it's different."

Bailey nodded. "We're beyond the veil. This is how we see it."

"I don't understand. Why are you bringing me here now? When I went to see Jessie—"

"Oh, that," Bailey sighed. "I guess I'm the source of her problems. I hitchhike sometimes."

"You're *possessing* her?" Natalie was appalled.

"Well, if you want to make it sound dirty," Bailey said defensively.

"Why?"

"I had to get the word out somehow, didn't I? Plus, she was my friend, and I get lonely. Sharing her thoughts is almost like having companionship again. Rather than sitting here in this bitch of a house to rot for all eternity."

"You mean like everyone else does?"

Bailey sneered. "I guess I'm more clever. I found a work around. Look, you don't have any right to judge me until you've run a mile in my shoes. Sure, I'm a ghost, a ghoul, some might say a demon, but that is *not* accurate. We may not need to breathe, eat, or sleep anymore, but that doesn't mean we can't feel. I long for friendship, touch, someone to just *talk* to. I can't even begin to describe how torturous it is to see everything with crystal clarity and be able to do nothing about it. Living in Blackwood Manor as a ghost is like living in a good storybook. I can see everything and know the way the place ticks. The problem is, I'm dead."

Natalie nodded as she considered what the girl was saying. "So, who else is still here?"

"Now hush up," Bailey snapped. "We're running out of time, and I do have things to say. You'll know all about golden warriors from your grandma. It's probably common knowledge now that I was the golden warrior back then. Now it's my brother."

"Yes, I saw the sparks."

"That's a blessing and a curse. He can make the property clean but not if he makes the same mistakes we made. If he does that, he'll fuel the bad ones."

"Is that what you did?"

Bailey nodded her agreement. "We took out most of the bad ones. A few still linger. It wasn't anything we couldn't handle at first. Until the tunnels. That awoke some of the dormant ones, and they're angry. The angrier they are, the more they fuel Lucy."

"Lucy Blackwood?"

"She absorbed her mother's power, as well as ours that night, and she is fueled by negative energy. She's getting stronger. You'll have a matter of days to prepare. If that. You need to prepare my brother, and you need to watch your enemies closely. Otherwise, it's all for nothing.

"Margaret sensed I could end her power and possessed me, trying to take me over so that she could control me instead of allowing me to vanquish her. Brock's doing it to Richard now."

Natalie remembered the way Richard shoved her and the hate she'd felt rolling off him recently. He'd even told her that story about the voice urging him to push Remi down the stairs.

"There are others that are more than willing to do the same. If they completely take him over, you've already lost. He must fight. Now come. Chuck's about to look up."

Bailey grabbed her arm, and they were swirling through the fog again.

Natalie's feet slammed back into the floor, and she was in Jessie's room once more. Jessie's eyes were back to their natural hazel, and she was looking around the room, confused, and then down at their joined hands.

"Who—who are you?" she asked, her voice shaking.

Before Natalie could answer, Jessie began screaming and threw herself down on the floor, thrashing uncontrollably. Natalie watched helplessly as feet thundered behind her.

# CHAPTER FORTY

Bates Photography was in the seedy part of Macon in a dirty strip shopping center. They drove past it at first. There wasn't a sign visible from the road. The only sign was a nameplate on the door, like what would be found in an office.

Richard pulled up in front, squinting at the sign to make sure this was the place. It didn't even have a glass door like most businesses of this kind did. It was a solid door and there were bars over the one tiny window next to the door.

"Are we sure this is a real business?" Rod asked, his face echoing the same uneasiness that Richard felt.

"According to Google," Richard answered. "Not gonna lie. I'm glad you're with me, man."

"Great," Rod gave a nervous laugh. "Two livers for the price of one. Well, let's go see what we can figure out."

They got out of the car and went straight to the door, walking into an office that was messy and dirty. The sitting area was small, consisting of only a small plaid armchair with rips and a table with a magazine tossed haphazardly on top of it.

The counter was stacked with files and fast-food containers, and the stench of old food was overwhelming. A middle-aged man with food in his beard sat behind the counter watching something on his phone.

"Excuse me," Richard said, placing a hand on the counter. "I'm Richard Price. You called and told me that my pictures were ready."

"Hmm," the man grunted and rose from his seat to disappear through a door behind him, not saying a word.

"The hell?" Rod whispered.

There was an uncomfortable silence that was probably only a minute but felt like an hour.

The man reappeared with a large manila envelope and tossed in on the counter. He typed on his computer for a moment and snapped a price at Richard.

Richard looked down at the pin pad and sent up a silent prayer as he swiped his card that his identity wouldn't get stolen.

"You could've told me it was Blackwood Manor," the man finally barked out. "Lots of people wouldn't have worked on them if they'd known."

"Oh, my assistant didn't mention it?"

"Nah. Just gave me your name and number."

"What did he look like?"

"You don't know what your own assistant looks like?" the man sneered. When Richard and Rod stared at him unblinking, he rolled his eyes and answered. "Man. White. Beard."

"Well, that's extremely helpful," Rod said sarcastically.

"It's fine," Richard interjected and grabbed the envelope. He thanked the man, and they made their way back to the car.

Once they were tucked back inside with the doors locked, Richard ripped the envelope open and pulled the photos out.

They were large glossy shots of Blackwood Manor and his family. His heart ached as he studied each one, peering into faces he hadn't seen since childhood. The initial flip through was for the sake of nostalgia.

Then he remembered Jessie's words. "Pay attention to pictures." At the time, he'd assumed she'd only been referring to Bailey's drawings. But what if she was talking about actual photos too?

Then he flipped through the pictures again. He went slower this time, and meticulously watched for the slightest details.

In several shots, Bailey's eyes were black. It was only Bailey's eyes, so after the third shot, he had a hard time believing that it was a coincidence.

The thing that disturbed him the most though, was that in every picture Callie was in, there was another face just over her shoulder, faint and subtle enough that it could easily be determined to be a flaw in the photographic paper, but undeniably there in every shot she was in. Always in the same spot, just over her right shoulder, peering out as though the owner of that face belonged in the picture.

The more he studied it, the more Richard was sure that face belonged to Lucy Blackwood.

The sound of his phone ringing filled the car and Richard pressed the button to connect the phone to the car's Bluetooth.

Before he could even say anything, the car was filled with the sounds of screaming and then Remi's chilling voice ignited a ball of panic in his gut.

"Richard! You have to help us!"

"Remi? What's going on? Where are you?"

"We're at the house. Me and Jamie." He recognized that she was sobbing, and his heart broke right in half. "We got separated. I don't know where she is. Please help. She's going to kill us!"

"Who?"

Before she could answer there were sounds of loud bangs and her shrill terrified screaming. Then the phone was silent for a moment. They heard a child playfully giggling before the line went dead.

Richard turned on the engine and sped out of the parking lot toward Blackwood Manor.

"Hold up, dude," Rod tried to calm him. "How do we know that wasn't a trick? We should go to the police station."

Richard furiously shook his head. "No time. Didn't you hear her voice? It might already be too late."

He silently prayed that he was wrong as he increased his speed.

# CHAPTER FORTY-ONE

Brad
Two hours ago

"You want me to do what?" Brad sat in the office of Heaven's Estate. His mouth was wide in shock at the task that Kate Wilkes asked him to do.

She looked across the wide desk at him and smiled widely. "I don't think I stuttered, Bradley."

"But why?"

His breath hitched as he tried to comprehend what was being asked of him. He'd always been loyal to Kate Wilkes and her entire family. They'd been there for him at a time no one else had. He could never repay everything she'd done for him. But this. He didn't understand this.

Kate sighed and sat back in her chair. "I should think it would be obvious. For Heaven's Estate to flourish, Blackwood Manor must be desolate. It was Rebecca's will."

"Well, yes, I understand that. But these kids aren't preventing that."

"They're nosing around in matters that would best be left alone," her tone was hard. "That Richard came over here asking questions. Not to mention they are harboring my grandson."

Brad gave her a look but didn't respond.

"Oh, yes. I know. Don't try to cover for them. Bradley, listen," she sighed again and batted her eyelashes at him a few times. "I admire your softness for children. Believe it or not, I do. But you must realize that they are no longer children and must pay the price for their actions. Now, I have it on good authority that everyone is out of the house today. You will call the two girls and have them come back to the house. Then we can set up for a strike."

"No," Brad said hotly. "Giving you information is one thing, but I will not set them up."

He rose from his seat and strode to the door.

"You will do this, or your daughter will die."

Brad's blood went cold, and he slowly turned back toward Kate. "What?"

Kate's smile only widened, revealing lipstick smudged on her teeth. "I will make certain of it."

He charged forward and brought a fist down on the desk. "That wasn't our agreement!"

"No? Agreements terms can be changed. After all, isn't that what you're attempting to do right now? You are indebted to me. The choice is yours, Bradley."

She held out a prepaid cell phone to him, and he snatched it out of her hand.

"I hate you for this, you know."

"Yes, yes, I know. But that's alright. As long as you're a good boy and do what you're told, you can hate me as much as you want."

# CHAPTER FORTY-TWO

They drove back to Blackwood Manor in just under forty minutes, an insanely quick amount of time. Natalie, Mel, and Gus were waiting for them next to the porch.

Richard was momentarily thrown by Natalie wearing an all-white uniform with bandages on her neck before being pulled back to the issue at hand.

Remi's car was in the driveway, completely abandoned.

As Richard and Rod ran up to the others, they saw Gus perched on the porch scrolling through something on his phone.

"Has anyone seen them?" Richard asked when he got close enough.

"No," Natalie answered. "We've been here about ten minutes, and we haven't heard anything. Gus is checking the footage on his phone to figure out what we're walking into."

"On his phone?" Rod asked, incredulously.

"I have the footage rerouted to my phone in case of a system crash," Gus answered without looking up. "I'm going back through the footage now to see if I can see them. It takes a lot longer like this."

"So, what exactly happened on this phone call?" Natalie asked him.

He'd called her when he was racing back and told her to compile the team and meet him at the house, but he hadn't given her too many details. He just wanted to concentrate on getting back as quickly as possible.

"It was Remi. She said that her and Jamie were in the house, but they got separated and someone was trying to kill them. She was screaming and there was a lot of banging and someone laughing."

"Alright," Natalie let out a big breath. "Let's go." She gestured for Richard to follow her around the back of the house.

"No fucking way!" he yelled. "Something is going on with Remi and Jamie, and we need to get to them as quickly as possible."

"We don't even know what we're walking into," her tone was level. "You are not going in there halfcocked. None of us are. There's something you need to know anyway."

She grabbed his arm forcefully and began to lead to the back of the house.

He hated her in that moment. Hated that she had such authority over him, hated that she was keeping him from Remi, hated that insufferable stubbornness.

Once it was just the two of them in the back fields, she quickly summarized her day at the psych hospital and conversation with Bailey. Then she pointed toward a rag doll nailed to a post about ten feet away.

"Now, give it a blast."

"But I thought golden warrior power didn't manifest until a time of need."

"The time is now," the certainty in her voice did something to his gut that he could not explain. "You've been showing signs they are attempting to possess you. They know you have the power. You need to learn to control it before we go in there."

"So, you're saying—"

She nodded. "It's eat or be eaten."

He turned toward the doll, his nerves wrapping his belly into a tight fist. Then he extended both his palms. His palms crackled with blue, but nothing happened.

"Think about it," she urged him. "Think about it with everything you have."

He closed his eyes and felt the warmth extending through his arms and into his open palms. He opened his eyes to see a blue light shoot out about two feet before dying out.

"Better!" her eyes danced with excitement, and she nudged him out of the way. "Much better! But you have to let it take you over."

She stuck her palms out and the white light shot out bright and hot over twenty feet. The rag doll strained backward against its nails.

"So, you're a golden warrior too?"

She put her hands down and stepped aside. "No, my power is different. It's tied to my psychic abilities. My grandma always said she and I are a little bit magical. I'm not sure if that was the truth or it was just the best way to explain it to child me. I don't use it a lot, but I have it pretty well controlled. It's a good defensive tool, but I can't vanquish like the golden warrior can. That's you. Try again."

He took his place back in front of the doll again and put his palms back out.

"Remember," she told him, "let it consume your whole body."

He nodded and did what she said. The warmth started in the pit of his stomach this time, then spread through each of his limbs in turn until it was pushing out of his palms.

The blue light shot past the doll, incinerating the rags of the dress it wore and the grass in the surrounding area. When he pulled back, there was nothing left of the doll.

"Yes! Yes! You did it!" Natalie was jumping up and down excitedly. "Now, just blast the hell out of anything that comes in your path in there, and we're good."

"Hey guys!" They turned toward Mel's voice coming from the side of the house. "Come on!"

They ran back up to the front where Gus was cursing in frustration and rising to his feet.

"Okay, screw it," Gus snarled. "This is pointless. I can work faster at the hub in my room. I can't see them on here. But the hallway is clear."

"Wait a minute. Is it safe?" Mel asked, concern evident on her face.

"We have to help the girls," Rod answered. "I say we just do it, but we all stay together. There's five of us. If we stay together, it should be fine."

Richard and Natalie exchanged a look, and he could tell by the look on her face she was thinking the same thing he was; large numbers don't necessarily mean anything at Blackwood Manor. After all, he had four people, he loved perish in a high stakes situation just ten years ago. At the same time, the two of them now knew the extent of their powers.

He wasn't going to risk Remi though. Or Jamie. He couldn't lose any more people he cared about. He didn't think he'd be able to take it. There had already been too much loss in his life.

Natalie nodded her understanding as if she could read his mind and wholeheartedly agreed with him. "Absolutely. We stay together. No matter what."

As a unit, the five of them made their way inside the house. It was eerily quiet. Richard had the momentary thought that it was even quieter than when he'd first arrived back at the house. The silence was deafening. It was like a huge, nagging bug burrowing its way deep down into his brain and eating away at the healthy tissue until all that was left was an overwhelming sense of wrong.

They moved up the stairs and down the hallway towards Gus's bedroom, looking in every direction and around every corner, looking for anything that seemed out of the ordinary and may be lurking in the shadows, waiting for the perfect moment to attack.

Once they were in the bedroom, everyone plopped down on the furniture, and Gus immediately went into the computer system to check the cameras, running everything back a little at a time looking for any sign of the girls.

After sitting there for about five minutes, he alerted them and pointed out something on the screen. Everyone gathered around the computer where he hit play.

The image was of the upstairs hallway. Remi and Jamie were coming up the stairs. They looked like they were calling for someone.

"Is there any audio?" Natalie asked.

Gus pressed a few more keys on the keyboard and then they heard a completely normal sound.

"Hello?" Remi was calling down the hall. "Are you guys here?"

"His car isn't here," Jamie said. "Remi, I don't like this. I have a bad feeling."

"Maybe we just beat him here," Remi answered. "It hasn't been that long."

"No, something doesn't feel right. He said he was already here. I think we should leave."

Before Remi could answer, there was the sound of a creaking floorboard and the girls turned toward the noise.

Ashley Bundy

Two figures appeared as if out of thin air. One was a young child who didn't look any older than six years old. It was clearly Lucy Blackwood. Her blonde hair and blue eyes were an exact match to the notorious painting.

Seeing her in motion like this made Richard's blood cold. Live action Lucy was considerably creepier than painting Lucy. Her eyes were vacant, and she wore an ominous grin on her face.

Standing slightly behind her was another figure. Time stood still for Richard. His chest was tight and burning and his vision started to go cloudy.

"Richard. Richard!" Rod slapped him on the back, and he came back to himself. His vision cleared and he pulled breath back into his lungs. He realized he hadn't been breathing.

"You okay, man?" Rod asked him.

Everyone was looking at him with extreme concern.

"I'm okay. It's just that's my sister."

"That's not Bailey," Natalie said, leaning in closer to the monitor to see her.

"No, not Bailey. It's Callie."

It was Callie, looking as much herself as she had the day she'd died. Her hair swooped lightly over one eye, tall for her age, skinny, and looking slightly unsure of herself. Her very body language was the same. But he didn't understand why she was here. She hadn't died in Blackwood Manor. It had been just as long for her as it had been for him since she'd set foot in this place. Why would she choose to spend her afterlife in the place where tragedy changed the trajectory of their lives?

"Umm...what?" Mel asked. "How is that even possible? Why would Callie be here?"

"I don't know," Richard answered.

"He's not high though," Rod confirmed, seeing disbelieving look on Mel's face, "That is Callie. No doubt."

Natalie placed her palm on the screen and then pulled it away as if suddenly aware that wasn't how her gift worked.

"I'm ready," Richard told Gus. "Go ahead and play it now."

Gus hit play, and everyone's attention returned to the screen.

"Callie," Remi said, surprised. "What are you doing here?"

Callie didn't answer, but she looked down at the ground.

"Like my trick?" Lucy giggled. "They took my sister, so she took her place." She jerked her head over her shoulder towards Callie, who tried to shrink back into the shadows.

"Who took your sister?" Jamie asked.

"Your people," Lucy snarled. "I get stuck in this place, and they take away the one person I have to keep me company. I think it's a fair trade."

"Callie," Remi took a cautious step forward and stuck her hand out. "Come on over here, honey."

"NO!!" Lucy growled, and she lunged forward, sending Remi into the wall, and the camera went black.

Everyone stood there for a moment looking at the screen, unsure of what to think or say.

Rod shot out of his seat and into the hallway.

"Rod, wait!" Richard called after him and everyone rushed after him.

Rod was in the hallway examining the area the camera had been focused on, where the interaction took place.

There was broken glass on the floor, and Natalie knelt over that area to place her palm on the floor. Everyone gave her silence to concentrate as she squeezed her eyes closed.

They stood there watching for about thirty seconds and then she shot to her feet and made her way to the wall, beginning to run her fingers over it.

"Natalie, what is it?" Richard asked. "What did you see?"

"A secret room," she answered. "The door is over here somewhere, but I'm not entirely sure where."

The group began to examine the wood paneling of the wall, running their fingers over every crevice and knocking in search of hollow spots.

"I have something!" Mel stuck her fingers inside a knot in the wood and a door popped forward about half an inch.

The group grabbed hold of the door and wrenched it open. Behind it was an extremely small room that was made up of exposed brick. There was a single chair in the center with Jamie tied to it, bound and gagged.

Rod rushed forward and pulled the tape from her mouth. Tears poured freely down her face, and she was crying hysterically.

"It was Callie. It was Callie and Lucy!" she cried.

"We know." Richard said soothingly as Rod undid her ropes. "Where's Remi? What happened to Remi?"

"I don't know," she squeezed her eyes closed. "Lucy attacked us, and I blacked out. I woke up in here, and Callie was tying me up and I couldn't see Remi anywhere. Trap. It was a trap!"

Once they had her ropes undone and pulled her from the secret room, they all returned to Gus's room where he went back to the cameras, trying to figure out where Remi went.

Jamie still sobbed on Rod's shoulder when they heard movement from downstairs.

"Hello?" Brad's voice traveled up the stairs and everyone let out a collective sigh of relief.

"We're up here!" Richard called down.

Brad's heavy footfalls carried up the stairs and then he walked into the room looking extremely confused. "What's going on?" he asked. "Why is everyone here?"

"Remi and Jamie got lured here," Richard told him. "Lucy and Callie attacked them, and now Remi is missing."

"Callie? What the hell are you talking about?"

Richard briefly got Brad up to speed by explaining what they'd seen on the cameras and finding Jamie in the secret room. Then he turned to Jamie, who had calmed down considerably. "Can you tell us exactly how you guys ended up here?"

"Remi got a phone call saying everyone was meeting here. That there was something we needed to see."

"Who called you?" Brad asked.

"Well, you," Jamie flushed and cast her eyes down.

"Me? I didn't call anyone."

"Well, she thought it was you. That's all I know."

"Look, man," Rod said to Brad, not unkindly, "I don't think anyone here thinks you would lure the girls here, but would you mind if we checked your phone? No stone unturned and all that?"

"Of course," Brad pulled his phone from his pocket and handed it over to Rod who pulled up the call log and briefly scanned through it.

Rod nodded and handed the phone back to Brad. "Well, whoever called it, wasn't him. Remi's number isn't on there. Too bad we don't have Remi's to see who it was."

"Guys," Gus's alarmed voice carried over to them and they all gathered around the monitor once again to see what he'd found.

The camera view was of the cellar, and Remi lay limp and unconscious on the ground as she was dragged by the two girls, one on each leg, into the tunnels.

"Great," Rod growled. "The fucking tunnels again."

# CHAPTER FORTY-THREE

Sheriff Thomas O'Reilly sat back from the computer monitor and sighed.

Richard studied the man, pudgy in build, receding hairline, and nervously contemplated what would come next.

Finally, after what felt like hours the man turned to face the group in Gus's bedroom.

"What are you all even doing here?" he said with an edge to his voice.

"What?" Whatever Richard had been expecting, it hadn't been that. "We live here. You told us we could come back. Now Remi is missing. In the tunnels! You can see it clear as day in the monitor!"

"I certainly did not give you clearance to come back in, Mr. Price," the sheriff bit out through gritted teeth, "because the property is still a crime scene that's being investigated. You weren't supposed to be here. By being in here, you may have inadvertently destroyed evidence, and now we have to halt the investigation to look for someone that never should have been here. I don't think you all understand how serious this is and just how much trouble you're in."

"You called me!" Richard was agitated. "You called me and told me the bodies had all been there awhile, and we were free to come back."

"Old bodies or not, we still need to properly investigate," the sheriff said simply.

Richard gave an irritated grunt and explained again about the phone call from Remi, and Jamie chimed in with her side that they were told to meet at the house.

Ashley Bundy

The sheriff didn't say whether this was an excusable reason to be in the house, but he set his mouth in a narrow line before responding to their explanation.

"Alright, well, I already have a team in route to search the tunnels. It hasn't been too long, so hopefully we can get her out fast enough."

"Great. Let's go," Richard rose to his feet.

"Absolutely not." It was clear the sheriff was quickly losing patience with him. "You all need to get out of the house now. Professionals will handle this."

"Wait one damn minute. This is my house, and she's my friend. I think I have a right to look for her."

"No, you wait!" the sheriff's voice boomed now. "It's bad enough you all are here to begin with. I will NOT be letting you down in those tunnels. That's what trained professionals are for. If I let you down there, you'd just destroy evidence, slow us down, and get yourselves hurt. Sound familiar? Sounds like the last rescue mission you conducted yourselves down in the tunnels. I'm having to pull valuable men off a kidnapping investigation for this. Get your ass out of here or I'll have you arrested for obstruction."

Brad grabbed Richard's shoulder and pulled him gently back toward the door. "He's right. You can't help her right now. Leave it to them."

Fury ignited inside Richard, and he lunged toward the sheriff, but Brad and Rod both had hold of his arms, their fingers grinding into his bone as they pulled him away.

Once they got outside, they saw police cruisers and forensic vans out front, already pulling out equipment and tools. At least the sheriff hadn't been lying about having a team coming.

They walked to the edge of the property and beyond the tree line where an officer was already setting up a barricade.

Richard shook with anger as he looked back up at the house and kicked himself inside for not going with his initial instinct to search for Remi himself.

It had been Brad to point out that they now knew how extensive the tunnels were and how dangerous, and that people were seriously hurt the last time—all very good points—and he'd agreed to call the police. He'd never imagined, though, that they wouldn't be allowed to help in the search efforts. After all, in this type of situation wouldn't more people be better? With every minute that ticked on by, he felt more dread in his heart that he may never see Remi again.

He felt a hand on his back and looked to the side to find Natalie standing there staring up at him. Her eyes were wide with concern.

"It's okay," she said gently.

He shook his head violently and felt the warm sting of tears on his cheeks. "No. Something's wrong. I can feel it. This is my fault. I never should have brought her here. I—"

"Richard," she squeezed his shoulder firmly. "This is not your fault. You had no way of knowing this was going to happen, and Remi knows that. She'll be okay. They'll find her."

"They should have at least taken you," he spit out in disgust. "You know where you're going. They're going in blind, and something is gonna happen. I just know it."

"Listen to me," she gave his chin a firm but gentle tug and forced him to look at her. "She's okay."

"How do you know?" he cried.

"I know," she said firmly. "You know I know."

Ashley Bundy

He didn't answer her, but he did allow himself to be pulled into her embrace. He stooped down to lay his head on her shoulder as she wrapped her arms around him, and he cried into her hair.

Rod fumed as he stood behind them, observing. Richard crying in Natalie's arms was such a nauseating sight. She was rubbing his back in small, tight circles that made his stomach muscles clench.

He looked over at Jamie who was pressed firmly to his side and exchanged a knowing look with her. She raised an eyebrow and looked away.

They both saw the signs and spoke of it frequently, but they disagreed on what it meant. Rod simply didn't like Natalie. He didn't trust her, and she rubbed him the wrong way. Sure, she said and did all the right things, but Rod just couldn't let go of this nagging feeling that she was completely fake. Even setting aside the psychic thing, he still believed that.

He firmly believed with everything he had that she was playing Richard, he just didn't know why, but he intended to find out.

Jamie completely disagreed with him. She liked Natalie. She thought she was nice, liked her spunk, and thought her gift was beyond cool, and she noted an attraction between the two of them. She didn't want them together; she'd pushed for him and Remi forever, but she didn't dislike Natalie in any sort of way.

There was a brief moment when Rod started to doubt himself. He was the only one that seemed to have any kind of issue with her, so he'd started thinking maybe he was just paranoid—that he'd just been put off by the whole psychic thing—but then she'd gone incognito after the tunnels, and his suspicions went right back through the roof.

Sure, it was half ass explained. She'd been quiet because she wanted to give Gus and Baxter an opportunity to come clean on their own. And it seemed like a satisfactory answer to everyone else in the interest of starting fresh and the silly "no judgement" rule.

That explanation had not put Rod at ease. If anything, it put his hackles up even farther. All that showed him was she was very capable of keeping secrets when it suited her.

# CHAPTER FORTY-FOUR

Mel's attention was diverted to the tree line at the edge of the property. There was the slightest movement that she caught in her peripheral vision. She bent to pretend to tie her shoe and cast her eyes up.

There was an elderly woman lurking just beyond the trees. She was wearing a baby blue pantsuit and was heavily done up. The woman turned and began moving in the opposite direction.

Mel stood up and nudged Natalie to get her attention. When Natalie turned, Mel jerked her chin in that direction and Natalie looked, then narrowed her eyes.

"Oh, really?" Natalie snarled. "What's that about? Let's see, shall we?"

She grabbed Mel's elbow who followed behind a couple of steps. They walked beyond the tree line, keeping a safe distance from the woman in the blue suit.

When the woman left the tree line on the opposite side, Natalie put up an arm to hold Mel back before they could emerge from the trees.

The woman walked across a vast, green property that was much better kept than Blackwood Manor.

"You've viewed the property records," Natalie whispered. "Is this Heaven's Estate?"

Mel nodded. "Yes. I didn't realize it was so close, but yeah, Heaven's Estate is the neighboring property on this side."

"Which means that was Kate Wilkes," Natalie smirked. "What would our friendly neighbor be doing lurking in the shadows of the trees if she didn't have anything to hide?"

"It does look suspicious." Mel agreed.

"Let's go see what she's hiding." Natalie made a move to emerge from the trees, but Mel grabbed her and dragged her back.

"No! Are you crazy? We'll be seen."

"Are you forgetting who you're with?" Natalie laughed.

"It's not Blackwood Manor," Mel hissed. "This place is operational. They have a staff. A large one."

"I can use my gift to find out where people are and make my way through the property. Stick to me, and we'll be fine."

"I don't know."

"Look, Mel. It's okay if you don't want to go. I understand. I'm not going to make you take that kind of a risk. But I'm going. I owe it to Richard. The choice is yours."

With that last statement, she bolted from the trees out into the open, strolling confidently across the luscious green grass.

Mel grunted in frustration and dashed after her, running to catch up. When she came to a halt next to her at the edge of a storage shed, Natalie had a grin on her face.

"I knew you wouldn't be able to stay away," she teased.

"Oh, shut up," Mel snapped. "What the hell are we doing at a shed anyway?"

"There's a gardener too close to the house so I detoured to here. Plus, it's not necessarily just a way to wait until the coast is clear. There could be a treasure trove in here for all we know."

She jerked the door open, and they went into the tiny shed. It had a musty smell and was dusty. While the rest of the property was well tended and gorgeous, this shed appeared long neglected. The dust on the ground was at least three inches thick, and there were holes in the walls from termite damage.

Not that she was judging. A maintenance shed probably wouldn't be her top priority if she were fortunate enough to own a property like this either.

There were gardening tools thrown inside, old broken-down furniture, and even a snowboard, of all the strange things.

Natalie sprinted straight to a chest in the corner. It was an old wooden crate of a box that had an old, rusted lock on it.

She grabbed a spade from a nearby gardening bucket and brought it down hard on the lock, busting it. The lock broke away and to the floor.

"Natalie!" Mel hissed in shock. "We can't just destroy their property."

Natalie didn't listen. She opened the chest and began to shuffle through it. She pulled out an old-fashioned black cloak and held it in her hands for a couple of seconds. She became very still and quiet, and Mel instantly knew she was having a vision.

She stayed as quiet and still as she possibly could be as she waited it out and Natalie began to move again.

"This is sick," she whispered. Her skin was gray.

"What happened?"

Natalie looked up at Mel. "This is where they keep it."

"Where they keep what?"

"The shit for their sick rituals," she let go of the cloak and let it fall to the floor, then rubbed her hands against her jeans. "They wear these cloaks during their ceremonies.

They kill animals. The dagger they use is at the bottom of the box, but I don't want to look."

Mel stuck out a hand to help Natalie to her feet. She didn't like the way the younger girl looked now. She was extremely pale, and her skin had a clammy shine to it. As Natalie took her hand, Mel also noted she was shaking ever so slightly.

"Are you okay?"

"Yeah. Just every time I get a peek into one of the ceremonies it's a weird little jolt. I hate it. It's necessary though."

Natalie put a palm to the door and then inclined her head. "Coast is clear. Stay close."

They exited the shed and darted towards a door at the back of the house. Natalie turned the knob to find it unlocked and they silently entered an immense hall.

There was gorgeous wainscotting on the walls and the lighting offered a warm, welcome glow. Natalie signaled for them to go left, and they tiptoed down the hallway.

Mel wanted to gasp and ooh and aww, but she didn't dare to make a sound. This was the most beautiful building she'd ever seen in her entire life.

Natalie held up an arm and Mel walked straight into it. It was hard enough to take her breath away, but she still somehow managed to keep from making any noise.

Natalie grabbed her arm and pulled her into a door. They had no more than closed the door behind them that they heard footsteps in the hallway and voices too near to risk going back out.

Mel stepped back from the door and surveyed the room they'd found themselves in. It was a small office. Jackpot.

Ashley Bundy

She made for the desk and immediately tried to get on the computer, but it was password protected. *Damn it.* She sat back in the chair furiously. They didn't lock their doors, but they had to go and put a password on the damn computer. She didn't have time to break into it. She could do it, but it wasn't her biggest strength. That was more Gus's area of expertise.

Instead, she began to open drawers and pilfer through them in search of physical files. She wasn't hoping for much. This was the digital age after all. But she hit the jackpot in the bottom right drawer. There were files lined up neatly in a row.

She glanced up to check on Natalie. She was still standing at the door with her palms to it.

Mel slunk down to the ground to better study the labels on the files. She wasn't one hundred percent certain what she was looking for, but her gut told her she'd know when she saw it.

Her gut was apparently right because she was drawn to the third file, labeled *Coven*. How obvious could they get? She pulled the file out and flipped through a couple of pages, eyes going wide at what she was seeing. She looked up again, trying to guess how long they'd been in this room and weighed her options. Could she stuff it under her shirt? She closed her eyes and squeezed the file at its binding, trying to gauge the thickness. No, it would be too thick, and besides, taking it all together would be too conspicuous. Probably wasn't a good idea anyway.

Instead, she pulled out her cell phone and took photos of each individual page before placing the file neatly back in its spot.

"Psst," Natalie hissed. "They're gone. It's time."

Mel scrambled to her feet and made her way to Natalie's side. They opened the door and silently slinked into the hall. Natalie guided them through one hallway and then another, she made to enter a large door and on the opposite side stood Kate Wilkes, smiling broadly. She was flanked on both sides by large, body building looking sort of men.

"Hello dears," she smiled. "Please, join us."

Each grabbed their arms and jerked them into the room, snapping the door shut behind them.

# CHAPTER FORTY-FIVE

"How did they best me?" Natalie wondered to herself. She was sitting with Mel in front of a large oak paneled desk. Kate sat across from them, stirring a cup of tea.

The woman was still smiling. The damn smile. Natalie was pretty sure it never left her face. She'd never seen the woman without the smile spattered across her face. It didn't come across as endearing. It was creepy as hell. It didn't help that the woman wore extreme make up like she thought she was a teenager or something. It didn't even look good. She always wore bright lips that smeared out of the lines. Natalie had always thought she looked crazy.

Ever since they'd been sitting here, she'd tried to figure out how they'd known she and Mel were in there. She'd been using her gift to see around corners, to see if people were in her path, as she'd done so many times before to sneak into areas she didn't belong. Her sight had shown her that room was empty.

They'd not only known she and Mel were in there, they'd blocked her sight as well, and she couldn't figure out how. She didn't even know something like that was possible. It baffled her.

Her concentration was interrupted as the door behind her opened and she jumped at the noise, turning around. Her father strutted into the room, and she had a strange feeling in her gut.

Her feelings for him would always be complicated. He was her father and a part of her would always love him, but she simply couldn't trust him. He wouldn't have been the person she'd choose to call in the event of an emergency.

"Bradley," Kate exclaimed in that bright, fake voice of hers. "I believe these belong to you?" She gestured her hand toward Natalie and Mel.

Natalie turned and shot the woman death daggers from her eyes, hoping with everything she had that she was being intimidating. Somehow, she knew she wasn't. This tactic didn't seem to work on Kate the way it worked on other people.

"I am so sorry, Kate." He strode to the desk and took one of the elderly woman's hands between two of his big ones. "I don't know what got into them. I appreciate you not pressing charges."

"Of course," she giggled and waved a dismissive hand. "Our curiosity gets the better of us sometimes. No harm, no foul. However, should I catch you on my property uninvited again, I will be forced to call the sheriff."

Her friendly tone of congeniality turned stone cold, and Natalie recognized a stoniness in her eyes that made her stomach turn.

"Understood," Brad said warmly to her and then gestured to the girls to stand up. "Natalie, Mel, let's go."

They rose to their feet and allowed him to lead them from Heaven's Estate, all the way to the property line of Blackwood Manor.

With each step they took Natalie's fury bubbled up inside her like a blister. The nerve. The actual *nerve* of this man to walk into the enemy's lair acting like he was picking up a couple of disobedient toddlers from daycare. He'd been so sweet and cordial with Kate when he knew exactly what she was. It was sickening.

Ashley Bundy

He didn't say anything until they were back at Blackwood Manor and then he laid into them.

"What in the Sam Hill did you two think you were doing?" he thundered.

Natalie reared back and swung with all her strength, smacking him clear in the face. Then she turned on her heel and headed toward her car with the others staring after her, slack jawed.

Natalie grabbed a bag of spicy chips, her favorite comfort, stress-relieving food, and tore it open as she plopped down at the kitchen table in her tiny apartment.

She hadn't spent much time here since starting the Blackwood Manor investigation, and she hadn't thought she'd be back until later, but she needed time away from the rest of the group to calm herself down and stuff her face.

She immediately regretted hitting her father in front of everyone. It hadn't been very professional of her, but she'd just been so overwrought with emotion toward him that she'd been unable to choke down the impulse.

Now, she was sitting here pouting alone, and shoving chips in her mouth like a petulant child.

She was contemplating whether she should call Richard and explain her actions when she heard the door to her apartment slam open. She was in a different room, but the sound was loud and deafening, and had clearly been opened with enough force to hit the wall. She scowled again. That better have not caused any damage.

"Natalie!" her father's voice thundered through the apartment, and she heard the stomping of his footsteps throughout.

Instead of getting up or calling out to greet him, she kept her ass planted firmly in her chair and shoved another handful of chips into her mouth.

After a couple of minutes, he stomped into the kitchen and strolled right up to the table, stood over her, and crossed his arms. "What the hell was that about?"

"Come right on in," she said sarcastically. "What did you do? Follow me?"

"You bet your ass I followed you. I've tried to be patient with you, but it's time we had it out. I've had about enough of your attitude, young lady," he growled. "I understand you're hurt, and you have a right to be. You do not have a right to be disrespectful or to hit me. You don't have to like me. You will start treating me with respect."

"And you don't have the right to try to play the role of a fucking parent! I'm grown. You missed your chance to raise me. Just because you weren't there then doesn't mean I'm going to stand for you ordering me around and lecturing me now."

"You were caught breaking into a major plantation. You are on security cameras. There is footage of you sneaking in there. Do you understand that? What were you thinking? If you wanted to see Heaven's Estate, we could've just called Kate and made an appointment. Why sneak in? Does it give you some sort of cheap thrill?"

"Okay, stop it," she put up a hand to shut him up. "What did I just say about lecturing me? Getting caught was stupid. I don't know how they caught me but that's my business."

"You are on camera. How many times do I have to say it? You're smarter than this."

She narrowed her eyes. "There are so many things wrong with that statement. One—I'm not referring to the fucking cameras. You should know that considering the family is full of the gifted. I'm talking about the fact that my gift showed me the room was empty. They were able to trick my sight. That's a problem. Two—how the hell would you know what I'm smarter than? You were never around."

"Cameras or not, you had no business being there. What if I hadn't known her? You could be in a jail cell, or worse."

"Again, that's my business."

"You're my daughter. It's very much my business. Why not just call her?"

"Why?" she laughed manically. "Why? I'll tell you why. I didn't make an appointment with Kate because I was there for information. I was there for the truth. I was there because Kate was lurking around the tree line at the edge of Blackwood Manor being shady as fuck, and I wanted to know why. If I'd scheduled a nice, polite little tour of Heaven's Estate she would have spun her own narrative, nothing close to the truth, and I think you know that."

They exchanged a look for a moment, and he didn't reply, but she could see it on his face. He was waging an internal battle, trying to figure out just how much she'd learned.

"I don't know why it's so hard for you to grasp," she spat out. "That I have a gift. It's not like I'm the first. This runs in the family. I see things. Did you not realize I learned the truth while I was sneaking around over there?"

He flicked his eyes up to a spot on the wall just over her shoulder, and she couldn't help but feel the rage deep inside her. The coward didn't want to look at her. Well, she wasn't going to let him get away with it.

"You've been helping her. All this time."

"You don't understand what you saw."

"I'm not a child who's incapable of understanding what I see with my own eyes. I had a vision. A long one. Their family dressed in those ridiculous cloaks, chanting, slitting throats of animals and even babies. You, sneaking over there in the middle of the night and giving her information. For years. Every weakness about residents that she could use, destroying lives. Even with Richard's family. Playing their friend, like an honorary member of the family, while you're telling her every little weakness they had? You were never my favorite person, but I never thought that of you."

"No one was supposed to get hurt," he said. His voice sounded low and strained, like a person who's tired and ready to give up.

"What were you doing?"

Brad grasped the back of a chair and slumped down into it, ran his fingers through his hair and finally made eye contact with her again. "Our family has known theirs for years. I can't remember a time when Kate wasn't around. She was like another grandmother to me, and I felt loyalty to her. I knew she dabbled in witchcraft, and I didn't see anything harmful in it. Then when Claire bought Blackwood Manor, Kate made me an offer."

He reached out to try to take her hand, and she jerked it away, shoving her hand back into the bag of chips, only to find it empty. "Fuck!" She crumpled the bag and tossed it toward the trash can, but it missed and hit the floor instead. "So, what was her offer?"

"She said she could probably save Caroline. All I had to do was give her information. She didn't want to hurt them. She only wanted to drive them away. As long as Blackwood Manor was empty, Heaven's Estate would thrive. No one was supposed to get hurt."

"And yet they died," she snapped. "And so did Caroline. She clearly didn't do what she said and yet you're helping her now, too."

"They died because of the choices they made that night," he said gently. "Kate didn't orchestrate that. It was a tragic accident. As for Caroline, she was too far gone."

"She might have convinced you of that bullshit, but she doesn't fool me. Why are you helping her now?"

"She told me our relationship would be repaired."

"Well, that's twice she's failed."

"Natalie, that's not fair."

"No, you know what's not fair? You thinking some witchy bitch can make me love you again instead of trusting I have a brain of my own. Get out."

"Natalie—"

"*Get out.*"

She stared him down with her best go to hell stare. He gazed into her eyes for a few seconds, and then rose to his feet and strode from the kitchen. She listened to his footsteps in the hallway and then finally the sound of her door closing.

She let out a shaky sigh and then rose to grab another bag of chips from the pantry.

A door opened down the hall, then there were soft footsteps in the hallway. Dani stuck her head tentatively around the doorframe.

"Is the coast clear?"

"Yeah," Natalie sighed, and sunk back down in her seat at the table.

"Who was that?"

"Daddy Dearest."

Dani's jaw dropped and she looked in the direction of the front hallway, as if expecting to see him standing there. "Oh."

Natalie felt a pang of guilt. She'd let Dani get too far out of the loop. It was so easy to do in an investigation. "He works for Richard. I just found out he's been helping the loony neighbor.

"How do you feel about seeing him again?" Dani took a seat opposite her.

"I feel like that hurt child all over again." That much was true. Her heart broke all over every time she saw him. "But I'm not going to run away. I made a commitment to helping Richard, and that's what I'm going to do."

"Well, do what you gotta do, babe. I'll support you no matter what."

"Yeah," Natalie muttered, and shoved her fist back in the bag of chips.

# CHAPTER FORTY-SIX

Baxter sat in a chair in the hallway of Heaven's Estate biting his cuticles. He'd screwed up. He didn't often screw up, and he wasn't sure what the consequences would be.

"Mr. Bronson," he looked up to see a maid approaching him. "Ms. Wilkes is ready to see you."

He followed the maid down a hallway and into an office. Kate Wilkes looked up from a computer and gave him a smile. He walked in, ignoring the maid who had brought him this far, trying to gauge the look on Kate's face.

"Baxter, dear!" She rose to her feet and rounded the desk to throw her arms around him.

Uneasy, he hugged her back. "Hi, Aunt Kate."

"So," she looked up into his eyes and firmly patted his arms. "Tell me about Natalie Morse."

Baxter wasn't sure what he'd been expecting, but it hadn't been that. "What?"

"Natalie. You've worked with her for a while." Kate turned and took her seat back at the desk, gesturing for him to sit opposite her. "You've been working with her awhile."

"Yeah, but she's introverted. I'd assume you would know more. Considering how involved you've always been with Brad."

"Yes, but ever since the divorce, Natalie hasn't been around me much. Even before, my interactions with her and her sister were limited. Sylvie never liked me. So, what can you tell me?"

Baxter let out a breath. "Well, let's see. She claims to have that sight. Maybe she does. I never believed in psychics or mediums and all of that, but I have to admit, sometimes the woman knows things she shouldn't. She gives me the willies. I've seen her uncover certain things and it just feels unnatural. She doesn't talk about herself though, so I can't tell you personal details. She does go by the last name Morgan. I never connected the dots until I saw her with Brad."

"How much does she know about us?"

"Well, she knows who I am. She knows about Josh. His venture into the tunnels kind of derailed the whole plan. I wouldn't be surprised if she knows more, but I simply don't know."

"Why didn't you tell me about Joshua?" Her eyes were suddenly cold and dark. Baxter literally felt a chill in the air as goosebumps rose up on his arms and the hairs on the back of his neck stood on end.

He swallowed, choosing his next words carefully. "You mean that he was on the paranormal team with us?"

"Don't play games with me, young man. You're not so big that I can't take you over my knee. Of course that's what I mean. Are you going to answer me?"

"Well, I figured it would be a good idea to earn his trust. Bring him back home voluntarily. For you."

"And yet, you didn't tell me immediately he was over there."

Baxter downcast his eyes. He wasn't sure how to respond to her. Kate Wilkes was the only person in the entire world that ever made him feel intimidated.

"Well, we'll get to that later," she ended up saying for him. "We have more important matters to tend to. Natalie was over here today snooping around the property. Her and that other girl from the group."

## Ashley Bundy

"Mel?"

"I think that's what Bradley called her when he came to pick them up, yes. Of course, I knew as soon as they were on the property. They couldn't get past all the protective enchantments. No one could. But one of them did steal a file from the office about the coven."

"You left that information out to where it would be easily accessible to an outsider?" That didn't sound like the Kate he knew.

She gave a devilish grin, the kind that always made his skin crawl. "Well, not the truly important things. Those are in the safe, of course."

"So, it's a dummy file?"

"No. Everything in it is true. I like to leave just enough information out there to screw with an outsider's head. Mostly, I keep it on hand in case the barriers are compromised. To have some idea of what my enemies are looking for to give myself a better defense."

"So, they managed to smuggle the entire file out even though you caught them?"

"Of course not, don't be stupid," she snarled. "But the hidden camera showed that Mel woman taking pictures of the pages with her cell phone. This electronic age, I swear. So unnecessary. Anyway, you know these girls. What are we up against?"

"Well, of the two of them I'd say Natalie is the bigger threat because of her 'gift'. Although Mel is smart. She's our researcher and can find out damn near anything with enough motivation. Natalie is the pushy, intrusive one. In fact, I can pretty much guarantee that Mel was only here because Natalie dragged her."

"Okay. I supposed that's good enough for now." But that wasn't enough. There was more coming. Baxter could feel her eyes burning into him with a great enough intensity that he could almost feel his skin sizzling.

"Are you alright, dear?" Kate asked him. "If you don't mind me saying so, you seem a little flustered."

"To be honest, when you asked me to come over here, I thought it was about that kidnapping. That you knew I was involved."

"Well, this boy is a bit older than we would normally go, but a child's a child." Kate shrugged her shoulders.

Baxter's blood ran cold. He'd taken the boy out of panic, not because he thought he'd be used in a ritual. "You mean…"

"Of course." Kate picked up her pen.

"Well, that's not why I got him," Baxter said, gently trying to break into the conversation. "You see, Gus, I mean Joshua, told the others our real identities. He told them everything and ruined everything. I went to his apartment to confront him, only it wasn't his apartment. The boy saw me. That's all it was."

"I see. Well, he'll still suit our purposes. It'll have to wait until the full moon though."

"Naturally."

"I'll send one of the guards to your place to pick up the child."

"Why?"

She gaped at him like he was stupid.

"You don't want to be caught with him, do you?"

# CHAPTER FORTY-SEVEN

Richard was sitting with his back to the edge of a tree, tapping his foot nervously. The sun was setting and the more time they sat here waiting for the police, the more restless he became.

Rod pulled Jamie's arm and the two of them walked over to sit on either side of him.

"I know you're worried, dude," Rod told him. "But you need to try to relax. You won't be able to do Remi any good if you give yourself a heart attack."

"She's okay," Jamie patted him awkwardly on the knee. "I can feel it."

"Well, you were in there," Richard straightened his legs and turned his body to better face Jamie. "You were in hysterics when we found you. The footage was scary as hell. What makes you so sure she's okay?"

"You know, as scary as that was, I felt like Callie was protecting me. Even when she was tying me to that chair, she was gentle. Lucy is batshit crazy. I won't deny that. But I feel like as long as Callie is there, she won't let anything happen to her."

"I didn't think about it like that," Richard gave an audible sigh of relief. "Thanks, Jamie."

"You bet," she reached over to give him a hug.

"So, what was up with Natalie and Brad earlier?" Rod interjected. "She smacked the shit out of him. What do you think that was about?"

Richard shrugged. He'd seen Natalie smack Brad, but he'd been too caught up in the situation at hand to give it too much thought.

"Hey, Mel!" Jamie called out. Mel was about twenty feet away, sitting on the hood of her car, working on her laptop.

Mel looked up towards them, and Jamie waved for her to join them. They watched as she closed her laptop, slipped it in her bag, and then came over to them at a casual stroll. Once she reached them, she sank down to the ground.

"Any news about Remi yet?" she asked.

"Not yet," Jamie asked. "So, what was up with Natalie and Brad? Why did she smack him like that?"

"Well, I'm not sure why she hit him, but he was pissed at us because we got caught sneaking into Heaven's Estate."

"What?" Everyone collectively bombarded her with questions.

She quickly told them about seeing Kate Wilkes lurking on the property, and Natalie insisting they go see what she was up to.

"Wow, and they caught you?" Richard asked. "How did Natalie not see that?"

"I don't know," Mel answered, "and I didn't get a chance to talk to her about it because Brad escorted us home like two kids getting caught shoplifting."

"So, what did you find in the office?" Rod asked.

"I'm not exactly sure what it means yet. But there's a whole lot of stuff in there about witchcraft and it was labeled, *coven*."

"Well, that makes sense with Natalie's weird visions," Jamie said. "Particularly the one out back with the baby and the fire."

"No," Richard shook his head. "I don't like it. It sounds too convenient to me. They have this secret society, and this stuff just happens to be lying around? How do we even know it's real?"

Mel nodded in agreement. "It bothered me, too, at first, but I took photos of everything and have been looking into it all since we got back. So far, everything checks out. I've found records of a family member, Rebecca Thompson, who came to the area suddenly and no one knew her background. She ended up marrying Reginald Thompson. The funny thing is, I also found record of a Rebecca Summers dating back to the Salem witch trials. She was a suspected witch and was scheduled to be hung, but she disappeared, never to be seen again."

"You think Rebecca Thompson and Rebecca Summers are the same person?" Jamie asked.

"I can't know for certain, but I strongly suspect."

"It makes a lot of sense," Richard admitted. "If she was a witch, that would explain where the rituals Natalie talked about came from."

"Just because that stuff happens to be true doesn't mean there isn't anything hinky about it. The whole thing just feels so convenient," Richard said. "How do we know they didn't leave that for you, hoping you'd drop everything? That they're still hiding something deeper?"

"I guess the real question is, what does them practicing witchcraft have to do with Blackwood Manor?" Rod added.

"Richard," Jamie nudged him and nodded toward the house.

He looked up, and his heart caught in his throat as he saw a stretcher being wheeled out with a person strapped to it. All he could see was the top of the head and a tuft of raven hair.

He shot to his feet and sprinted over the barrier toward the stretcher, ignoring the officer who called after him.

He skidded to a stop next to the stretcher and exclaimed, "Remi! Remi!"

Her eyes were closed, and she was extremely pale. She didn't stir when he called her name.

"She's alive," Sheriff O'Reilly said. "But she was unconscious when we found her. We're going to take her to the hospital to have her checked."

Two hours later, Richard sat on the end of Remi's bed, holding her hand. Rod and Jamie were sitting at a small table near the window playing a card game. She still wasn't awake, and Richard felt like he was going crazy.

The doctors said her vitals and labs were fine, but they were still waiting for the results of an MRI, which might tell them why she was still unconscious.

"Come on, Remi," he whispered, giving her hand a gentle squeeze. "Come back to us.'

There was a knock on the door and Richard looked up to see Brad stick his head in. "Can I come in?"

Brad came into the room, and Richard couldn't help but notice how haggard he looked. In the few short hours since he'd seen him last, Brad's eyes darkened, and his cheeks sunk in.

"You, okay?"

"Physically," Brad pulled up a chair to sit on Remi's other side. "Going through emotional hell though. Natalie. It's not important right now. How's she doing?"

"We're waiting on an MRI, but the doctor thinks she's okay."

"Has she woken up at all?"

Richard shook his head. "There's not much to talk about right now as far as she's concerned. So, let's talk about you and Natalie."

Brad sighed and shook his head, as if to avoid the subject.

"Brad, I care about you. And I care about Natalie. I want to help you guys fix whatever it is that's going on. I can't do that if you don't talk to me."

"She's upset with me because I'm friends with Kate Wilkes. She sees it as a betrayal. But I've known Kate my entire life, and she's always been good to me. It didn't help that Kate called me to come and pick her and Mel up after they snuck into Heaven's Estate."

"Mel said they did that because they caught Kate sneaking around and spying at the tree line. It could be argued she did it first."

"Kate's nosy. I won't deny that. But to be fair, whenever something happens at Blackwood Manor, everyone in the area becomes intrigued by it. It's the 'it place' of the county. Doesn't excuse them breaking into her house though. My friendship with her is the only thing that saved their asses. After all, Kate might have been rubber necking, but she didn't trespass."

"That might be true," Richard agreed, "but I trust Natalie's instincts. Mel found some pretty fucked up shit while they were in there."

Brad threw his hands up and shook his head. "Whatever it is, I don't want to know. I don't like feeling like I need to pick sides between all the people I care about."

Richard paused for a moment and then asked his question, careful not to make his tone sound too confrontational. "Why do you have so much loyalty to Kate? I mean, you have to admit something weird is going on, and she's right at the center of it. Between Natalie's visions and Gus telling us what he saw, it's creepy."

Brad sighed. "You know how I'm loyal to Claire's memory? How I would have done anything for that woman?"

Richard nodded.

"That's because she was good to me. Even though she made mistakes, I know she was a good woman, and I will always defend her memory. I feel the exact same way about Kate. She was there for me at a time when no one else was.

"Because of my family's tendencies to have supernatural gifts, we were often shunned, but she was always kind to us. She would invite us to functions, involve us in the community, talk us up. When I got locked up, she was a character witness. Of course, it didn't change things, but she did it, and that meant the world to me. When I got out, she helped me find work, because without her involvement, no one wanted to hire me. When Caroline got sick, she helped my family as much as she could. It was a combination of Kate's and Claire's kindness that got me through that terrible time. And when I started drinking, Kate's the one that helped me stop.

"Yes, she's absolutely weird, and she can be a bit nosy. She sometimes sticks her foot in her mouth, but she is a good person. That witchcraft stuff? It's something that interests her. We all have interests. It doesn't bother me. Shunning her because she believes in that stuff is no different to me than shunning someone of a different religion or sexual orientation."

Rod looked up from his game. "Yeah, but when it hurts other people, it should bother you."

"How is she hurting anyone?"

"You're kidding, right?" Richard asked, incredulous. "If the Thompsons are practicing witches and they're cursing Blackwood Manor, then they are responsible for every death and injury that's ever happened there."

Brad waved a dismissive hand. "That's silly. We have absolutely no proof that they've cursed Blackwood Manor or caused harm to anyone."

Jamie stared at him. "Natalie had a vision of them killing a baby."

"Yes, our family's gifts are helpful, but they aren't completely infallible. We've been wrong before. My grandmother got things wrong. Maybe Natalie saw a baby because that does sometimes happen with that kind of ritual. It doesn't necessarily mean that Kate or her family did that."

Richard was about to argue but was cut off as the door opened and a doctor walked in.

Richard shot to his feet and shook the doctor's hand. "So, are the test results back yet?"

"Yes. There is no brain swelling or injury that could be determined. She does have a cracked rib but that shouldn't be causing her unconscious state. More likely, it's the shock of whatever happened."

"Is this a coma?"

"It doesn't appear to be. It's only been a couple of hours. All we can really do is wait it out. She'll most likely wake up on her own sometime today."

# CHAPTER FORTY-EIGHT

Natalie pulled up into the parking lot of the rundown apartment complex and automatically wished she'd brought reinforcements with her.

After the confrontation with her father, she'd showered, finally stripping out of that silly uniform and been prepared to take a long sleep before her phone had rung. It was the mother of the missing boy, returning her phone call. She'd requested for Natalie to come out immediately.

Natalie was tired and becoming more and more drained from Blackwood Manor, but this was an innocent child, and her gut was telling her this was somehow connected to Blackwood Manor. She just wasn't sure how yet. It couldn't be a coincidence that it was Gus's old building. She wouldn't be at all surprised if it was his exact unit.

A pretty Hispanic woman sat on the bottom step of a crumbling staircase nervously tapping her feet, and it was obvious she'd been heavily crying. She had to be the mother.

Natalie got out of her car and hit the door lock before approaching the woman. "Mrs. Ramos?"

The woman looked up at her. "I'm Natalie Morgan."

Mrs. Ramos shot to her feet and threw her arms around Natalie, hysterically crying. "Thank you. Thank you so much for coming. I'm Anna Ramos."

Uncomfortable by the flood of emotions that were swirling through her, Natalie waited for the distraught woman to pull away first. Before she was even out of her arms, Natalie knew the woman was innocent.

"I'll be honest, I didn't know if you'd be receptive to my phone call. Not everyone believes in what I can do."

Anna reached for a cross hanging around her neck. "I believe in the spiritual realm. If one side is possible, who am I to say another side isn't? And I'm willing to try anything. The police are suggesting I had something to do with this."

"What? There was security footage showing someone lurking around your building the same time."

"They think I may have hired someone to take him. That I was struggling and couldn't take care of two growing boys anymore. Because there wasn't forced entry. I love my Benito. I would never hurt him."

"I know you wouldn't." Natalie smiled at the woman and gave her shoulder a reassuring pat. She looked around the area, trying to get her bearings, and her eyes focused on the row of cars that were slightly catty cornered to the staircase, and realized from the angle that was where the mystery person from the footage had been crouching.

"Okay. So, my gift works primarily from touch. When I touch an object, I can often see things attached to it. I can pick up on emotions and thoughts when people touch me. I'm not going to lie, sometimes if multiple hands have gone over an area, it doesn't always work the best because there's too many to pull just one out of the fold, if that makes any sense. But I promise to do my very best. We'll start here and then move up to your apartment if that's alright."

Anna nodded. "I just want my Benito back."

Natalie nodded toward the line of cars. "I know this is a long shot, but do you by any chance have assigned parking here?"

"No. I wish."

Ashley Bundy

Natalie mentally concluded there was no point in touching the cars without knowing if they were the same ones that were parked there that night.

Instead, she moved to the staircase that Anna had been seated on and touched the railing. She was flooded with flashes of people coming and going from the first floor to the second in various states of dress. Just residents. She jerked her hand back to stop the visions, shook her head at Anna and gestured for her to go up the steps first.

She followed Anna up the steps and up to the door of her apartment before gesturing for her to stop. She put her hand to the closed door and squeezed her eyes shut.

She had a flash of a large, dark figure pulling a key out of their wallet, and opening the door with it. Definitely not Anna Ramos.

"By any chance, does anyone have a key to your apartment?" she asked her. "A family member or friend that maybe feeds a pet while you're out, or stays with you from time to time?"

"No, it's just me and my boys."

Natalie nodded her acknowledgement and followed Anna into the apartment.

The apartment was small but tidy. She immediately touched the back of the door and was transported to the same apartment in the dark. She immediately felt the disgust of the dark figure at his surroundings. He felt he was above where he was at.

"Mama?" a small voice asked. Benito was in the hallway rubbing his eyes. He looked toward her (him), and Natalie was flooded with panic and horror from the figure in black.

The little boy's eyes went wide, and his little jaw dropped. He turned to run back in the direction he'd come from.

The figure strode across the room in two big strides and snatched the boy into his arms, plastering a big hand across his mouth. The moonlight from the window lit up his face, and Natalie could see that it was Baxter. He looked just as terrified as Benito.

"Anything?"

Natalie was pulled out of the vision by Anna putting her hand on her shoulder.

"You've been standing there a few minutes. Are you okay?"

Natalie nodded. "I think I know at least part of what happened. A man came in. He had a key. He thought someone else lived here. He panicked because Benito saw him."

Anna's hand flew to her throat. "Oh God."

"I can't promise anything, but from what I'm seeing your son is alive."

"But you can't promise?"

"All I can see is he didn't do anything to him here. But I'm not getting a malicious vibe off him. I'm getting a knee jerk reaction."

"How did they leave?"

"From what I can see, right out the front door, then locking it. What doesn't make sense to me is they should have been seen on the security footage."

"Well, if you follow the breezeway to the back, there's another staircase back there."

"That would explain it then. They went out the back."

Ashley Bundy

Anna collapsed onto the couch. "So, we don't know too much still. The cops think I let someone take him. How am I going to prove this man took him?"

Natalie knelt and took Anna's hands in hers. "I think I might have an idea of where to start."

# CHAPTER FORTY-NINE

Remi's body may have been asleep in a hospital bed, but her mind was completely occupied. She was trapped in a whirlwind of swirling fog.

One minute, she'd been standing in the upstairs hallway of Blackwood Manor with Jamie talking to Lucy and Callie. The next, Lucy was attacking them. She'd been hit in the head at some point, her vision exploding into a cacophony of colors before all feeling floated away.

When she'd come to, the world was different. It was as though all the vivid, bright colors had been sucked out of the world with a syringe. It wasn't that there was no color, it was just dark—blacks, and grays, dark, dull greens, and mustard yellows. She was completely enclosed in a haze of smoke and fog, surrounded by loud, spooky noises that came from every direction.

The fog was so thick, it was hard to see what was right next to her. She would occasionally catch a quick flash of a shadow moving in her peripheral vision, but by the time she would turn to it, whatever it was would be gone.

Her chest felt tight, the air smelled metallic, like blood and every nerve was on edge in her body. She was scared. Fleetingly, it occurred to her that she'd never been this scared in her life. She wondered if she was dead, and this is what death was.

She couldn't visually place where she was, but her gut told her it was not in the physical realm. She got the distinct impression that what she was experiencing was Blackwood

Manor beyond the veil. If that was true, she would finally get it.

This was why Blackwood Manor was filled with angry, sad, and trapped spirits. If this was all they ever saw, it was no wonder. If she had to be surrounded by this overwhelming darkness for centuries, she'd be pissed off too.

Hell, she was already getting there, and she'd just been plopped down into this existence.

*"Am I dead?"* she wondered to herself as her panic began to rise. *"Will I have to spend the rest of eternity like this? What did I do to deserve this?"*

There was another flash of movement to her left, closer this time, and she swung her arm out, making contact with something for the first time.

"Little bitch," a voice growled out, and she felt a great force hit her chest. The air left her lungs and left her with an overwhelming burning sensation as she hit the ground.

She took slow, deliberate breaths, pushing through the pain. Surely, she couldn't be dead. She wouldn't be able to feel this kind of pain if she were dead.

She looked up and focused as a figure materialized from the shadows into her circle of fog.

It was a woman. She wore all white, had skeletal hands, and no facial features. Josie.

"And everyone says you're the nice one," she croaked out.

"Maybe I'm tired of waiting for you people to get your act together. I've wasted away, rotted away, waiting for help. It's getting a little ridiculous the way people in the living realm need to be spoon-fed everything."

"How are we not helping?" Remi asked. "We've been working nonstop to figure things out. So did Claire and Emma. What more do you want?"

"Yes, but you don't *see* what's right in front of you. That's how so many lives end up being lost. You don't see, then you lose your life, and you end up trapped in here with us."

"What are we not seeing? The pictures? The cameras? We found those and studied them carefully."

Josie snorted in contempt. "Please. Donovan had to take the pictures to a photographer. You all weren't going to do it on your own. It's just sad."

"Then what is it we have to see?" Remi was distressed. "We know Callie is here. We know that Lucy is manipulating things. We know that Blackwood used to be part of Heaven's Estate."

"And yet you've ignored an extremely crucial piece of evidence practically given to Richard on a silver platter from his sister."

"What?"

"A certain piece of artwork."

"You mean from the psych hospital?"

"What do you know? You're learning."

"I really don't appreciate your tone."

"I really don't care."

Remi glared at Josie but decided to not push the issue anymore.

"So, there's something in the picture that Bailey drew at the hospital that we missed? What was it?"

"Do I have to do everything? Reexamine it."

Ashley Bundy

Before Remi could throw out her own retort, she was hit with a heavy feeling in her chest once again. The fog engulfed her once more and all she saw was darkness.

When Remi opened her eyes again, she was welcomed by a very different scene. The first thing she saw was the white squares of the ceiling and then she heard the steady hums and beeps that were immediately familiar. Hospital. She was in a hospital.

She went to turn but was amazed by how extremely stiff and sore she felt. It was as though she had fought and won a thousand different battles.

Richard was sitting in a chair next to her bed. He was asleep, but his head was slumped down on his chest at an awkward angle, and she knew he'd have a horrible stiff neck when he woke up.

She was overcome with emotion as she watched him sleep. She hadn't seen him since they'd made love, so they hadn't had a chance to discuss what it meant. Were they together? Was it just one, passionate night? She knew what she wanted, but she wasn't so sure she knew what he wanted. She didn't know what had come over her. It was like she hadn't been in control of her own body. She'd watched herself all over Richard, like a movie, unable to stop herself.

She didn't know whether to be offended or flattered that he hadn't stopped her.

"Richard. Richard," she croaked out and tapped his hand, which still rested on the edge of the bed.

His head snapped up, and he opened his eyes. She was shocked by the dark shadows that bagged beneath his eyes, and how bloodshot they were. It was like he hadn't slept in days. How long had she been here?

"Remi," surprise and relief were evident in his voice, and he smiled at her.

She smiled back and opened her mouth to speak but before she could, he leaned over and kissed her openly, and warmly on the mouth. *"Well. I guess that answered my question,"* she thought to herself.

"You found me," she said simply.

"I wish I could take credit for that, but the fucking police wouldn't let us help search," he rolled his eyes and squeezed her hand.

"Callie," she said suddenly, as the memory came back to her. "Callie was there—"

"I know," he nodded in agreement. "The cameras picked it up. Jamie's okay."

"Thank God. When we got separated, I was so worried. Brad called us and when we got there, it was like an ambush."

"Brad didn't call you. The house tricked you. We checked his phone."

"Why though?"

"I guess it just needed you to be there. I was going to ask if anything special happened while you were in there alone."

"The weirdest thing, actually."

Quickly, she told him about the experience that she'd just had with Josie. The fog, the darkness, and the overwhelming feeling of dread. More importantly, she focused on Josie's annoyance that there was something of importance in Bailey's drawing that they hadn't picked up on.

"What was so important about it?" Richard mused. "The only unusual thing that I noted about it was the lack of color."

"You said she was leaning up against one of the columns of the porch, right? Was that somewhere that she used to hang out?"

"No. I never saw her on the porch longer than it took to walk through the front door."

"Well, maybe the clue lies there then. Maybe we just need to check the columns. And the only color being the blue in her fingertips and the blue of her eyes must mean something. I'm just not sure what."

He looked down at his own fingertips, which were glowing blue and sucked air through his teeth. "Of course. It's been there all along, and we missed it. How stupid are we?"

# CHAPTER FIFTY

"We'll do it tonight. It's supposed to be a full moon. We'll deal with Blackwood Manor today. The circumstances will be perfect for the child." Kate grinned. "The harvest will be so beautiful this year."

Baxter gave her a tight-lipped smile and turned toward the basement to check on the boy.

Benito looked up from his spot in the corner. His eyes were red rimmed from crying. He pulled his blanket up around him like it would protect him from the figure approaching him.

"Hey there, buddy." Baxter set down a tray of food in front of him. "I'll bet you're hungry."

The boy's eyes darted down to the tray and back up to Baxter as he let out a tiny whimper.

"Come on, man," Baxter sat down on the ground, crossing his legs under him to look less intimidating. "You've got to eat. You want to grow up to be big and strong, don't you?"

Benito stuck a tiny arm out of his blankets to snag a piece of bread and pulled it back quickly.

Baxter smiled at him. "There you go. Look, I'm sorry about all this. It wasn't part of the plan. It'll be over soon. I promise."

"Mama?" Benito asked. It was the first time he'd spoken since Baxter grabbed him.

"You'll see your mama real soon," Baxter answered grimly.

Ashley Bundy

Later that morning, Richard faced the front porch of Blackwood Manor. The rest of the group stood behind, ready to further engage in the mystery.

As soon as Remi's doctor said she could be released from the hospital, he'd called everyone and arranged for them to all meet at Blackwood. He'd explained what Remi told him about her conversation with Josie, and how they'd concluded that the columns must mean something.

Once the group congregated, Natalie told them about the visions she'd had while working at the psych hospital. She'd been in a colorless fog like Remi described experiencing during her conversation with Josie. Richard was convinced that Bailey's picture was the key somehow.

He eyed the column that Bailey stood next to in the picture. The one closest to the door on the left-hand side. He strolled up the steps, the rest of the group following closely. He examined it carefully, running his fingers over the wood, knocking randomly to see if there was some kind of hollow spot, as there had been in the wall upstairs. All he found were paint chips and splinters. Until he got toward the bottom of the column and pushed aside some ivy that had been covering the base.

He noticed something etched into the wood, nearly invisible. The cuts were so light and shallow that they were barely more than scratches.

He knelt closer to see what it said and furrowed his eyebrows in confusion. It wasn't English. It wasn't any language as far as he could tell.

"What is it?" Remi asked.

"I don't know," he answered honestly. "There's something here, but it doesn't make any sense. It looks like gibberish."

Everyone knelt to look at the etchings over his shoulder. Natalie placed a palm to them briefly, then shook her head. She wasn't picking anything up from it.

"That's ancient runes!" Mel exclaimed. "I've seen them in tons of books."

"So, what do they say?" Richard asked her.

"Well, I'm not fluent in runes," she chuckled. "I don't know what it says by looking at it, but I can figure it out."

She pulled out her phone and took a picture of the ruins, then walked down the steps, trying to find a spot with a strong enough signal to do a Google search.

"You really couldn't get anything off that?" Rod asked Natalie incredulously.

She shook her head. "No. I don't know why."

"Hmm. Let's think."

"Rod, don't start." Richard shot him a pointed look.

Mel came rushing up the stairs. "Okay. I think it says *'The haven stone brings blue blissful salvation.'*"

"What does that mean?" Rod asked.

"When I had my vision, Bailey was holding a small blue stone when she was standing here!" Natalie announced, her voice excited. "Tell me that shit's a coincidence."

"Oh my God," Jamie exclaimed. Without a word, she raced for the house, threw open the door, and ran straight for the staircase.

"Jamie!" Rod screamed out; the panic evident on his face as he took off after her.

Everyone ran after them all the way to their bedroom. They'd all made a pact to not leave anyone alone until they got to the bottom of everything that was happening.

"Jamie, what is going on?" Rod asked her.

Jamie was digging around in her nightstand. "Yes!" she pulled her hand out of the drawer to reveal a blue stone about the size of her palm.

"What is that?" Richard asked.

"I found it in the garden and thought it was pretty, so I cleaned it and brought it up here. I completely forgot about it until now."

Natalie stuck out her hand, and Jamie held it to her chest possessively.

"Babe," Rod said gently, rubbing her back in a circular motion, "we need that stone."

"I've never owned anything this beautiful before," she said simply. Richard's heart instantly ached for her. In his own way, he knew what she meant. When you grew up being treated like trash, it was easy to become attached to the smallest things that brought you comfort. Even stones.

"We'll give it back," he told her firmly.

She looked up into his eyes, and he nodded at her, a silent message passing between them before she pressed the stone into Natalie's palm. Natalie immediately hissed in pain and dropped the stone, grasping her hand. Richard reached out and grabbed the stone before it could hit the floor with cat like precision.

"Natalie, are you okay?" Remi asked, her eyes wide with concern.

"It burned me." Natalie still stared at her hand, which was already breaking out with an angry red burn.

"I think I saw some salve in the bathroom," Gus said, and he and Mel went to look for it.

Rod's eyes squinted as he stared at Natalie's hand. "Why would it burn you and not Jamie?"

"I think it's pretty obvious," Richard said. "It's because of her gift. There must be something powerful about that stone."

"How are we supposed to figure out what, though, if she can't touch it?" Remi asked.

Gus and Mel reentered the room with burn ointment and bandages and went to work on applying first aid to Natalie's hand. The bandage was pretty thick, and she reached for the stone again.

"Do you think that's a good idea?" Richard asked. "I mean, it already burned you."

"I have no idea," she answered honestly. "This is new territory for me. But we have to try."

Richard nervously handed it back to her. There was tension in her arm as she took it, but after a few seconds, she relaxed.

The bandage appeared to prevent her skin from burning but she didn't have the intense face of concentration that she normally had during a vision.

She closed her eyes, wrapped her fingers around it, and squeezed. Then she opened her eyes and grunted in frustration. "The bandage is too thick. I'm not getting anything off it."

"What are we supposed to do?" Jamie asked.

Suddenly, there was a loud cracking sound, and books flew off a shelf. Rod shoved Jamie out of the way seconds before they would have hit her.

She pressed a hand to her chest and tried to control her breathing from the shock. "Thanks," she finally managed to whisper.

"No problem," Rod said. He bent down to begin to pick up the books.

"Wait!" Remi exclaimed and grabbed his arm to stop him. "Remember what Josie said. We don't see what's right in front of us. That happened for a reason."

They all leaned down to study the fallen books. One of them lay open.

"Wait a minute," Mel said as she studied the leather-bound book. "Is that Josie's diary?"

Richard picked it up and brought it closer to his face. "Yes, it is. What's it doing here?"

"Didn't you leave it in the cottage?" Remi asked.

"I did. Brad made me promise not to read it. I figured it would be less of a temptation out there."

"Read the entry it's on," Natalie said to him.

He nodded in agreement. He struggled to make out a couple of the words at first, since the writing was so faded from age. Then he caught his groove and began to read aloud.

*March 22$^{nd}$, 1863*

*The days are becoming harder and harder to bear. I'm constantly in dread for the day to come. Every day seems to bring with it a new disaster. Miss Margaret is completely unrecognizable from the woman I know. Even her eyes are wild and crazy. She hates the poor child.*

*I understand the shame she must feel. Our attacks were a horror no woman should bear, but it is not the child's fault. I hate seeing the harsh behavior she aims toward her. It really scares me sometimes.*

*Then there is Miss Lucy. I know all children are a gift from God, but something is wrong with the girl. I caught her with a dead kitten this morning. She drowned it in the bathtub and told me it was because 'the girl told her to.' I would think she's telling falsehoods except she has talked about this girl from the time she was quite small. I'm starting to believe she actually sees something and it's no longer childhood imagination.*

*I tried to punish her for the kitten, but Margaret threw a fit and sent me to bed without supper. She's spineless when it comes to the children, except for the baby.*

*Today I believe I found the haven stone. It's been a legend that I've heard of for generations. I never believed it but thought it was a fun story, nonetheless.*

*Legend has it that a good witch created the stone with a potion to combat evil. But it only works in magical hands. There is only one stone currently in existence, and it is in my possession. I haven't figured out how it works, but I did notice that it glowed when I held it to the strange etchings on the column at the front of the house.*

Richard furrowed his brow. Something about the entry felt familiar, as though he'd read it before. But he'd kept his promise to Brad and locked the book away in the cottage. *Our attacks were a horror no woman should bear.* Where had he heard that before?

"I've read about a stone like that!" Mel's eyes brimmed with excitement. "I'd never heard the name, but I heard the legend. To an ordinary person, it's nothing more than a stone, but to someone with magical abilities, it makes them the master of good vs. evil."

Everyone's eyes flitted to Natalie. "I can't even touch the damn thing."

"She's got a point," Jamie nodded. "If she can't even touch it, and she has a gift, then how is she supposed to use it to combat evil?"

"Maybe it's not the right kind of gift," Gus suggested. "Maybe it has to be someone who's actually magical. Not just someone who happens to have a gift."

"You mean like a witch?" Jamie asked.

"Maybe."

"That would be you then," Rod said. When everyone stared at him with confusion he went on. "Not you. Your family. If your family really is part of a witch's coven, then you would have magical blood."

"I can give it a shot." Gus shrugged.

Everyone rose to their feet and made for the door.

"Natalie, can you hang back for a minute, please?" Richard asked. When everyone turned to look at him, he said, "We'll meet you out there. This won't take long."

As everyone else left the room, Natalie looked at him with confusion.

"Look, Natalie," he began and looked down at his feet as the heat creeped up into his cheeks. "I wanted to talk to you before you heard it from someone else. Since everything happened in the tunnels, Remi and I have bonded, and we're kind of a thing now."

She furrowed her eyebrows. "Okay."

"I just wanted you to know that it's nothing personal. I've just known her longer, and we have a deep bond. I hope we can still be friends."

Her mouth turned into a wide "O". "Oh, Richard, did you think that we—?"

"What?" this was not the reaction he'd been expecting.

"Richard, I'm a lesbian."

The heat in his cheeks was a fiery inferno and his chest suddenly felt like it was in a vise. "You're—"

"A lesbian," she inclined her head. "I have a girlfriend."

"Well, I think I've officially discovered the meaning of 'foot in mouth.'" He gave a nervous chuckle. "I thought I detected something between us. You know, flirty."

She smiled. "Oh, that? I'm like that with everyone I like. I do like you, Richard, but like a friend. I'm sorry if I misled you. I never meant to."

"It's not your fault. It's mine. I find you attractive, so I chose to interpret your friendliness that way. I'm sorry. I'm trying to not be disrespectful."

"No, no—" she smiled and stepped forward, placing her hands on his arms, and giving them a gentle squeeze. "Are you kidding? You are the exact opposite of disrespectful. You have misinterpreted what I was feeling, but that's partially my fault. In fact, I think the way you're handling this whole thing is nothing less that chivalrous."

"Really?"

"Really. This works out for the best. You want Remi anyway, but you're so considerate of the way it would make me feel. I love that you chose to tell me yourself instead of letting me find out from someone else. If I'd been in love with you, that would have cushioned the blow. That's very chivalrous."

Ashley Bundy

He reached out and took her in his arms in a warm, friendly hug.

"Hey guys!" Rod's voice travelled up the stairs. "You coming?"

They broke apart and headed for the stairs.

# CHAPTER FIFTY-ONE

When Richard and Natalie joined the rest of the group on the porch, Gus took the stone in his hand and instantly screamed out in pain. Jamie grabbed it from him and watched as blisters sprung up on his skin. They were even more gnarly than the ones that plagued Natalie.

"Good thing we brought this," Mel sighed and took his hand to begin applying the burn ointment.

"This stone is supposed to combat evil," Jamie said as she hugged it possessively to her chest. "Maybe it's burning our evil people."

"Oh, come off it, Jamie!" Mel snapped, looking up from Gus's dressings. "Do you seriously think Natalie and Gus are evil?"

"Maybe we got it wrong," Richard mused. "Maybe it's not someone from a witch's bloodline. I mean, if it was created from a good witch who wanted to fight evil, maybe there's something in there that recognizes a bad bloodline. No offense, Gus."

"Well, what about Natalie?" Jamie demanded. "What do they even have in common?"

Remi chewed her lip. "It doesn't even matter right now. Our magical people can't touch the stone. If Josie wanted us to use the diary, she should have given us better instructions."

Jamie turned to her. "You talked to Josie on the other side. Maybe it's you."

Remi cautiously took the stone. She was visibly braced for burns but relaxed when they did not come.

Ashley Bundy

She knelt in front of the runes and held the stone before it. There was a soft glow, but nothing happened.

"Do you feel anything?" Rod asked.

Remi shook her head. "No. Not even a tingle."

"Should we go back to the drawing board?" Richard asked.

Natalie looked him square in the eyes. "You know it's you."

Richard nodded. He suspected it too. No one explicitly said this was a job for the golden warrior, but it was becoming explicitly clear it was.

When he took the stone in his hand, he felt the slightest warmth in his palm and blue bolts of electricity shot out of his fingertips, making Remi gasp.

It briefly occurred to him that he'd actively been hiding his hands. He was pretty sure that the only person that knew was Natalie. Possibly Brad. Brad seemed to know everything. He'd think more about that later.

He held the stone to the etchings and the glow coming from it intensified until it was bright as the headlights of a car, causing them to avert their eyes.

Richard, however, felt immune to the light. It wasn't too bright for his eyes, and it didn't make him unable to see. His sight was drawn to the etchings themselves, which were glowing blue. The symbols began to swell and then split apart, splintering the wood underneath, creating a door in the column.

Through the doorway, Richard could see golden light, and he stepped forward, as if he had no control over his own feet.

Once he stepped through the barrier, his entire body filled with a spectacular warmth. He was instantly enveloped with smoke and fog and thought of the experience Remi and Natalie described to him. They'd made it seem dark and drab, an endless pit of despair. He experienced lightness, brightness, and a hope that he couldn't remember ever feeling before.

He was aware of the silence and spun around. The others hadn't followed him through. He didn't know if it was a conscious choice on their part, or they'd been unable to, but he didn't want to be alone.

"Richie."

The voice was instantly familiar. Up until this moment, he hadn't been able to remember the sound, but now it came back like no time had passed.

He turned to see his mother smiling at him. Her skin glowed, and her eyes twinkled. She was even more beautiful than he remembered.

"Mom?" he whispered.

"Come here to me, boy," she opened her arms and pulled him into a tight hug. Her body was soft lines and warm. How was this possible? She was dead. She'd been dead for ten years.

"Am I dead?"

"No," she shook her head and ran her fingers through his hair. "You've just stepped over the line for a minute."

"Why?"

She sighed. "It's time. I'd hoped you'd never come back here. But you're here, and it's too late to turn back now. It's time to fight."

"How? I don't know what to do. I get more and more lost the more I learn."

"You know what to do, sweet boy. You need to give your friends the option to turn back though. It could be a bloodbath."

"What am I even fighting against?"

"A cruel, cruel curse. The only way to save yourselves and anyone else that comes after is to break it."

"Mama," he whispered. "I can't do this alone. My friends are great. They're extremely supportive, but they can't stand up against what's here. I'm scared."

"Don't worry, we're all on your side here. You'll have backup."

"Who's we?"

"Your father, sisters, Aunt Claire, Josie. Plus, a few others you won't know. We all have the same goal. To put an end to this." She kissed his cheek. "Go on."

The doorway that he'd entered through began to glow once again and he walked toward it.

"Richie." He turned toward her voice. "One last thing. Keep an eye out for that Natalie."

"What do you mean? I can't trust her?"

"No, no. I don't mean that. Just proceed with caution. She's in deeper than she knows, and her gift could be a liability. I love you, son. Good luck."

"I love you too, Mom."

Richard stepped through the doorway and was immediately met by a fist to the eye.

"Shit!" he screeched, clutching at it. His vision was spotty with a sharp pain.

"Oh, my God," Rod grabbed him and led him toward the steps to sit. "I'm so sorry. You disappeared into the fucking column, and we were trying to figure out how to get you out. You reappeared right as I was swinging at it."

"I know. I know. It's not your fault." The pain was already starting to subside a bit. He pulled his hand away from his eye and blinked a few times. "I disappeared?"

"It closed behind you," Remi said. He looked over and saw terror evident on her face. He longed to hold her, but there wasn't time for that.

He explained briefly about his experience with his mom. "She said to give you guys the option to leave. It could get bad, and you may not be able to defend yourselves."

"What did we say on day one?" Rod smirked "We're not going anywhere. We knew what we were getting into when we came here with you."

"So, what exactly are we supposed to do though?" Jamie asked.

As if in answer to her question, the sky darkened into a deep purple and bolts of lightning shot down. Dark masses rose from the ground, deep moans emitting from them.

"I guess that's our answer." Richard answered.

"Here we go," a voice said from behind them.

"Shit!" Richard exclaimed and jumped around. Standing in a throng behind them were spirits in various stages of disfigurement. His family. Plus others he couldn't recall ever seeing. They were walking out of the column as though it were an endless pit. They stood along the porch, in a configured line like an army. Others moved to take position along the property line on each edge.

"Begin," Josie stated.

As one, the spirits raised their hands and bolts of vivid color shot from their palms. Richard clumsily mimicked their gesture and was shocked to find blue bolts shot out with even greater intensity than when he'd been practicing on the doll. His body tingled all over with the warmth and intensity of it.

Richard fanned out, shooting his bolts at every shadow he could see from the corner of his eye.

The creatures howled and screamed. Horrible sounds that made him want to cover his ears, but he pushed through.

Five figures in black cloaks emerged from the tree line. The one in the middle lowered her hood, and Richard saw that it was Kate Wilkes, her make up projecting the madness within. On her left was another woman who lowered her hood. Richard didn't recognize this one, but he gasped when the third lowered theirs. It was Brad. He looked solemn, not smirking as the two women were.

Then it occurred to Richard why the diary entry seemed so familiar. *Margaret and Josie went through a horror no woman should bear*. Brad said that on the first day he'd come back. When he'd been trying to convince Richard not to read the diary. He'd lied. He'd read it before. Richard looked between Brad and Natalie. The fury on her face made it clear she didn't know about this, but now he understood why she'd been burned by the stone.

The rage that radiated through Richard's body was indescribable as he looked at the man he'd trusted, that his family trusted. He'd seen this man as a father figure, and to see him standing on the other side was a betrayal like no other.

The fourth figure was a smiling Baxter. Richard had never seen him smile before. He'd always thought Baxter to be a rather sullen person, his nose always wrinkled up as though he smelled something foul. It turned out that was a far superior sight to smiling Baxter. His eyes were wild, and his teeth were bared as though he were preparing to rip out some throats.

The fifth figure was a man in his late twenties. Like Brad, he didn't seem particularly thrilled to be part of the line up, but he was there, nonetheless. Richard guessed this was most likely Gus's brother.

Kate screeched and shot out a fireball from her mouth, which rocketed straight toward Gus. Richard dove in front of him and the fireball hit him square in the chest. His light went out, and he dropped to the ground. The fire engulfed him.

"Richard!" Remi screamed.

He rolled on the ground until the flames went out, and momentarily laid there, enveloped by the pain. It was everywhere. His muscles screamed as he tried to move. He cast his eyes toward his friends, who were huddled behind a group of spirits looking terrified. Jamie and Remi had their arms around each other, their eyes wide with terror. Natalie was the only one who was moving, charging down the steps, appearing to see none of the chaos going on around her.

"Get in the house!" he tried to scream at his friends. All that came out of his throat was strained cracking. They still seemed to understand him and ran for the steps. For a moment, Richard couldn't help but see the irony of the situation. For centuries, people fled from Blackwood Manor, and now a whole mass of people was seeking it for shelter.

Richard struggled to his knees and took in his surroundings. His family was surrounding him on every side, protecting him like a shield until he was able to fight again. But that left his friends vulnerable. The sky was ablaze with lights of all different colors.

He stuck his palms out in an attempt to assist, but no light emerged, and he dropped back to the ground, exhausted from the effort.

"You bastard!" Natalie screamed at her father as a golden light burst forth from her chest, and she levitated off the ground.

Brad whipped toward Natalie; his face lined with sorrow. "Stand down," he ordered.

She shot a whip of white light toward him that cut into his shoulder. His cloak tore, and smoke rose from his shoulder. He hissed at the contact. He then flicked a firm hand upward, and Natalie shot back about two feet.

"Stand down!" he shouted more insistently. "I don't want you hurt!"

"You are such a coward!" She shot more light at him, but he dodged it and threw up his own hands, hitting her with a purple light in the leg, causing her to drop back down to the ground.

She crumpled on the ground and seized the leg, which was broken. Brad rapidly approached her, and Natalie threw up both hands, let out a mighty scream, and a brilliant light poured out of her. The light was brighter than the sun, burning Richard's retinas, and he had to turn his head into the dirt. He felt blind.

There was a loud explosion and the sound of sirens getting nearer and nearer, but he still couldn't look. Even with his eyes closed, the lids burned.

"Holy mother!" he heard a voice exclaim.

The light lessened as the pain in his eyes let up, and he opened them.

Natalie was in a heap on the ground, sweating profusely, with the faintest blue light surrounding her. He felt the crackle in his fingertips once again, and instinctively knew that the light was back.

Many dark figures had been destroyed, leaving piles of crumpled ash and bone in heaps around the property.

Sheriff O'Reilly and a throng of officers appeared in the distance, their hands on their weapons and shock on their faces, stunned by the scene before them.

The door to the house opened, and Richard flipped around to see all his friends emerge.

"Is it over?" Remi asked.

A fireball appeared from the bushes and hit Rod in the face, knocking him off the porch. He screamed shrilly and began to roll on the ground.

Richard tugged his shirt off and ran toward Rod, jumping on him with the shirt, beating at the flames. Panic enveloped him as his friend's pained screams thundered in his ears. He beat at the flames with all the strength of his body.

"Rod! Rod!" Jamie screamed out.

Richard finally managed to beat the flames down, revealing ruined skin beneath, and Rod lay lifelessly on the ground. Richard rolled him over and checked for a pulse. There was none.

There was an indescribable anger in his gut and coursing through his body when he heard the cackle. He looked towards it and saw Kate peeking out from behind a bush with a sick smile on her face that revealed the lipstick on her teeth.

He shot to his feet and his entire body went hot. Blue shot out of every part of him. He threw up his hands and gave out a great roar as he aimed. He saw the smile fade, and her eyes go wide before she ran. It was too late. He was much faster. When his light slammed into her, she began to disintegrate before his eyes.

The purple sky deepened and there was a loud, almost mechanical sounding hum that filled the air. It pulsed out, going as far as the eye could see. Then it was gone.

The pressure in his chest was gone, and so was the pain. The air felt lighter. He surveyed the grounds. There were piles of ash and bone in every direction.

His family stood mere feet away as other spirits walked into a large, white opening in the sky. His mother's head rested on his father's shoulder, and Aunt Claire stood nearby, a pained expression on her face as she watched him.

"Help me!" he called out desperately.

"We can't," Aunt Claire told him with a small shake of her head. "No spell can reawaken the dead."

Richard crumpled to the ground and howled in agony. He couldn't take any more loss. He just couldn't.

He felt himself being pulled up into strong arms and he wept on his father's shoulder.

"It is not your fault, son. Do you hear me? You fought so bravely, and you accomplished so much. Unfortunately, loss is a part of battle."

He shook his head but found himself unable to respond from crying so hard. There was a light pressure followed by a warmth on his forehead. He opened his eyes to see his mother kissing him.

"I'm so sorry, my dear boy."

"Emma, Michael. We have to go." Aunt Claire was looking in the distance at the opening in the sky. It was getting smaller.

"Do you have to go?" he asked, feeling like a child once more.

"It's better if we do." His mother gave his hand a gentle squeeze before they all turned and walked through the opening a mere second before it closed.

He couldn't even feel them anymore. He knew deep down that they were gone. They'd passed over. Sitting on the ground near the trees was Brad, his arms over his head, as he rocked in defeat, tears streaming down his face.

Richard's anger was reignited as he stared at this traitor. He marched toward him, and Brad lowered his hands to look up at him.

"No! Richard, please!" he pleaded, but Richard ignored him, kicking him squarely in the face.

"You son of a bitch!" he growled, grabbing the older man's cloak with both of his hands, and hauling him to his feet, before punching him in the face again.

Brad howled in protest as blood spurted down his face from his destroyed nose. "We trusted you! They trusted you!"

"No one was supposed to be hurt!" Brad screamed. "They were just supposed to leave!"

"Richard! Richard!" A voice screamed at him, and his arms were jerked behind his back. "He's had enough."

He breathed heavily with exertion, his heart beating wildly in his chest. An officer pulled him back, and Sheriff O'Reilly stood over Brad, surveying the scene around them.

As Richard regulated his breathing, he took in his surroundings. Ruin was everywhere around them. Burned etchings and ash, Jamie's pained wails in the background. Life would never look the same again.

"His people are responsible for the kidnapping of that boy," Richard told Sheriff O'Reilly. "Where is the boy?" he snapped out and went to hit the older man again, but the sheriff held him back.

"I never saw him," Brad said as he tried to wipe the blood from his face. "But Baxter spent a lot of time in the basement."

"At Heaven's Estate?" the sheriff asked.

Brad nodded and officers ran in that direction.

# EPILOGUE
## THREE YEARS LATER

Richard sat on the porch of Blackwood Manor, looking out over the expanse of land. He was amazed at the difference the last three years brought.

The grounds were a lush, rich green that seemed to go on forever. The plantation was thriving for the first time in forever.

"Hey you."

He looked up and smiled as Remi took a seat in the chair next to him. He took her hand and squeezed it, gently running his fingers over the ring on her hand and glanced down to the generous bump her other hand rested on.

"How you feeling, babe?"

"Tired, but basically okay." She was only about three weeks from her due date, but she was taking it like a champ.

"Where's Emily?" he asked, referring to their oldest.

"She wanted her aunt Natalie to read her a story. I wasn't invited." They both laughed.

Three years ago, they never would have entertained the idea of living in Blackwood Manor with one point two children, but everything had been blissfully quiet since that day that felt like a lifetime ago. No spirits, no moving paintings, or creepy messages. Instead, they were surrounded by majestic beauty. It was a house. It was their home.

Once they'd felt sure that nothing continued to lurk on the land, they'd gone to work on restoring it. The grounds were stunning, and the house was perhaps the most beautiful one he'd ever seen. The paintjob was meticulously white, and the windows glowed like dancing lights. No matter the time of day, Blackwood Manor reached out with a healthy, welcoming glow.

The sun was quickly setting, and Richard looked down at his watch. "We better go in. I want to say goodnight before she knocks out."

They rose to their feet and entered the house together. Gus looked up from the podium that stood at the foot of the stairs. He waited to check people in, into the bed-and-breakfast that they'd opened a few short months ago.

They'd built a wall, closing off four of the bedrooms for the upstairs, which was the family wing. The rest were all guest rooms.

Gus grinned. "Bedtime already?"

Richard and Remi squeezed hands and nodded their agreement. "How many guest rooms are occupied?"

"Four. A fifth is on reserve. Young woman coming in on the red eye."

"Alright, well, you know where to find us if you need us." Richard gave him a fist bump, and he and Remi headed up the stairs toward Emily's room.

Their adorable two-year-old was propped up against pillows and laying in the crook of Natalie's arm. Natalie peered up over the edge of the book she'd been reading and gave them a quiet grin. "Emily was just asking about Cinderella's fairy godmother."

"Yeah? What was your question, baby?" Richard asked as he plopped down on the foot of the bed to tickle her feet.

She squealed in delight and pulled her feet away from him. "Was she real?"

Richard's eyes met Remi's first, and then Natalie's. "Yeah. I like to think so. We all have a fairy godmother out there somewhere who will show up when we really need them."

"Even little girls?"

"*Especially* little girls," he agreed, then leaned over to kiss her forehead. "But they won't be afraid to tell them it's time to go to sleep."

Natalie hopped up from the bed, and Richard pulled the covers over Emily. Remi reached down to kiss her and before she could stand all the way up, Emily reached over to kiss her bump. "Night, baby."

"Good night, angel," Remi smiled, then shut off the switch as the adults exited the room and closed the door.

Emily rolled over in the bed and smiled. Illuminated in the glow from the nightlight was her friend. The little blonde girl with the juice on her nightgown.

She stepped out of the closet and plopped down on the edge of the bed. "Is it a boy or girl?"

"Mommy says sister."

"That's good," Lucy gave her a big grin. "So, Emily, do you want to hear a story?"

Thank you so much for reading! If you enjoyed this book, please consider leaving a review. Reviews help authors be seen, and therefore, make it possible for us to keep making books possible for readers.

**Want to know more? Stay tuned for the spinoff series,** *Beyond Blackwood Manor*, **coming in 2025.**

# Acknowledgements

There are so many people that made this book possible. Thank you to my grandmother, Kathryn Frayne and Lou Ann Taylor for believing in this series, and more importantly, me. Thank you to my boyfriend, Don, for standing by me through the deadlines and endless late nights.

I've learned so much on this journey and enjoyed every single minute. This is such a rewarding experience, and I'd like to thank every single reader, whether you enjoyed the first book or not. Your feedback was instrumental in making this one what it is now!

To every single critique partner and beta reader for not being afraid to tell me when I wasn't performing at my best, you are rock stars, I couldn't have done it without you.

A special thanks to my editor Jenny Sliger of Owl Eyes Proofs and Edits and cover designer Kelley York of Sleepy Fox Studios, who thankfully agreed to return to my little series. You ladies are lovely, and your work is stunning.

Lastly, I have to give a special thanks to fellow author, Debbie Hyde. In addition to being an amazing author herself, Debbie runs an incredible reading/writing group on Facebook, The Fireside Book Café. This group is a wealth of knowledge, most of which is shared by Debbie herself. I've learned so much there and continue to do so every day! You really should mosey on over if you haven't already!

Thank you, readers! I hope you all will follow me throughout the rest of my author journey. These worlds wouldn't be possible without you!

Ashley Bundy

Hi there! I'm Ashley Bundy and I'm so happy you picked up my little book baby. I enjoy a good spellbinding mystery, so I thought it would be a good idea if I wrote a few! I like to weave fictional stories with my real-life experiences to make them feel more raw.

The Blackwood Manor duology is based on a couple of haunted houses from my childhood. One was my childhood home, and one was my best friend's. Between the two of us the houses told endless stories. Some of our actual experiences are in these two books, but I'm not saying which ones. You'll just have to guess!! Happy reading!

## Where to Find Me

Join my newsletter at: https://ashleybundy.wixsite.com/my-site-1

Facebook: Ashley Bundy Author

Twitter: https://twitter.com/bookloverbundy2

Instagram: https://www.instagram.com/ashleybundyreads/

Tiktok: https://www.tiktok.com/@ashleybundybooks

Goodreads: https://www.goodreads.com/goodreadscomashley_bundy

Bookbub: https://www.bookbub.com/profile/ashley-bundy

Amazon: https://www.amazon.com/stores/Ashley-Bundy/author/B0CPTG44TK

### Miss Blackwood Manor? Find it here
www.books2read.com/blackwoodmanor